Life, Love, and Lupus

Stevie Beth

authorHOUSE®

AuthorHouse™
1663 Liberty Drive
Bloomington, IN 47403
www.authorhouse.com
Phone: 1-800-839-8640

First published by AuthorHouse   09/28/2011

ISBN: 978-1-4567-5144-9 (sc)
ISBN: 978-1-4567-5146-3 (hc)
ISBN: 978-1-4567-5145-6 (ebk)

Library of Congress Control Number: 2011903853

Printed in the United States of America

Contents

Buttercup

I am a simple buttercup
who has often contemplated
the inconsequentiality of my being.

I heal no sick,
I raise no dead,
I give no sight to the blind.

Yesterday, a passerby stopped,
smelled my fragrance,
and whispered, "Thank you."

Catheryne

The Diagnosis

At birth, my parents must have known and named me Mary. When I began this excavation, I was twenty-three years old. Today, I am twenty-five. This story has been a lifetime in the making. All of one's life experiences shape who you are and what you will become. I was diagnosed with lupus at the age of seventeen. That diagnosis and my penchant for melodrama have played a surprisingly large role in my current predicament. That probably sounds strange, and perhaps it is, but being diagnosed with lupus somehow made me feel vindicated.

Imagine an overweight seventeen-year-old with no real self-esteem -just a talent for making people laugh. Laughing always seemed to make the hard stuff easier. I had always been told that I was lazy and a hypochondriac, but I did not mind the criticisms because I often felt the same way about myself. My legs ached all the time. Whenever I walked, there was pain. Many times, invitations were declined because the energy needed to engage in the various activities was not there. After years and years of pain, I began to accept the pain as a normal part of my life. At this point, it never occurred to me that this was abnormal.

In my senior year of high school, I was in a school play. During a break, the cast sat on the stage to discuss aspects of the play. I noticed that while everyone else was seated on the stage, I was sitting in one of the chairs in the stands. I had not even really thought about it, but I realized at that moment that I had chosen the seat because the stage was very low and it would have been excruciating to get up. This realization made me consider that something may be wrong with me.

It was later that year when I noticed that I avoided going to the bathroom. I would hold it until I couldn't anymore. I hated sitting on the toilet, because getting up was painful. This discovery sent me to my parents and then to the rheumatologist.

It was at this point that several tests were done on me and I was given the diagnosis of lupus. Suddenly, I had a new "L" word to describe myself. I was not lazy at all - just sick.

I spent the next few years getting used to different medications and surviving one health crisis after another. For some reason, I was not frightened of the disease; perhaps because I was so accustomed to it by then. I had not had a name for it, but it had always been there.

No amount of pleading, willing my body, or promises made under duress make my body move when it decides not to. Fearing that if I sat on the floor I might not be able to get up; refusing to go to the bathroom because it was too embarrassing to admit how excruciating it was to get on and off the toilet; growing to be resentful of loved ones who didn't have to deal with constant pain; wishing daily that I could be someone else; hating my life but – at the same time – fighting like hell to stay alive: this is my life.

In weak moments I think, "Why me?" These moments are short-lived because I try to remind myself that my life is not a tragedy. The murder of innocent people on September 11, 2001, was a tragedy. The brutalization of millions of Jews in concentration camps, or the Challenger exploding in the eighties: those were tragedies. My pain is just life; it's my life. Perspective is important in coping with my disease.

In the beginning, I had an insatiable appetite for information on lupus. I decided that if it was going to be with me for the rest of my life, I might as well learn as much about it as I could. I told myself that everyone has burdens to bear and that this disease was mine.

My decision to put a positive spin on things was short-lived. At the time, it felt like I was the only one my age who was suffering. I knew that friends and relatives were in pain, but nothing seemed equal to what I was bearing. It got to the point where I could not see past my own pain. It consumed me, and soon it became me. I guess this is when denial became a friend of mine. I decided to take medicine only when I deemed it necessary or remembered. I told myself that I wasn't sick. I started missing appointments, letting prescriptions expire, and challenging death to take me out. I yelled at death; I berated death; I challenged death.

One day, death responded; and as a result of its ominous presence, I was stricken with a third blood clot and had to have a blood transfusion.

The weight fluctuation caused by the steroids prescribed for the lupus painted stretch marks liberally all over my body. The psychological impact of the excess weight went unnoticed for quite awhile. Suddenly I realized that I was shying away from affection from males and hated to be touched.

The sight of myself naked in the mirror is more than I can stand. The thought of having someone I care about reject me is truly terrifying. I can't imagine any other reaction to my body than utter disgust. My body is hideous. I preferred the idea of death over anyone seeing me naked.

With lupus, the fatigue is the most consistent problem. At twenty-five, you get no sympathy for being tired - lupus or not. My friends know that I'm sick, but sometimes they still get frustrated when I tell them that I am too tired to go out or that I am turning in early. During really intense flare-ups, every part of my body hurts; just lying in bed hurts. My body is sore to the touch, and any stress – major or minor – can trigger flare ups. It's hard for healthy people to understand. Lupus is such a random and unpredictable disease, and it can affect each and every part of the body.

My list of ailments (from joint and muscle pain to blood clots, fatigue, and obesity) would not be complete without the inclusion of migraines. Most people don't believe me when I say this, but I would take lupus two times over if I could rid myself of the migraines. Imagine the most excruciating pain possible: that's what my migraines are like. When I am stricken with one, I want to die. I have never experienced another pain that is anything like it.

The doctors don't know if the headaches are linked to my lupus or not. The number of migraine visits I have made to the ER far exceed lupus-related ones. In addition, many times I have been treated badly by hospital staff members who assume I am only there for the medicine or narcotics. Their bedside manner is often atrocious, if they have one at all.

I have around seven or eight doctors and take about twenty-nine pills a day as well as a weekly injection, and that's just when nothing's wrong. On many days, I feel resentful and hateful about how much I have on my plate. The majority of my time is spent in doctor offices and hospitals or sorting out my medication.

It doesn't seem fair to be so young and be so sick. I take more medication than my grandmother. She was amazed when I told her how much medication I'm on. Some days, I just want to quit taking the medicine, just to see whether anything would happen to me. It just all feels like too much some days. It's hard not to want to give up, and on those days I remind myself that it could be worse. I know that compared to many people in the world I have it easy, but every now and then I grant myself a five- to ten-minute pity party; and then I go on.

It has become necessary for me to wear a medic alert necklace now. If that isn't the pinnacle of all things cool and in vogue ... but I digress. Anyway, I have had so many people stop to compliment me on my necklace and then become mortified when they get close enough to see that it is a medic-alert necklace.

I also have lots of trouble with my knees. While I was in college, I got a handicap permit so parking on campus would be easier. The permit was permanent, so I can still park in handicap-spaces now. The worst part of this is the stares I receive because I don't look handicapped. I often feel as if I should limp and grimace as I get in and out of my car. I know I am really attractive at twenty-five, being this fat girl with a medic-alert necklace and a handicap-parking permit; I just can't understand why men aren't falling all over themselves to greet me at my car door.

I do a lot of reading on the disease, and there are many support groups around Alabama. I have been telling myself for years that I am going to join a group, but I never do. At least four friends have offered to go with me. Once, I managed to volunteer at the Lupus Foundation. I went in for two days, stuffed some envelopes and other chores, and then never went back. I don't know why I was intimidated, but I was. The women at the foundation had specifically told me to let them know if I changed my mind about volunteering and not to just stop showing up, but the latter is exactly what I did. I'm deeply ashamed of that. The worst part is I don't even really know why I did it. I just did. I have this tendency of doing things that really don't make any sense – even I don't know why I do them.

Most days, my attitude is that I have a disease and not that a disease has me. I don't think about lupus every day. Taking the medication is just part of my routine. I no longer feel depressed about being sick, and I am past being angry; now I feel as if I am just coping.

As far as diseases go, I must say that lupus hasn't been as vicious as some diseases are, or as vicious as it could be. I still try to gather as much information about the disease as possible. Since being diagnosed, I've noticed that lupus isn't as recognized as other diseases are.

The scariest part of the disease so far has been its impact on my kidneys. Lupus has stopped my kidneys from working at full capacity, and I may need dialysis sometime down the road. For a few months last summer, I received chemotherapy as a powerful attempt to slow down lupus' damage on my kidneys. It was very scary, but I made it through. For now, the treatment seems to have been successful.

I worry sometimes that as I get older, the disease will get worse. I wonder, if I met someone and got married, what kind of a burden I would be on my husband. I know it's normal for people to enter relationships with baggage, but I come with a Samsonite store.

Since being diagnosed, I have had kidney interaction, and I wonder whether I will be able to have children when I am ready. Right now, lupus has not interfered too greatly with the plans I have made for myself, but I worry about the future and what is yet to come.

On the other hand, having a disease has made me more appreciative of good days and good health. I am thankful for days when my joints don't ache or when I have more energy than the day before or when I able the bend a little further than I could the last time I tried. Many people my age don't question their own mortality or value life, but I think about life and death a lot – so much so that I am not afraid of death. I think in order to really live, a person has to deal with death.

Thank You Laude

Just before graduation from high school, I was hospitalized for four weeks with a blood clot in my leg. A second blood clot was found in the other leg in the summer before I was to leave for college. My parents insisted that I take the first year off and then look at going to college.

The idea of not going to college had never occurred to me before. I had read about many different schools and decided that Bowdoin in Brunswick, Maine, was the one for me. While I was accepted into five of the six schools I applied to, acceptance at Bowdoin was a dream come true. I now look back on receiving Bowdoin's acceptance letter as one of the most exciting times of my life. The college sent me a plane ticket and invited me to visit. I fell in love with the campus and made up my mind to leave Campbellton, Georgia, and go to Maine.

I was determined to start college when my friends did and Bowdoin was my destiny. However, the summer was rough on me health-wise. I depended on my parents so much that the thought of being so far away from them crippled me in a way the disease never could.

I had also applied to my mother's alma mater, a Christian University in Alabama. It was only a four-hour drive from Campbellton, while Maine was a twenty-hour drive. I wonder what my life would have been like had I gone to Maine. I decided instead to go to school in Alabama. That decision led to some of the best years of my life. In August of 2001, I received a bachelor's of art degree in, no surprise, English.

College was an experience for me. I did not want to tell anyone I met that I was sick. That first semester, I would drag my aching body to class and stay up late, studying and finishing homework. I wanted to make every class, but I was running my body into the ground. Finally, I decided that letting people in on my sickness was a good idea. My professors understood and that made an indelible impression on me that has lasted until this day. It was at this stage of my life that I learned that informing people of my illness was not a plea for pity but rather a way for people to understand what I deal with on a daily basis – and a way for me to cope and survive.

My college experience cannot be adequately understood without introducing Samantha, aka Sal (don't ask why it's Sal and not Sam). To neglect mentioning Sal would be to leave out a tremendous part of my college experience. Sal and I met in our freshmen year. We were both assigned to the same dormitory. We talked briefly one afternoon in front of the dorm, exchanged phone numbers and that was about it. Days later, a creepy guy, we named 'the pheesh' from our freshmen class asked me to lunch. I was terrified about dining with him, so called Sal and asked her to go to lunch with us. She accepted, and that marked the beginning of an amazing friendship.

Sometimes, I think about our friendship and marvel at it. In senior year, we lived together for a while off campus and for a few years after we graduated from college. All these years later, she is still the first person I talk to in the morning and last person at night.

Samantha has been there for me during some of the roughest periods of my life. Sometimes it feels strange to me that we have only been friends for thirteen years; I feel like I have known her for an eternity. She knows me better than anyone. She can tell what I am thinking and feeling by the tone of my voice. I hate that I cannot lie to her. Don't get me wrong, I try; but I am always unsuccessful at getting her to believe me.

It is scary sometimes how well we know each other. Somehow, laughing with her makes everything funnier. We have concocted some of the craziest schemes together. She has supported me through the ups and downs of my sickness and refuses to ever let me feel sorry for myself. She has always been the practical one, and I have been the feeler. She has tried to show me the importance of taking charge of my life and not lying stagnant, waiting for life to happen to me. Right along with thanking God for my parents, I also thank God for her and our friendship.

At times, I feel as if I have taken more from this friendship than I have given. I cannot imagine my life without her. I have had lots and lots of friends over the course of my life, but it was not until I met her that I understood the meaning of best friend. She has not only been a best friend but a best sister, best support network, best counselor, and all-time best partner in crime. When I look back over my college experience, she is what I think of first.

I have bored her many times over the years talking to her about my crushes and the unrequited love that seems to follow me to relationship after relationship. When I was being foolish, she would tell me, of course; but when I was happy and excited about something one of my love interests had said, written or done, it was Sal that was genuinely happy for me – even when she thought the guy was not worth all of the pomp and ceremony.

My friendship with Sal has taught me a lot, but I think the most important thing I have gleaned from it is how to be a friend. However, to just say we are friends is hardly accurate. We are family; we are sisters. There is absolutely no one on this planet who can infuriate me the way she does. Sometimes, we get on each other's nerves so badly that we cannot even stand the sight of one another. Then, when we are just at that boiling point, one of us will say something ridiculous and we will begin laughing and forget we had just been about to come to blows.

I cannot forget to mention the movie quotes. I think between the both of us, we have seen every movie ever created. We have this annoying talent of using quotes from movies in normal conversation. The real sick part is that the other one will follow suit with the next line from the movie. This is something we still do to this day. It is always the most obscure of lines that we tend to remember. It is amazing how the same lines stand out for both of us.

Sal once told me that she prays for me at night, and when she does she even prays that things will work out for me and *him* – him being Paul, the second man I tell myself I have ever loved, the one who I ran off, screaming, and who now hates me … but I'm getting ahead of myself.

I met him my senior year. I fell for Paul Hughes fast. In some weird twist of fate, we were placed in the same senior seminar group. He was kind to me. That is all it took for me to be hooked.

My biggest fear then and now is public speaking. I can't stand attention of any kind. The insecurity I feel regarding what people must be thinking makes me crazy. I really don't know if this is due to low self-esteem or whether it is a weird brand of narcissism.

Each seminar group had to present on a topic, and each of us received ten minutes to present. Our topic was King Arthur. Preparing for those ten minutes made me physically ill. I called Paul more times than I am willing to admit to get reassurance that I was not going to embarrass myself in front of the seminar group. We met briefly one evening to discuss the project and watch a video at my apartment. After talking to him for just a few moments, I knew that this night would mark the beginning of my newest crush. I did not know then that I would consider him one of the great loves of my life, which is tragic when you learn how this story ends.

I discovered that he had a love of films, especially Hitchcock films. I do not remember how we got onto the subject of movies, but he began telling me about the Hitchcock film *Rear Window*. His voice and the story he told mesmerized me. He got almost to the end and then abruptly stopped. He refused to continue with the story and told me I had to watch it to know how it ended. This marked the beginning of my curiosity with him and the film.

Our involvement in senior seminar made it necessary for us to exchange email addresses, and his address was to become one of the most important pieces of information that I became privy to. After senior seminar was over, I asked Paul if he minded if I continued to email him. He was very receptive to this, and I have been obsessed with emailing him ever since.

The emailing was ridiculous while we were in school, but after we graduated and he moved back to a small town in Alabama, it became out of control for me. Email became the only way I could communicate with him, so for a while it became my life. Then AOL instant messenger became my new best friend. It would make my whole day to receive an email from him. We got to the point where we emailed every day and sometimes more than once a day.

Now it's a few times a week. This is not my preference, or my doing, for that matter. I still email him daily and each day desperately hope for a reply. He always gets back to me, but it is not always as immediate as I wish. Even as I type at this very moment, I am hoping to receive an email from him. It has been almost a week now and I am anxious to hear from him.

Nothing has changed in three years. When I think about the time that has passed, I feel so pathetic and weak. Pathetic, yes; ready to quit, no. As hard as I try to push him out of my mind, he is always there. He is so witty and so insightful, and that makes me love him a little more each day. I love him in all the ways you can possibly love someone. I love how he makes movie-watching scientific. I love that he is a *Star Wars* and *Lord of the Rings* geek. I love that he becomes vexed at my mistreatment. I love his reverence for the spiritual and his love of music, and of films.

He is so caring and compassionate and seems to really care about my feelings, even though he can do nothing about them. I feel like I can tell him anything. I truly believe that he reads every desperate word that I send him, although he seldom – if ever – responds to my declarations of love. If he does address them, he makes his responses so vague and broad that it is impossible to really understand what the hell he is talking about. He does not like discussing his feelings or the painful events that have happened in his past and that have shaped the man he is - the man that I love.

I yearn for the days on the playground when you could just pull a guys thumb back until he called "uncle!" and agreed to be your boyfriend before you relented. Some days, I just wish I could make Paul realize how good we could be together, and make him want to be with me. It seems so unfair that I could want him this much and yet it so impossible for us to be together. Why is it impossible? What would have to change for this work? Who would I have to be for him to love me? Why must everything come down to me changing? Why is it that it never crossed my mind until now that the problem might be his?

I can't gauge my relationship with Paul, or maybe it's that I don't want to because I don't like what is being communicated. We are friends; that is what I know for certain. We have been able to maintain this weird relationship for over three years, seeing each other only once. We send each other birthday and Christmas gifts every year, we email consistently, and that's about all we do.

One night a few years ago, I was online and decided to write him. I wanted to say a lot, but I was not woman enough to say these things in a real way; so I wrote this poem and sent it to him.

Intrigued by what is hidden,
completely inspired by the forbidden,
I dare to excavate the caverns of your mind.
Heartache has created walls,
walls that serve as protectors
against pain and disappointment.
Past pain and old haunting hurts have banded
together to stop any reoccurrence of heartache.
As a result of this alliance,
the core of you has been locked away.
I want to know you.
I want to know that which is concealed.

11

I love the part of you that is free to be loved,
I desire to love the part of you locked away.
More than experiencing the intense joy of
having you love me, I just want the intense pleasure
of you letting me love you.
What pain has created this enigma?
What disappointment led to the construction
of this wall?
Why is it so hard for you to let yourself fall?
Hearts racing as a result of extreme emotion;
your pounding heart likened
to a smarting thumb.
Why does feeling cause you to become numb?
Dreams of crumbling walls and mysteries
solved are all my mind can fathom.
More than you revealing secrets from within,
I just want to be let in.

Paul told me later that he liked the poem and was a little blown away by it. He went on the say that it was so incredibly good that he read it to his roommate. I could have lived without knowing that piece of information, but I was glad that he liked the poem. I naively believed that he would not realize the poem was about him.

Looking back, I realize how stupid I must have been. The poem hits on everything that I have ever thought of him. It was written at the beginning of my infatuation, and this next one was written some years later in this insane, one-sided love affair. The sad aspects of our "relationship" were beginning to come into focus. The denial I was feeling was beginning to wane. I was beginning to let my frustration show a little more. There were times when I actually let myself get angry over the fact that he was not in love with me. I believe this poem was also sent to him via email.

Moments of clarity hurt like hell,
unable to stand the ache,
I attempt to remain in what is not real.
Realities shrill rings loudly in my head.
Leaving only inward cries to tell the tale.
Hiding to not be noticed,
enraged at being unseen,

desperate for you to know,
terrified that you know,
I am secretly banging my head against the wall,
kicking, screaming, using clinched fists to
beat anything in my reach.
Grasping at straws, struggling to smell smoke
where there is no fire.
In an attempt to make you real.
All the while hating how that makes me feel.
Still unable to heal,
screaming so loudly from the inside,
convinced that you can hear.
Feeling real in the surreal,
viewing life through a kaleidoscope,
where run of the mill people,
monotonous situations are suddenly
distorted into masterpieces.
An average boy made into a hero,
everyday friendships are altered into
breathtaking romances.

I endured lupus' ravaging of my body and mind, and I won - graduating Thank You Laude in August 2001.

Romantic Propaganda

I've tried so hard to wash him away, and I just can't. I hate how he leaves a place and his scent and presence surround me hours after all other traces of him are gone. My body may leave him, but my thoughts and heart remain with him. I've watched him sleep and have longed to stroke his back and run my fingers through his hair. His intellect, his wit, his bad-boy nature, and the quiet brilliance that surrounds him arouse me. So many women have adorned his bed and then been left broken hearted and quivering in his wake. And yet still I desire him. I crave him like my next breath, yet I am afraid to inhale.

He is so real. A flesh-and-blood man, not a figment of my imagination. His realness is intoxicating. His ability to inspire me frightens me. I have reveled in the pain that loving him has caused me. I have written horrible poetry on nights when I am alone and craving him. I envy how he lives his life so freely, so uninhibited. My attempt to feign indifference around him has managed to do nothing but make me anything but indifferent to him. He is so much better than his lowest moment and capable of so much more than his greatest. Whenever I am in his presence, I long to be someone else, someone who was not afraid to kiss him or make love to him, someone who felt free enough to run their fingers through his hair, someone who acted on their urges, someone who actually lived life as opposed to observing it.

I love loving him. I even love hating myself for loving him. I love how insane I feel for confessing all this. I see so many relationships where couples have lost that feeling: that exhilaration; the feeling where your heart stops when he enters a room; the joy you feel when you hear the sound of his voice; the feeling where the anticipation of his touches drive you wild; that moment where you are left breathless by simply looking at his face or remembering his smile. I want the rush. I am hooked on those rushes.

Common sense tells me to mistrust him, but somehow I look into his eyes and I believe him. When we are together, I feel like I am on the cusp of ascertaining something that I have coveted for so long. I cannot explain the gentleness I see when I am brave enough to look into his eyes. There are no words to describe the feeling of trust that his touch inspires. And there's absolutely no way to express the sincerity I hear in his voice when he speaks of silly things. I've heard that "love is friendship set to music." Even if that is not so, the very possibility of it is worth the trouble.

He is a sensation that can only be felt and not explained. I want to trust him. I want to have that "make love for the first time with the lights on" kind of trust with him. Sometimes, this infatuation has felt like a farce of some sort while at other times, depending on the time of day, it has seemed like a Greek tragedy. I find myself somewhat comforted by the deafening silence he has brought into my life. He looks at me with such intensity that I fear he sees my deepest secrets before they are even created.

This sort of romantic propaganda has plagued my adolescence and has bled into adulthood. My quest for a soul mate, and a Hepburn/Spencer romance …

Each time I believed it was the real thing. I allowed my heart to get swept up in a tidal wave of emotions, and each of my three relationships bordered on obsession, with my being unable to think of anything else. The tragic part of this story is the fact that, of my three loves, not one of them ever reciprocated my affection, and I never realized it until the bitter end of each relationship. My love life has been a testament to insanity. I have played out the same scenes over and over again. The only thing that has ever changed is the thespians. Do I discount my love and experience because of this technicality? Not in the least.

I have loved with all that I am and with all that I have to give. I am now in love with two very different men. Much of my life is spent in deep contemplation over these two men, neither of whom loves me. They both love me in that "love thy neighbor" way but not in the way that I long for them to. I am accepting a challenge from myself to find what makes me happy. I am struggling to love myself a tenth of how much I love these two men.

I started a personal journey to discover love. Do I truly understand what it means to be in love? Could I possibly? I am desperate to have love find me, to caress me and keep me close. Are there some people who aren't meant to be loved? If so, perhaps I am one of these unfortunate souls. Maybe love eludes me because I so desperately seek it. My own desperation could possibly be my own worst enemy. It seems as if love should be one of the few things in this complicated world that should be simple and free, but alas, love is far from simple and does not come without a heavy price tag. It seems as though we are built to need love, as we need oxygen. Love seems to be a necessity.

My life would be so much easier if I could just neutralize the part of myself that craves closeness with another person. I have been so consumed with finding a man to love me that I have forgotten to love myself. It's been so long since I have even attempted to do this that I am afraid that I wouldn't even know where to begin. There are just so many things about me to loathe and be ashamed of.

Are my thought processes that of a normal twenty-something-year-old woman? My guess would be probably not. Where did I take a detour? I never set out to be different. I just want normal. I want average. I say that I want to find the love of my life and get married and have children, yet I fall in love with men who don't want relationships. I get fixated on these relationships that can never be and waste years daydreaming about the impossible.

Maybe it's not love that I am looking for; perhaps it is something else entirely. This could be the cause of my frustration. I just might be looking for all the wrong things. Maybe happiness is something else for me. I keep telling myself that falling in love and being loved by another will make me happy, but maybe that's not it. That can't be right, because a person's happiness can't be derived from another person. That doesn't make any sense, does it?

Previously

I have always been able to say anything through a poem. I show tremendous courage in my writing. If ever I was face to face with Paul again, I do not think I could muster up anything other than a quick and shallow "hey." I have said some things to him over the last few years that have shocked the hell out of me for being brave enough to confess. I have even been fool enough to make sexual innuendoes through my emails to him. He strategically ignores them. He has turned ignoring my romantic overtones into an art form.

I have seen him once since we graduated from college. We agreed to meet at the largest city near his small town. He treated me to a movie, and then we went to lunch and had a three-hour talk at Barnes and Noble. It is no exaggeration to say that it was one of the best days of my life. The three-hour conversation is what I remember most. I feel like I could talk to him forever. He is so funny, and I laugh so much at the things he says. There is no one else who makes me feel the way he does.

I think of him, or talk to him, or email him, and I cannot help but imagine us together and married. He is the kind of man I want to marry and raise children with. I wonder how I could love someone so much and yet find the love so unrequited. The sound of his voice is like home for me. I could have a love affair with just his voice. My dream is to have him read to me. I wouldn't care whether it was Dr. Seuss or Browning; his voice is poetry.

When I found out my father was gravely ill, I wrote Paul about it. He was so compassionate and caring in return, and sent me the following email.

Mary,

I just want to respond in some way, and it's either going to be a quick "I'm here for you, but I don't know what to say," or something rambling and incoherent. I'm going to try for the latter with a bit less of the incoherence.

First off, your dad thinks you're strong, and you shouldn't doubt him there. He's wiser than you and I, I'm sure, and yet I know for a fact he's right about this one. Your life isn't easy; did you ever really consider that? You're strong for getting up in the morning. You're strong for going to work. You're strong for being there for all those kids and mothers and fathers. You're strong for knowing you shouldn't take your work home with you and doing it anyway. You're strong, Mary. No doubt.

I'm not going to say, "If God wills it ..." or anything like that. I hate that when people try to reassure people, especially people of faith, that it's all about God's will. Where's the consolation in "the design all around us" when we are pissed off and scared to death? Whether it is or it isn't God's will, it's OK to be scared and to be sad and to pray in desperation and to cry your eyes out. You can be the strongest woman in the world, as you say your mom is, but don't be surprised when you find out she's not all stone. Don't let that be a shock to you because this is her husband, and this is your dad, right? You guys love him, and he loves you, and you have to remember that what's happening to you is what happens. It just is. I don't know how else to put it. Cry, and don't feel guilty. You're scared, and it's normal to cry and be scared, isn't it?

I think of you all the time, and now I'll keep you and your dad and mom in my prayers, I promise. If the doctors have faith, you should, too, and your faith should supersede the doctors' anyway. However trite and self-righteous and "Christian-y" that sounds, I think it still holds true, but it's really, really, really hard, I know. I believe that I'd just simply fall apart if my mom or dad were gone, and rare has been the time that I thought that might happen. Deep down

I know that I'd make it, and that something would sustain me. But damn it, it'd be hard, and I know it.

I guess what I mean to say with all this matter-of-fact garbage is this: take it as it comes, murmur your frightened words to that always open ear, and know that your dad loves you, that he knows you love him, obviously, and that whatever happens, you're going to make it. Your dad says you're strong, and you are.

Love ya, Mary.

Paul

Whenever I am hurting and need to reach out to someone, he is the first person I think to call. He makes everything better for me with little to no effort on his part. There is something about him that heals me. He will always address my feelings as long as they don't relate to our relationship. He loves me but he is not in love with me. It was during this time of my father's illness that he finally told me that he loved me. After three long years he finally said it in the form of a salutation: "Love ya, Mary." I'll take that. Sadly, I will take that. It took a near-death experience with my father for him to give me a "love ya." I knew it, but it was reaffirming to hear it. He meant nothing other than friendship by it, but he still wrote it. He wrote it, and I will treasure that he did, even if it is the only time.

One Saturday night I sent him a poem I had written on the way to dinner with my cousin, Rhoda. I knew the poem was a little too honest and revealing, yet I sent it anyway. He responded and told me that when he received emails and poems from me such as the one I had sent, he felt overwhelmed and – if I am remembering correctly – he also stated that he found it exhausting.

That had a profound effect on me. The last thing I ever wanted to do was burden him with my feelings. I say that with all sincerity and without malice. I just wanted to share every feeling I had with him. I know now that he was right and that my need to share probably was exhausting and overwhelming at times. I had just wanted him to know how I felt. Now I realize he would have to be a complete idiot not to know. I have done everything short of tattooing "I love you" on his body.

Sometimes I reason with myself and discuss how ridiculous this relationship is and encourage myself to move on and accept that we are friends and that's all we will ever be. Then I remind myself that he is everything I have ever dreamed of, and it's hard to let go of dreams. I think people lose a part of themselves when they let go of dreams. Wherever broken dreams go, I imagine there are pieces of people's souls there, keeping those fragmented dreams company. Giving up on Paul would be confessing that I no longer believe in fairy tales and happy endings. I would not be me if those characteristics suddenly abandoned me. My dreams, hopes, and aspirations make getting out of my bed in the morning a little easier.

Over the years, I have become more and more infatuated with Paul. It got to the point where I could not be receptive to anyone else because of how deeply I was pining for him. The reality that we are not going to end up together comes to me in waves.

I was having a reality moment when Alistair came into my life. Alistair was supposed to be fun. He was supposed to help me forget Paul or at least to love Paul a little less than I do. I was not supposed to fall for Alistair. He is not the type that you love. He is a ladies' man who considers monogamy a terminal illness and who is sexually indiscriminate. His lovemaking is equal opportunity to all women.

When I first met him, I was not at all interested. He became a new experience for me because he sort of pursued me at first. He was the most obnoxious and persistent person I had ever met. I found him rude the first couple of times we were together. He would touch me and say crass things. I had never been around anyone as forward as him.

At first, I would fool myself into thinking that I hated the touches and attention; but then, like a bolt of lightning, it hit me: I liked the advances. The rudeness and the affection intrigued me. He is very good with women and has had more than his fair share of lovers. He is also very good with the lines and the moves, but for some reason, when he told me I was beautiful, I believed him. At least, I believed he thought so. I had never considered myself beautiful - in fact, I had never considered myself much of anything.

One summer a few years ago, when Sal and I were living together, she started dating Eric, Alistair's roommate. She was spending all of her free time with him, and I felt like I only saw her when she came home to change clothes. One night she was at Eric's and had forgotten something. She asked me to bring it to her at his house. I was at home watching movies, and as I was in a hurry to get there and back, I did not bother to change out of my shorts and a t-shirt before I left.

When I got there, Eric's yard looked like a used car lot. There were so many people there. Almost immediately, I was embarrassed. I walked into the house and saw Alistair. He was very nice, as always, and helped me locate Sal and Eric. As soon as Eric saw me, he started making fun of my outfit and asked me if I was on my way to PE. I laughed, but I was embarrassed and felt so out of place compared to the other females there. Looking back now I can see that it had nothing to do with what I was wearing; it was something else entirely: I was in a different league.

While there, I was offered a drink, and another, and then another, and soon it became clear that I wasn't going anywhere. Before I was talked into staying the night, I started searching the house for my keys. The lights were all off and people were strewn all around the house, passed out for the night. There were several keys along the mantle, so I started searching through them to see if mine were there. All of a sudden, I felt someone behind me. I turned around quickly and saw it was Alistair. He pressed so tightly against me that I was pinned against the fireplace.

Slowly, he started to run his hands up my shorts. Usually when he started to touch me I would grab his hands or tell him to stop, but for some reason I didn't; I couldn't. I couldn't, because I didn't want him to stop. At first, neither of us said anything, but finally he spoke in a whisper, in a voice I haven't heard since: "This is the first time you've ever let me touch you like this."

I took a deep breath and tried to say something back, but nothing would come out. It was at this time that one of his girls came over to us, wanting him. He turned to her while his hand was still up my shorts and said, "Could you give me a minute? I am having some Mary-time right now."

Suddenly, I remembered why I had never let him touch me like that. After our brief but oh-so-memorable (at least for me) moment ended, he went off with one of his merry maids for fucking, and she ended up in his bed that night while I slept on the futon in the den – a scenario that would play out countless times during the course of our relationship: him in the bedroom with some random woman, and me on the outside, wishing it was me on the inside.

Oh I am a lonely painter
I live in a box of paints
I'm frightened by the devil
And I'm drawn to those ones that ain't afraid
I remember that time that you told me, you said
"Love is touching souls."

Surely you touched mine,
'Cause part of you pours out of me
In these lines from time to time
Oh you're in my blood like holy wine

Having lupus does make me different from most people my age, but I think the real story here isn't my ups and downs with an autoimmune disease; rather, it is my ups and mostly downs with life and love. At twenty-five years of age, I can honestly say that I have never had a boyfriend or a first kiss; and yes, that means that I am a virgin at twenty-five. I'm not exactly sure what you'd call the relationships that I have been in other than dysfunctional, one sided, imagined, humorous and sad. OK, well I guess I did know a few descriptive words.

This is a firsthand account of how I ruined the best relationship I never had by never being satisfied and by accepting the relationship for what it was, which was a great friendship – and sometimes that's enough, or at least it has to be in order to keep the good thing you've found.

Alistair

> "The only people for me are the mad ones, the ones who are mad
> to live, mad to talk, mad to be saved, desirous of everything at the
> same time, the ones who never yawn or say a commonplace thing,
> but burn, burn, burn, like fabulous yellow roman candles exploding
> like spiders across the stars and in the middle you see the blue center
> light pop and everybody goes "Awww!"

from *On The Road* by Jack Kerouac

For some reason, I cannot recall what events led up to me spending the night with Alistair. It was the most uncomfortable and beautiful night I have ever spent. Nothing sexual happened that evening. We talked until we fell asleep. We gently caressed each other in our sleep. He slept so soundly that night, while I was wide awake, just lying there watching him sleep and listening to him breathe. He snored a little – not loudly, but it was very consistent. In his sleep, he placed his arm around me. I was very conscious of everything he did that night. I remember having to go to the bathroom and not wanting to go because I did not want to move his arm from around me. I feel so alive when he touches me. I feel like silk when he touches me.

I have never been one to sleep late, so I was up early the next morning. He was still lying beside me sound asleep. I eased myself out of his bed and took a long look around his room. I noticed that he had a copy of Kerouac's novel *On the Road* on his shelf. There was also a copy of JD Salinger's *Catcher in the Rye*. He had lots of paraphernalia from the Beatles.

I was so intrigued by what I saw that later I decided to write him a letter consisting of the observations I had made while in his bedroom. I remember mentioning that I too was a Beatles fan. It was at this time that I was completely enamored with their song "Something." I told him that my favorite Beatles song was "While My Guitar Gently Weeps." I thought it was interesting that he liked *Catcher in the Rye*. I could see a little Holden Caulfield in Alistair. It was obvious to me why he might be drawn to that book. The perfection of his name was not wasted on me.

Sometime later, Alistair told me that he had read the letter and really appreciated it. I felt good about it. I had just done it on a whim.

Months later, Alistair's grandfather died. I didn't know what to say to him because I had heard he was really torn up over the death. I decided to send him a quick note saying that I cared and would be praying for him. Apparently, this note meant a lot to him, because he called me the next day at work to thank me. He told me that he had had an awful evening the night before and had been tired and cranky from the long flight back from England, but the note had turned everything around for him. I could tell that he was being sincere – more sincere than I had ever seen him. This episode marked the beginning of a series of love letters that he received from me over the last couple of years.

My letter writing to him became a love affair for me through letters, like in the novel *Desiree* about Napoleon and one of his loves. I confessed things to him in these letters that I had never revealed to myself. He made me feel sexual, and I liked it. I loved how passion felt so real with him, not just real but possible. It made me feel desirable that he wanted me. I got a rush from knowing that the only thing that stood in the way of being intimate with him was my refusal to be with him. I know that he knew there were parts of me saying yes. I had never been made to feel sexy before, and he did that for me. I told myself that if I were not a virgin, I would have given in. Giving one's virginity to someone is a big deal. Sex for Alistair is recreational, but for me it is everything.

I cannot help but wish that we valued the same things in life. He is this reckless soul with no real plans – just a mission to have as much fun as humanly possible. He once told me that he did not want to have children or get married. When I asked him why, he told me that he was already ruining one life so why destroy two more. That conversation made me so sad for him. Of all the things that I could wish for – that he loved me, that

I was someone different or that we could be together, like in my dreams – what I wish for him is that he finds that peace that they say passes all understanding. I do not know the stuff that his dreams are made of, but I hope that he finds what he searching for. I believe he is seeking that peace through his countless sexual encounters with different women every night, and through drugs and alcohol. I pray that his restless soul finds peace before it is too late for him. Sometimes, I think about him and what he is doing with his life, and my soul cries.

When I am honest with myself, I can admit that secretly I am waiting, praying, and wishing that he finds his way and that somewhere along this journey he decides to take me with him. I say that he is not the monogamist type, but I cannot help wishing that this might change. Begrudgingly, I will admit that I am one of those clueless women who believe her love can change a man. I keep hoping in the tiniest vessels of my heart that he will change and that I will be the woman who makes all the difference.

Even as I type, I feel myself becoming ill over this confession. I loathe being pathetic, and there is no fate worse than being clueless and pathetic over a man. Sometimes, I fool myself into thinking that I see something in him that is not visible to anyone else. I feel as if I am privy to the real man. He is one of the smartest people that I have ever encountered but, for some reason, he keeps that part of himself concealed. He has no problem with having people believe that he is an asshole, a drunk, and a pothead. He is definitely all of those things, but there is more. There is so much more.

I found out recently that we are both fans of the song, *Abraham, Martin and John*. Whenever I hear that song and it gets to the part where he says "the good they die young..." my mind and heart always flashes to Alistair. I cannot help but wonder why he likes the song. Does he feel a connection to it? His callous disregard for his life breaks my heart.

Alistair once told me that he sometimes has to reread my letters and double-check that they are addressed to him, because he cannot believe all the nice things I have observed about him. I thought that was the saddest admission I had ever heard. I guess the negative is easier to believe. I guess in some ways we are kindred spirits in this belief. Honestly, I think I am more in love with the idea of Alistair than the actual man. When I envision what I want in a mate, Alistair is not him. I wish desperately that he were, because then my affection for him would make sense.

I want to save Alistair from himself and I want to shield Paul from the pain of his past. Lucky thing for me neither of them is in love with me. The last thing either of them needs is a girlfriend with a savior complex.

The dumbest thing about my infatuations is that if either of them ever seriously responded to me in the affirmative, I would probably run away screaming. I am strange like that. Most people my age are out engaging in fun activities on a Friday evening, and I am here thinking about life, thinking about love, never actively doing anything about it. It is my hope that these ridiculous experiences will one day prove to have been worth it. It is also my hope that purging will somehow be cathartic and rid me of the desire to send out ridiculous love letters and desperate emails.

As of late, I have not written Alistair. I think I am slowly coming to my senses. Alistair has this way of letting me distance myself from him, but just when I am about to really rid myself of him, he calls and reels me back in. Just when I think I am finally disgusted with him, he does something out of character, and I am all fucked up again. I want to be friends with Alistair, but I am just tired of feeling crappy due to all of the drama that accompanies believing you are in love with someone who does not reciprocate your feelings. These things are never easy and hardly ever make any sense. Perhaps it's best this way.

Dancing For Rain in the Sahara

He touches me, and suddenly I am in a place that cannot explain. He kisses me, and I levitate all the way back to my car. I gasp for air and lose my breath when he is near. My heart feels so swollen and bruised inside my chest, and breathing becomes too painful. I look at him and dream about all the things that could be. I see him and am heartbroken by what is actually there. I am dying for answers that I am sure he cannot give. I love him so much sometimes it feels as if I may explode.

This all feels so unfair. I feel as if I understand him on so many levels but I cannot read him at all when it comes down to me. I don't know why, in the midst of beautiful women throwing themselves at him on a dance floor, he is focused on the one that says *no*. Does this mean something to him? Do I mean something to him? Am I some kind of conquest or does he truly want intimacy with me? I want to believe that, but I want it so desperately that I am scared I am seeing only what I want to see.

I want to ask these questions but I fear that probing will push him away. I wish I could cut out the part of my heart that loves him and weeps for him. I hate how deep I have let this get. He means so much more to me than he or I can explain. I want him to a better man for me but more importantly for himself. I want him to see what I see, love what I love. I hate how much energy I have put into loving him. I fear that there will be nothing left when it truly happens. In the deepest caverns of my mind I know that my fantasy will never come to fruition, yet I still love with the strongest and deepest part of myself.

Just when I think I have cleared my body of all toxins, Alistair re-enters my system with greater intensity. I am never truly rid of him. This is so unfair, to love him so much and know that we will never be together. I try to act nonchalant about his flirting with prettier, livelier women. I have gotten pretending not to notice down to an art form, but I see every smile and every close embrace. I wish that I did not tense up whenever he touched me or was close to me. I wish that I could be the person he wants me to be; but I cannot, no more than he can be the prince in my fairy tale. What good is it to be together and spend the whole time wishing we could be somebody else? I know that I will never be able to give it a chance, because I could not recover from the heartache that accompanies loving a man such as Alistair.

One of the worst pains for me is feeling jealous. I found out from Eric that Alistair was facing some serious issues and was drinking a lot to deal with the stress. Immediately, I lost my breath and thought, "I will die if he has gotten another girl pregnant." I do not know why this struck me with so much intensity. I actually felt tears welling up in my eyes as I waited for the news to fall from Eric's lips. It was as if the whole world stopped.

Finally, he told me that Alistair was in some legal trouble with past issues that had finally come back to haunt him. He might have to spend 45 days in jail. As soon as Eric told me this, I smiled. I could not stop smiling. I was giddy with happiness. I was a happy fool. Why was his impregnating another girl so potentially fatal for me? How sick is it to prefer that someone you love goes to jail rather than fathers a child with another woman?

I hate to admit this, but I think I would want to be that pregnant woman. I can never have him in the way I desire – or deserve, for that matter – and in some sick way, having his baby would be always having a connection to him. And suddenly, I have just become a potential guest on the Jerry Springer Show. I don't want to have a baby to keep him; I just want a way to keep a part of him that I will have forever. I am terrified that my memory will not be enough.

I write him letters because I am afraid to touch him with my hands, so I do it safely with my words. I dream about him because I am too afraid to let him touch me and too afraid to like it. I lie to myself because I am afraid I will lose whatever it is I have with him. I crave him silently because I am afraid to captivate him with my voice. I am afraid to do any of the things that really matter with him. I am afraid to truly love him, because that would mean I would have to trust him. Strangely, I trust with so many things except the most important part of myself: my heart. When I am around him, I feel as if my heart is on the outside of my body, visible and susceptible to harm.

The most frustrating thing of all is that I don't know what, if anything, he thinks or feels about me. I know he is not in love with me, but do I intrigue him? Does he notice me immediately, the way I do him? Is there a weak part of him, however small, that I have been able to capture? Are there times when he desperately tries to not think about me? I just want to know what questions keep him up at night. I want to know if there is a connection, or if I have made the whole thing up. Could I do that? Sadly, I think that I could, oh so easily.

It is as if the more I want Paul, the more I want Alistair. I am somehow in a romantic triangle with myself. When I am with Alistair, I feel as if I don't have a care in the world; but with Paul I feel it's OK to worry and to be afraid. I feel as if I will slowly go insane. It makes absolutely no sense for me to love them the way I do when we are nothing more than friends. Sometimes I think that if I had the option to travel life's path with one of the other, it would not really matter which one I chose; the destination would not ultimately mean happiness.

I seem to be this constant seeker of unrequited love. I do not know why this is the theme of my life. I really do think I know what it's like to be in love, but I can't know for absolute certain because I have never had anyone love me back that way. Can a person know what it's like to be in love without knowing what it feels like to be loved by someone romantically?

I felt all of this on a different scale with Constantine— *Record scratches and stops.* Who the hell is Constantine, right? Bear with me and we will get to him.

My feelings for Alistair and Paul are so out-of-control crazy, they are like nothing I have ever known before. As I sit here and ponder this, I feel tears beginning to form in my eyes. I want someone to fall in love with me. At least, I think I do. Do I follow hopeless causes because this is all I know? Do I feel safer in these types of doomed relationships? Am I doing all of this on purpose? Or do I just really suck at finding the right guy? Do I have some sort of pheromone that alerts men with any potential to steer clear of me? As ludicrous as this may sound, I honestly wonder at times. I feel like a deflated flotation device.

When others are patient enough to listen to me, I am always asked, "Well, do you put yourself in situations where you can meet men?" Every time I hear this, it confuses the hell out of me. Are they suggesting that I set up shop in a men's restroom? I live my life, I go where I want to go, and I go where I need to go. It seems like a person such as myself should run into an occasional man or two without advertising in a men's locker room. I seem to be a very friendly person. I have always had lots and lots of friends. Generally, people tend to like me. They just don't seem to love me *in that way*. I'm twenty-five years old and have never had a boyfriend. Either I'm doing something wrong, or there is something wrong with me. I just don't get it. It has to be me. Other people don't seem to have these problems.

I want to be an independent woman. I don't want to be the type that is dependent on a man for happiness or to feel important. I want independence, but I want to choose it; I don't want to be that strong, sophisticated single woman by default. I don't want to be alone because there were not any other options. I just want a man to love me. That seems so basic and simple. People walk away from horrible car wrecks, women conceive at 50, someone was actually able to teach a chimp sign language, and men have been able to walk on the moon; and yet a man can't walk to my door. I don't get it.

The Child

Recently, Alistair and I were together for a function. Lots of Alistair and Eric's friends had gathered downtown to watch Alistair's brother, who is the lead singer of a band. After the event, everyone headed to Alistair and Eric's. As is his fashion, Alistair had let himself get inexcusably inebriated. Most of the people at his home were high or drunk or both. As the evening slipped away and the morning crept in, all were still up dancing.

Alistair and I often have the same argument over and over again. He will continually ask me to dance with him and then become agitated when I refuse. We have known each other for almost three years and this scenario has never changed. On this night, on around the fourth time he asked, I decided to oblige. We started dancing, and he got a little too close for comfort, so I asked him to back up a bit. He got a little upset and said that I made him feel like a child molester. That comment hurt me badly. I was so upset that I slept with Eric and Sal that night, even though three in the bed was a little crowded.

I awoke to go to the bathroom and noticed that Alistair had passed out on the sofa. I took this opportunity to sleep in his bed. Later, he joined me. While lying in his bed with him, I told that he had really hurt me with the comment he made. He apologized and explained that he just wanted me to enjoy myself and that he gets frustrated when I keep to myself.

I told him that he had many character flaws, and I liked him despite those. I just wanted him to do the same with me. He rolled up close to me, and we just lay there listening to each other breathe. I wanted to tell him that I was ready and wanted to make love to him, but instead I just remained silent, hoping the moment would never end.

Finally we started to talk, and he spoke about his family and about how much he loved his mother. We discussed this feeling of emptiness that he felt and how he used drugs and alcohol to fill himself. He said all of this in a joking manner, with a dash of sarcasm added. I laughed aloud with him, but inside I felt my soul crying again. As he went on discussing various topics, I couldn't help but imagine what it would be like if something miraculous happened and we could be together and really make it work.

I want us to be together but I also want everything to change. I want him to be different, me to be different, and the timing to be different. Unfortunately for me, things are how they are; all I can do is accept what I cannot change and find the serenity I seek within that.

I love being around him. I love hearing him say my name; seeing him use his charm to make some random female feel sexy and beautiful; smelling him when he reeks of liquor from the night before or when he is wearing his best cologne; watching him dance while listening to his brother sing; hearing him say something obnoxious while intoxicated, and then turn around and say something meaningful the next day that makes the night before forgivable; feeling privileged when he lets me in just a little bit; lying next to him, trying desperately to fall asleep and not being able to help myself from watching him; hearing him discuss a movie or a song that means something to him; just feeling him close to me, those few moments when I am brave enough to look into his eyes, the moments when my heart skips a beat just from seeing his face: these are the things that I love. This is my Alistair experience.

He tells me all the time that he feels like I am two people. The person who writes him letters and the shy virgin he comes into contact with. I know this must be confusing to him. Every single time I have told him how much I want him it was the truth, but every time I have explained to him that I am different and that I don't act on desires was also the truth. The things I confess to him are the truth. These things are not hollow. I cannot explain the depth behind these thoughts, feelings, and urges. At times, I am more honest with him than I have ever been with myself.

He wants the kind of woman who will tell him what she wants and how she wants it. I am not her. I want to be, but I am not. No matter how many different people reside in my head, all of them just want to be close to him (I stole that from the Carpenters). This relationship has taught me to expect nothing. As soon as there are expectations, I will be disappointed.

I want to be able to accept him always, just the way he is. I want to love that person, even when he is self-destructive, reckless, insensitive and in need of prayer. He doesn't understand that a few uninterrupted moments with him is everything to me. Those seconds of real intimacy between us is what I live for.

The touches, the stares, the words, the memories that drive me crazy. In love and longing for what could be instead of dealing with the harsh reality of what actually is. This obsession has been cruel, poetic, haunting, unforgettable, unforgiving, unyielding and my own. I look at his picture with my eyes closed, and I stare through the darkness. The pain is a sick pleasure I revel in. I have swooned over his callousness, written poems regarding his indifference, wept for his reckless disregard and had beautiful dreams about the demons that haunt him – all in effort to not forget how it feels.

I wait by a phone that never rings; I have heard things that he has never uttered. I have wished that I could cut out the part of my heart that belongs to him but fear there would be nothing left. How did a few magical moments become everything? I've watched him sleep and desired to lay my hand across his chest and feel his heartbeat (just to make sure that it's there). I've been intoxicated by his smell. Somewhere between that place of consciousness and sleep, his aroma is strong and comes to me, comforting me like an old friend. I smell him so as not to forget how it feels.

He's on my mind even when he's not; he's always there, like some phantom. I hate myself for becoming so weak. I hate myself for falling for him. I walked into this with my eyes wide open. He never made any secret as to who he is. He's a playboy, a hedonist – irresponsible, inconsiderate, and also the man I dream is holding me as I sleep. He is my addiction. One hit of him is never enough; a little only makes me crave more.

I've always longed for the impossible; I love him solely because he's unattainable. I fill my veins with him - to not forget how it feels. I find reminders of him everywhere. He's in every song I sing and lies between the words of everything I read – everything brings me back to him. The farther I run from him, the closer it seems to bring me. He's inescapable. I cannot breathe deeply without breathing him in. I inhale him - to not forget how it feels.

The letters, journal entries, and poetry are all there so as not to forget how loving him feels. I never want to forget the pure exhilaration his touch brings, the joy his humor brings, or the passion he inspires in my dreams – or how his intellect intrigues me and loving him makes me feel alive. I live when I think of him, I live when I cry over him, and I live when I allow myself to admit I love him. To forget how it feels would be more than I can bear.

Nothing this painful has ever proved worthwhile in the way this has. I've given up on a lifetime for fleeting moments. I have let myself lose all control and direction when it comes to him. When it comes to him, I never know where I'm going until I am there. I have always hated being lost, but I feel found in the chaos that is his life. I want to be a part of his life. I want a place in his upside-down world. I want to know that I matter and that he does think about me in weak moments. I want to know that I creep into his mind at random times during the day. I need to know that I matter to him in some way. I need to know, to not forget how it feels.

Eric, one of Alistair's closest friends, told me that I needed to stop loving Alistair and stop longing to give him my virginity. He went on to say that I needed to find a good guy – someone as wholesome as I am. I know all of this.

I know how pathetic this relationship is. I have to live it day in and day out. I know that Alistair is a cad and will always be one. I know that he doesn't fully appreciate the person I am. I know that he is on a downward spiral. I know that he can't possibly love me when he hates himself so much. I don't want this to end with me hating him, but I do want this to end, because it is painful and useless. All this has been is fodder for this story I am attempting to tell. I don't know what I want out of all this, and that is the honest truth.

I don't know how this will end or where it will go. I have no clue how this story will end. I just take it one day at a time. Whatever the truth may be, I know that he has ignited a flame in me that I hope will never die. I keep hoping that one day this will all make sense. There has been too much for it to have meant nothing. I believe that everything happens for a reason, and if I were simply brought into his life to tell him that he is better than he knows, or if he was brought into mine to give me those rushes I had only read about before I met him, I would take that happily. Our two very different lives have collided for a reason. This I know without question.

I don't know what I am doing. I don't know what is happening with my life. I spend more time daydreaming about what my life could be than I spend focusing on what my life actually is. I don't even know now who I love more: Alistair or Paul. Forever, it was Paul hands down. He is a good person with quiet demons that he wards off by keeping himself very closed off from any sort of intimacy.

Alistair's demons are monstrous, haunting and cruel; he finds his escape through the alcohol he drinks, and through the faceless and nameless women that he fucks, and through the drugs that levitate him to his own special and serene place.

Paul is dependable and honest. Alistair is not. If I were with Paul, I would always feel secure when we were apart. If I were with Alistair, my heart would ache and be fearful whenever we were not together. The last thing he wants to do is hurt me, but this is bigger than him now. He couldn't help but hurt me. This is all so clear, but God help me I love them both. I have spent countless hours obsessing over them. This has been a gross waste of my time, considering that I will really never be with either one of them. No amount of hoping will make it so. It all seems so unfair. I am screaming inside, wondering what I have done wrong. Why am I so hopeless?

I keep wondering why this is how it has to be. I love with everything that I have, and I can't seem to have that reciprocated. Maybe I am too romantic and not realistic enough. Is it ridiculous to believe in soul mates? Does being in love really exist? Is being in love just something that one person made up and everyone else has sort of jumped on the bandwagon, claiming to have had the same experience? Or have I just missed it entirely?

My solace has been found in these two men, and maybe that's what I am finding so hard to give up. Many times, I have prayed, said, or yelled that I want that peace, which they say passes all understanding, to wrap around Alistair and hold onto him for dear life; but maybe that's what I need to find for myself. Maybe I am more like Alistair than I have ever admitted. He fills his voids with drugs and alcohol, and I fill mine with romantic fantasies. We are all looking for something and not having any luck finding it.

Last night, a great friend of mine called and asked me to be in her wedding. I was taken aback. I knew she was dating someone, but I hadn't expected to hear they were getting married in four months. She is one of my best friends, and I am very happy for her; but I am so jealous I cannot even breathe. She was the friend I commiserated with over our pathetic love lives, and now our club of two is down to one.

I feel so left behind. I have known both Alistair and Paul longer than she has known her future husband. This realization slapped me in the face. I have wasted years of my life rallying behind lost causes. What would my life be like right now if Alistair and Paul hadn't been at the center of it? Damn me for wasting this time and energy. Damn them for letting me.

Rage

I'm pissed off, vexed, in a fit of blind rage. I am mad as hell. I am so mad that I cannot see straight. What have I been thinking? When I think about the amount of time I have wasted lusting after a loser and Mr. Emotionally Constipated, I want to spit and slap the hell out of myself. These relationships were doomed from the start. Alistair is never going to settle down, change his life, and stay committed to one woman; and Paul considers intimacy a death sentence. Why have I been hoping these things would change? I could remain in this hell for a decade and nothing would come of it but wasted time – *my* wasted time.

In some ways, my life has been on hold. I had been convinced that one of these relationships would pan out and I would be with either Paul or Alistair, but the blinders are starting to fade. Slowly, I am realizing that this was all made up, a fantasy of some sort. My love doesn't have the power to change these men. It never did. Wishing like hell for something doesn't make it so.

I know that I am not going to end up with one of them, yet I still love both of them with every fiber of my being. How can this be? Maybe I am in love with the pain and reveling in my own misery. Maybe I can't differentiate pleasure from pain; perhaps they are the same experience for me. Some months ago, I had a bladder infection. It took me a while to figure out whether the sensation I was experiencing was pain. I knew something weird was going on, but I couldn't decide whether I liked the feeling or not. Finally, after a few days, I realized that I was in pain. Maybe the Paul-Alistair infection has taken over my body, very gradually, gently teasing and caressing my heart and soul pretending to be a friend instead of a foe. Penicillin cleared up the problem with my bladder, but as far as I know there is no known elixir to fight an infection of the soul.

When I am in the presence of these men, I feel fine. All is right with the world while I am with them or communicating with them in some fashion. But out of their presence, I am in a constant state of rage thinking about the fool I have been. I could write hundreds and hundreds of pages on how I have wasted my life and why I am too good to wait around for them to realize what a great find I truly am. But at the end of the day, I will rock myself to sleep with visions of them dancing around in my head.

No matter how clearly things are shown to me, I keep going back. I keep putting myself in places where I might run into Alistair. I send him one pathetic love letter after another. I continue to email Paul daily in a desperate effort to ensure that he never forgets me. Sometimes, I feel that this whole ordeal should be a level in Dante's Inferno. **To forever pine for those who will never love you in return.** My own personal living hell. The worst part of all of this is that I have done it to myself. I am here by no one's hand but my own. No one is forcing me to stay here. My refusal to let go of Alistair and Paul is my crime and consequence. Neither one of these men has led me on in anyway. I have led myself astray.

I keep trying to figure out why I have done this to myself. My close friends and family are perplexed as to how I have let things go on this long. I have no way to explain any of this to any of them, because I don't understand. I sometimes wish they would both decide not to speak to me any longer and stop responding to my letters and emails. Maybe that's what it will take for me to get myself back. I am not strong enough to let go of those sparse moments of pure joy that I derive from simply talking to them or being in their presence. I cannot let go, and that scares the hell out of me. Being out of control is not something I ever wanted. I just can't stop myself from thinking about them, dreaming about them, and longing to be with them. I just need to be slapped hard and consistently until the spell is broken. I need to be able to let go and move on. I am not growing in this box I have placed myself in.

I cannot even imagine my life without the two of them in it. How did I get here? It is as if my life prior to them doesn't exist. There was a time when I was an interesting person. I used to be able to engage in conversations in which their names never came up. What happened to that girl? I liked that girl. Why didn't I tell her that I liked her? It took her disappearance for me to realize that she was interesting, smart, and worthy of being noticed by equally charming men. I hope I can find her again and that she hasn't been lost forever in the chaos I have created.

I am burnt out on love at twenty-five. If I focused as hard on my aspirations for law school as I do with these men, I might one day find myself on the Supreme Court. I wish I were this committed to some worthwhile cause. The deeper I fall into this, the harder it will be for me to climb my way out. I have tried shaming myself publicly in the hopes that I would somehow come to my senses and let go, but nothing has worked. I am trapped.

I have contemplated calling Paul and putting everything out there and letting him tell me once and for good that we are just friends and he does not love me and never will. That might work, but I haven't been able to muster up the courage to make that call. I guess that means that on some level I want to continually mislead myself. Fantasy is so much better than reality; at least, it is in my world. When I am not hurting, I am angry; and when I am not angry, I am sublimely happy – until that starts to hurt, and then I start to hurt all over again. The pain always seems to last so much longer that those exhilarating moments I spoke of earlier.

I am more concerned with obsessing over whether or not they are thinking about me than I am with my health challenges caused by my lupus. I check my email daily, like clockwork, to see if Paul has written me, yet I cannot remember to refill medications that I take for my disease. I have got to start loving myself. If I could love myself the way I love Alistair and Paul, I would be one self-assured woman. Perhaps I love them because it is easier to shower affection onto them than onto myself. As anyone can see, I could write hundreds and hundreds of pages on why I love these two very different men. I don't even know if I could muster up a paragraph on what I love about myself.

Maybe I have stumbled onto something. Could all of this be a clever ruse to escape having to deal with myself? I have made Paul and Alistair's non-interest in me my fault. I have translated their less-than-romantic feelings for me to mean that there is something wrong with me. I have felt like I am not enough for them – that somehow something was wrong with me. I kept thinking that maybe, if I corrected some character flaw, they would deem me worthy to love.

How can I expect someone else to love me when I so clearly do not love myself? How can I sell a product that I don't believe in? People are attracted to confidence, and so the opposite must be true of people who are lacking it. I have spent more time than I will admit feeling insecure about my body and intellect. I feel too dumb for one and too hideous for the other.

Alistair loves to touch me, and I love those moments, but they are ruined by my insecurities. I tell myself that we haven't made love because I am waiting for marriage and to meet the right man, but really I am disgusted by my body and am horrified to share it with anyone. He asks me all the time why I care so much about what other people think. I always shrug my shoulders. I don't know why.

I have heard somewhere that being shy and self-conscious is a form of narcissism, because the individual feels as if people are paying more attention to them than the people actually are. It's weird to think of myself as a narcissist. Most times in crowds, I wish that I could shrink so small I would not be noticed by anyone. I hate people paying attention to me; there are many times that I have wanted to be invisible. I sometimes feel as if the whole world is watching me and laughing. I don't know why I always feel like I am the punch line of some joke. The sad thing is that I am the one, for the most part, who is telling the joke.

No one loathes me the way I loathe me. Don't get me wrong, I have a lot of good qualities; but it's the bad ones that somehow stand out the most. I have always heard so many more good things about myself than negative, but it's the negative things that stay with us forever. Deep hurts are the worst kind of hurt; they are the ones that never heal. Sometimes I wonder if people ever consider the weight of their criticism of others. If only we understood how much we damage and hurt each other with the things that we say. A person is always their own worst critic; another negative voice is the last thing any of us need.

I know that over the course of my life, I have said something pretty hurtful things to people and never thought twice about the impact my words have had on those individuals' lives. I know that I will forever be sorry for some of the things I have said to people which have left painful scars on their lives. We never know how much we hurt one another.

Cervantes' Windmills

I have played out this drama of complicated love scenarios more times than I care to admit. I have had my heart broken repeatedly throughout this staged event. The only difference between other people and me is that I have lived this through my dreams and imagination. I have agonized over loving two men who do not love me – who do not really *know* me, for that matter. My imagination has led me down a dangerous path.

I have created non-existent problems and have come up with futile solutions. I think I have been in love with the idea of being in love, as opposed to actually being in love with either Alistair or Paul. I have made connections that haven't really been there; I've engaged in intimate moments that we haven't shared. This experience has been a mirage of some sort. I have been so thirsty that I have been willing to quench that thirst at any cost.

Things in my life have not been easy but never unbearable. I know what it is like to hurt; I know pain; I am no stranger to disappointment; but I have never truly suffered. I perceive this aching in my heart as my biggest pain, the tragedy of my life. Slowly, however, I am realizing that this pain I am in is not insufferable. There are times when I feel so unbelievably alone and am desperate to be comforted, but I am never truly alone. I have a host of relatives and close friends that are never too far away. If ever I truly needed something, I know that someone would be there for me in an instant. I have spent far too much time focusing on who doesn't love me instead of being thankful for those that do.

I blame my vivid imagination on the fact that I am an only child. Only children have no choice but to be creative. I also blame my obsession on romantic movies, songs, and books. Since I was a small child, I have envisioned intricate, complicated tales of romance. I have grown up believing in Prince Charming. In my mind, being in love has always been the best part of being alive. I guess making sure it isn't the *only* reason to live becomes increasingly more important over time. I have never wanted the mundane. I have always had caviar dreams on a sardine budget. I have sought after the fairy tale my whole life – damn that Walt Disney.

I know that I am going to have to realize that life isn't a movie or romantic song; sometimes life is ugly, sometimes it is hard for no apparent reason, but most times it is worth living. The ugly somehow makes the pretty beautiful and the suffering makes the joy phenomenal. The pain I have experienced seeking love has been real, making me real and the experience real. This journey would have not been worthwhile if it had all been perfect. How do you appreciate the good times if there have never been any bad times?

This is how I should feel. I know what to say, but the only problem is that I can't make myself feel that way.

I do not know how long my love for these men will go on; perhaps it will never end. I truly believe that when you genuinely love someone, no matter what separates you, you will love him forever – if you're lucky enough to find him. If there was no other choice and I was forced to name one thing that I like – well, love – about myself, I'd have to say it is my ability to feel. I excel at feeling. I love my ability to feel deeply; it is what I do best. I am not ashamed of loving Alistair or Paul. I'm really not all that regretful about it either, even though I have said otherwise in the past. I am confused about a lot of things, but I know that I care for them deeply.

Oddly enough, I have never spent a great amount of time with either of them prior to falling for them. It was something immediate that attracted me to both of them. Loving them has been so innate for me. I feel as if all of this was meant to be, in some weird, convoluted, deranged way. Nothing makes sense and for a while that bothered the hell out of me. I guess I am learning that not everything has to work out like some algebraic equation. Sometimes you just have to take things as they are and be thankful for what you are given.

Sal has tried so hard to understand my infatuation with both Alistair and Paul. She probably knows me better than anyone, but on this issue she is just a perplexed as the next person. People tell me all the time that they cannot imagine wasting as much time as I have trying to figure out why I have such a yen for these two. I think the answer to that question lies somewhere with Jimmy Hoffa's remains, or it could be hiding somewhere with those weapons of mass destruction … who knows? I have learned some valuable lessons throughout this soap opera. I know that I am braver than I've ever realized. I understand myself a lot better than I thought I did.

I let Paul read a good portion of my writing, and he told me that my writing became weak and I lost my power when I wrote about him. He also told me that I put myself down a lot when I write about him and that I make him out to be this angel. He wondered if I wasn't seeing him correctly, or if he had done a poor job of accurately presenting himself to me.

I responded by saying that I was of the opinion that my writing about him was some of my better work. I also informed him that I did not see him as perfect or without flaws; I considered him not being in love with me a huge character flaw on his part.

He has not yet responded. His refusal to respond to any of my questions related to anything remotely intimate is normal for our relationship. When he does not know what to say, he says nothing. I do find his method frustrating but also a bit freeing. I feel free to tell him anything about my feelings concerning him, because I know he will not respond to me and this eliminates any fear of being embarrassed. We've both learned to play these little games with one another. He ignores me when I tell him that I love him, and I attempt to become more and more outrageous with my declarations of love for him. I have gone from telling him that he is going to marry me, come hell or high water, to making not-so-cryptic sexual innuendoes to him. Paul's safe; he is a place of refuge.

He is so easy to be friends with. He doesn't require anything of me and never tries to change me into his ideal. He just accepts the obnoxious person that I become when it comes to him. I know that on a lot of levels, he wishes that I didn't think I loved him. He doesn't think I am truly in love with him. I know it must be hard for him to tiptoe around my emotions because he is such a nice guy. He seems to appreciate all of the eccentricities that accompany me. He appreciates that I love the Carpenters, that I cry at romance movies and sometimes even sitcoms, that I have already picked out names for my (our) children, that I call his cell phone to hear his voice on his voice mail, that I could be in love with someone I haven't seen in almost three years, and that I write love letters to men I am too afraid to talk to. I feel good in the skin I am in when it comes to him.

I feel as if it is possible for him to love me right now, at this moment, just as I am. I don't have to wear a mask with him. I can be the shy virgin who is fearful of her feelings and desires, and that's alright with him. I think part of the reason that I love him so much is because I feel free to be myself with him. I feel as if he truly sees fat me, insecure me, big-hearted me, super-sensitive me, seeker-of-miracles me, believer-in-soul-mates me, ugly me, pretty me, the real me. I find some comfort in the fact that it's been about four years and he is still in my life.

I often remind him that if I didn't write him or call him, we would have no relationship, and this usually strikes a nerve with him. That statement is only partly true. This emailing thing we have going couldn't have lasted over the years if he wasn't writing back, so I guess on some level he is getting something he needs out of the relationship. We have been friends for awhile now, but I still practice what I am going to say when I call him on the phone. There are times when I make notes. Somehow, that doesn't sound as ludicrous in my head.

He is always so patient with me. Even when I can tell that I have pushed all the wrong buttons with him, he is always kind and reassuring. I love him to death, but it really pisses me off that he is not in love with me. I am so ridiculous at times, I do realize this. Paul never makes me feel pathetic or desperate. He just makes me feel good. I like who I am for the most part when it comes to him. He truly cares about me, and when he tells me that he prays for me, I know that he honestly does. He could pray for God to intervene and stop me from harassing him, but he prays for my health and well being. He is such a good friend to a person who doesn't truly appreciate what a gift that truly is. I still get these rushes when I check my email and he has written me. I am always hoping that the email I receive will be the one where he says everything I have been longing to hear for far too long. Unfortunately, that email never arrives.

I've Let Him Places Deeper than My Vagina

There is nothing left to say, nothing left to hide. Everything is out and exposed. I finally came clean with Alistair about the real reason we have never made love. In the past, I have told him that I was waiting for marriage, or at least waiting to fall in love with someone who loved me in return. This was all true until I met Alistair.

Since my senior year of high school, I have been taking steroids to help control my condition. Since that time, I have gained around eighty pounds. I hate my fat body. I am disgusted with myself and couldn't stand to share it with anyone. My insecurities keep me from Alistair. I have tried to put myself in situations with him and hope that the insecurities melt away, but they never do. I know that I have to learn to love myself before anyone else will.

I keep thinking that Paul could love me like this. I think this is why I hold onto him with everything in me. I have made him this perfect being and made myself believe he is the only man who could ever love me. That's why it is so excruciating to even contemplate letting him go. I feel that if I lose him, I lose my only chance to have someone love me – the real me. He doesn't understand what I have made him mean to me. How did I get here? My problem is me, not the men that I love. I am the problem. I turn kindness into romance, I turn attention into affection, and I turn a kind word into love. The question I must answer is, Why?

I hate what I have done to myself. My low self-esteem is ruining my life. I won't be happy until I learn to make myself happy. I can't find my own happiness through other people, through a man. I have to be happy alone to be happy with someone else. That's the journey that I need to make - the journey to self-discovery. I have to fall in love with myself. I have to know that I am someone who deserves to be loved. I am someone, regardless of whether I have a man in my life. When I really learn this, I think the road to recovery can't be too far off.

I am good at loving another person – I *excel* at loving another person – but I need to shower that affection on myself. When I think of all the time I have wasted musing over Constantine, Paul, and Alistair, I feel ill. I could have used all that wasted time to get through law school, lose weight, strengthen my relationship with God; instead, I used it sending emails, writing letters, and swooning over fantasies. The lost time is what hurts the most: all those years, months, weeks, days, hours, minutes and seconds are lost to me forever. I will never get the time back. I have to turn this sinking ship around. I am the one in control. I have to remember that. If I don't want to be the *me* of the past, I just simply have to stop. If I don't change soon, the damage will be irreparable.

I found out recently that Alistair's computer was stricken with some brutal virus meaning he has been unable to check his email. I guess I have been given a sort of stay of execution. He is still in the dark as to why I cringe when he touches me, even though I love his touches. I am thankful for the extra time, but I wish there were a way I could get that email back. I don't think I am ready to be that honest with him. I'm not ready to be that vulnerable. I wish this thing with Alistair was just physical, but it's so much deeper than I ever dreamed it would be. Even though it may seem that I use the L-word loosely, I really do believe that I am in love with him.

Alistair is not the sort of man you fall for. He is the kind of man who shows up on your doorstep at 3 AM with lovin' on his mind. He is the sort of man who will make love to you all night long and then forget to call the next day. In some ways, I think that all people desire to know someone loves them for no other reason than them just being themselves. Alistair is strange there. He seems to prefer people who do not love him or give a damn about him. All that does is make me want to love him all the more.

I love everything about him: the good and all the bad. I fell in love with all his sinister habits, his sarcasm, his salacious sexual appetite, his reverence for sin, and his amazing ability to leave a woman broken-hearted. What a pair we make, the virgin and the rebel.

Both Alistair and Paul act as if loving them is some act against nature. They are both perplexed as to why and how I claim to love them so much. Loving them feels innate to me. I do it without even trying. It's like breathing for me. It was easy to let them in so deep, but it seems to be impossible to remove them. Sometimes I wonder if laziness is why I continue after these two men. I mean to put all this energy into another man, but it just makes me feel tired to think about it. I feel as if I could never bring another man up to speed. These two know so much about me; I have invested so much of myself into them. I don't know if I'll be able to do that again.

When this is all said and done, I don't know what I will have gleaned from the experience; but I hope it makes me wiser. I don't want to fall in love like this ever again. I don't even know if want to fall in love again at all, period. I don't know if my poor, poor heart can take this again.

I sit here, thinking about all of this, listening to the Bee Gees singing "How Deep Is Your Love?" and wonder when I became so melodramatic. I wonder what Alistair is thinking about at this very moment. I can't help but wonder if I have come across his mind at all today. I just wonder. Does he only think of me when he sees me? I want to die when I think about how many times he crosses my mind. I don't help myself by having pictures of him all over my office and in my apartment. He is literally everywhere I turn.

I've looked at these pictures millions of times; I have every trace of his face burned into my memory. I am aware of every curve, eyelash, and even the shape of his eyes. I know his face better than I know the back of my hand. I am so familiar with every part of him, and yet still when I look at a picture of him or see him, he still manages to take my breath away. Every time is like the first time with him. I never seem to become jaded by the experience. How does he do it? I'm dying to know. I've let these two men into the deepest part of myself.

I try to reassure myself by saying that these experiences will help me grow as a person. Each page I type, or poem I write, helps me to understand myself so much better. I don't always understand why I feel a certain way, but I always know what I am feeling. I have tried to compare this to other people's experiences, and it never adds up. This used to alarm me, but now I find comfort in the discrepancies. I like to think that this is a unique situation. This perspective helps me to accept that things don't always have to make sense. It doesn't make sense, and that's all right with me now.

There are rare moments when I feel fortunate to know what it is like to truly love a person. I can't help but sometimes wonder what it feels like to be loved so deeply by another. I think Paul finds the affection overwhelming at times. I think he feels a lot of responsibility when it comes to my feelings. He owes me nothing, but the person he is makes him feel some level of obligation to me. I don't know why. He hates that not loving me causes me pain. He can't make himself feel something for me but he can't bring himself to ignore me either. Alistair does not feel this same level of obligation to me. When we see each other he's sweet to me, but in the meantime he doesn't give me a second thought. He doesn't love me and has probably never taken the time to realize what that does to me or how it makes me feel.

I don't want anyone talking to me or spending time with me because of a false sense of obligation. But at least I know that Paul cares about how I feel. I know Paul values me as a person and a friend. I don't have a clue as to how Alistair feels about me. I almost don't want to know. I can continue on in this fantasy as long as I don't let reality creep in.

I haven't seen Alistair in a few weeks and, surprisingly, I have been doing well with the time apart. Well, I was doing fine, until I heard *Abraham, Martin and John* the other day in the car. Ever since then, I have been craving him like crazy. It's weird how simple things can trigger such strong emotions.

I think what I want most is to find someone, get married, have children, and lead a simple life. Family is very important to me. Neither Alistair nor Paul has any desire to get married or have children. In all honesty, I think Paul is starting to feel that tug. He likes kids, and I know he wants to have children, even though he claims that he doesn't. He does want these things, just not with me. He'd make a wonderful father.

Alistair told me once that if he had a child, he'd have to clean up his act. He couldn't be someone's father and be the burnt out, alcoholic pothead he currently is today. In some sick way, that made me happy. I was glad to know that he would clean up his life for a child. It also made me sad that he is so aware of his hedonistic lifestyle and yet makes no effort to live a safer, more responsible life.

Sometimes, I wonder if I would love Alistair as much if he were less reckless. I'm afraid that's what might be attractive to me. Alistair is the first "bad boy" I have ever had any sort of relationship with. Alistair has this way of charging up all of my sexual energy. He is the first man to have had that sort of affect on me. It's frightening, but most times it's exciting and unpredictable. He makes me want to do things that I've never dreamed I'd want to do. Most times, I can't tell if this is love or lust. I keep telling myself I want a family with Alistair, but maybe it's just passion I crave with him.

He has the same affect on me that a flame has on a moth. I know he will burn me, but I can't help myself from moving closer and closer to him. The more he pisses me off, the more passionate I feel about him. My fixation with him is a sick one – one that I have more than enjoyed over the last three years. Three years, I can't believe I have had this yearning for him for this long and have not acted on any impulses.

A few months after graduation, Sal and I attended a Sugar and Spice Party, which are parties attended by women only where the sales person demonstrates what's new in the land of sex toys. Actually, we went to several. It was at one of these parties that I decided to let go and make a purchase. I choose the silver bullet. As a twenty-five-year-old virgin, I wasn't exactly sure what to do with the contraption, but it looked less complicated than the "wasically wabbit."

One long, curious afternoon, I decided to pull the bullet out and experiment with it. The first thing I did was make sure that I was home alone. When I was sure I was alone, I pulled down my panties to my ankles and got into my bed. Initially, I turned the bullet on and put it near my vagina; then slowly, I let the bullet touch my parts of my vagina. I slowly moved it around and turned it up, which made the bullet move faster and throb harder. It wasn't long before I realized I had the bullet right where it was supposed to be. My heart began racing, my lower extremities were pulsating. My head flung back and my toes began to curl. I felt this deep itch inside me; it was so deep. I knew if I could reach it something spectacular would happen. I knew if I could hit that spot, there would be an explosion. After many more minutes, I hit that itch; and as expected there was an eruption. There was liquid everywhere that had been expelled from my body. My moans had turned into screams. And there, at twenty-five, I had my first orgasm – and I had given to myself. Why had it taken me so long to figure this out???

It's funny how I turn twenty-five and suddenly I'm obsessed with marriage and having a family. The logical part of me knows that twenty-five is not old, and being single at this age isn't going to doom me to a life of spinsterhood; but in weak moments, being single depresses the hell out of me. Twenty-five seemed to come so fast, and I am terrified that the next twenty-five will come just as fast. I know you can't rush these things, but I am running out of patience. I am a nice person and fairly intelligent, but I can't seem to make that connection with anyone. People seem to appreciate family but are not as into having one of their own. Alistair and Paul both seem to value family – both in their own way, of course. Paul would sacrifice his whole life for his family, a sacrifice that he has already made for many years now. To see the pride in Alistair's eyes when he watches his brother perform gives me chills every time I see the two of them together.

Paul reminds me so much of George Bailey from *It's A Wonderful Life*. Paul, like George, has the hardest time leaving his own personal Bedford Falls. Paul is very committed to his family. He seems to plan his life around how he can best serve them. A few months ago, Paul's grandmother died. He took it very hard because they were close. While grieving for her, he mentioned that it might be time for him to move out and venture on his own. He had been helping his parents care for his grandparents for many years. Paul has two brothers – one older, one younger – but he seems to be the child who has heaped all the familial responsibilities on himself. He has this strong commitment to his family. I love this about him, but I can't help but wish that he would try to carve out a separate life for himself. Most everything I know about Paul comes from me piecing together the little pieces of his life he gives to me. I have no clue if any of these assumptions are accurate.

One of the few things that Paul and Alistair have in common is how much they love their mothers. Alistair told me once that if his mother died, he'd have no reason to live after that. That really scared the hell out of me, because I knew he was telling the truth.

I know from some of the things Paul has told me that he has gone through some rough times with his mother and older brother. He has never discussed any of this in detail with me. I know that the man he considers his dad is not his biological father. From past conversations, I get the impression that his biological father is a jerk who Paul has no desire to see much less have any sort of relationship with.

Alistair has never mentioned his father to me. I know that his father is British. I saw a movie recently where the leading man said to the leading actress, "I want to love you past your pain." What a great sentiment I thought to myself. I wish I could communicate that to Alistair and Paul. None of this information came from Alistair but from random people that know him a little better or maybe a little longer than I have. Alistair seems to have this fear of people finding out that he is not a complete moron. He seems to be more comfortable in that skin.

I know that I will never be as important to them as their family, but I am desperate for some place in their life. I just want to be special to them. I want to know that all of this didn't just mean something to me but meant something to the two of them. I am learning to accept that friendship is going to have to be enough for me. It is a hard lesson to learn, but I realize the importance of mastering this. I can't ever be happy if I continue to wish for something that won't ever happen.

My relationships with Alistair and Paul did not happen in a vacuum. I had some practice in pathetic behavior with someone while in high school. My history is one of loving men that won't – or can't; I'm not sure if there's a difference – love me. His name is Constantine and I think he was really the first person I ever loved romantically. Remember earlier I mentioned there was a third guy? Well, this was him.

Where It All Began

I mentioned at the start that there were three great loves of my life. It was my intention to finish this story without mentioning the third, but I realized to leave him out would be dishonest, and that this connection meant more to me than I have ever wanted to admit. Those feelings have been so buried for so long that to exhume them will be a hard undertaking for me, but I feel it's important to look at all the twists and turns my low self esteem has taken me in pursuit of love.

There is no point in my life where I have felt beautiful or special or worthy of notice. He made me feel visible at a time when I thought the world was ignoring me. It all started the summer before my junior year of high school. When I first met Constantine, I was not at all impressed. He was a nice guy but there were no immediate fireworks.

That summer, he and I and two other friends had to go on a retreat with a summer internship in North Carolina that we were all involved in. It was at this retreat that I really got to know him. He had a girlfriend at the time and spoke of her often.

One night, we were all awake very late, sharing stories and laughing about the happenings that had occurred during the school year. I do not recall why he began to speak of his girlfriend, but I will never forget what he said. He told us that his girlfriend was not the prettiest of girls but that she was a beautiful person on the inside, and that was what he was attracted to.

My whole life I had wished that I could find someone to love me for the person that I was on the inside. I felt as if no one would ever love me because they lost interest before they got to see the person I really am.

On the last night, we had a bonfire. Everyone was to write down a wish or a worry and burn it, and that was supposed to make our wish come true or give us an answer to something we were seeking. We had to walk a long way to get to the bonfire. After I burned my piece of paper, I was ready to go back to the cabin. However, my two girlfriends were not ready to go and wanted to send me on my way by myself with just a flashlight. Constantine told them that he would go back also, because he did not want me to go back alone.

I cannot for the life of me remember what we talked about on the way to the cabin. At one point, he rushed ahead, and I was little ill about it but as soon as he came back into focus I saw he was there to help me cross over a difficult part of the trail. He had gone ahead because he didn't know exactly where the spot was and didn't want me to get hurt. Everyone knew that I had problems with my legs; no one, including me, knew that lupus was the culprit. As we walked, I remember studying him and realizing how good-looking he really was. I had never noticed before.

When we returned to school after the summer, Constantine and I were closer than ever. We talked on the phone all summer and met up a few times to hang out. By the time school started, I was deep in this crush. We ate lunch together, we sat next to each other in all the classes we had together, we talked on the phone every evening; he would call me and we would talk right before I fell asleep. I would sleep with the phone under my pillow so I would be sure not to miss the call. The feelings began to build and build in me, as if I was about to explode.

We went out one afternoon, and as the day ended we sat down on a park bench and talked. He asked me if there was anyone in our class that I had a crush on. I wanted to lie, but I decided to take a chance that maybe he was asking because he wanted me to say it was him. I told him that indeed there was someone I was infatuated with.

He begged and pleaded for me to tell him. I laughed and laughed as he named the boys in our class. I noticed that he never mentioned his own name. He asked me questions about himself indirectly. He'd say, "Is the person tall?" "Is it someone I'm friends with?" "Does the person have a girlfriend?" I knew the truth would be a dead giveaway, so I lied and said the mystery man was not attached to a girlfriend. He looked me in the eyes and asked if that were the truth. I told him that it was, and he said I was lying and he could tell.

We were on a park bench waiting for my mother to pick me up at a neutral meeting spot. We lived far from each other, so it was easier for my mom to get me after we were finished hanging out. When I saw my mother starting to turn into the parking lot, I told him that I would tell him what he wanted to know, but if I revealed my secret crush he could not speak to me for a whole week to give me time to recover from the embarrassment – and even then I might need more time.

We were both silent as my mother's car approached us, and then he told me, "Mary, if I can't talk to you for a week, I don't want to know."

I looked at him and smiled and floated all the way to my mother's car.

Weeks later, I decided that I had to tell him because I was dying. One night, I psyched myself up to confess all when he called me. Like clockwork that evening, he called.

I took the call in my bedroom and shut the door. I quickly told him to not say anything and that when I was done, I was hanging up right away. I started by saying, "I go to school sometimes when I am sick, because I want to see you. These phone calls are the highlight of my evening. I think about you all the time, and I don't know why. Sometimes when I am with you, I feel like I cannot breathe. My night is not complete unless I hear you tell me goodnight. I have never ever felt this way about anyone before."

I was already to hang up when he said, "Wait, Mary, please. I feel the exact same way."

I felt as if I was dreaming. Had I heard him right? I do not remember how that conversation ended, but that night changed my whole life. I had never been special to a man before, and I was seventeen years old – better late than never, I guess.

We were inseparable after that. The phone calls increased, the outings increased, and the feelings increased. I felt as if I loved him, and that terrified me. I remember one night it got really late and I figured he was not going to call so I fell asleep.

Late that night, the phone rang, and it was him. He said, "Mary, it's really late and I'm exhausted, but I just couldn't go to bed without saying goodnight to you. Good night, and I will see you tomorrow."

I couldn't believe that someone had to talk to me before they could fall asleep. No other person has been able to make me feel like that since.

Time passed and graduation was upon us. I remember that we decided to take each other's yearbook home to write something in them and bring them back the next day. I decided to make mine meaningful but not overly sentimental. I figured he would probably do the same.

I remember getting my yearbook back and being in complete shock over what he wrote. His message went as follows,

Mary,

With everything that has happened over the last year, I'm sort of at a loss as to what to say. I could start somewhere in North Carolina, or at the start of the school year, or at the end, but nothing could really sum up what you've meant to me. I know I'm not the greatest at showing emotion, but I am never lacking it. Don't ever think that I was oblivious to you, because I wasn't. Even if I looked like my eyes were straight ahead and you were on the side, I never lost sight of you. You've taught me a lot about what it means to listen, about what it means to care about someone and care for them, what it means to have a soul mate, what it's like love, and what it's like to be loved. All the ups and downs, criticisms, comments and opinions really don't mean anything now. The way I figure it, people who want to judge will not mean anything later on, but our relationship is something that can never be lost, or dropped, or stopped. Some bonds mean too much, and some mean more than any word can describe. I will always carry you in my heart. I love you.

Constantine

This message meant the world to me. This was verification that I was not alone in the feelings I had. After reading this, I knew it had all had been real and not in my mind.

The summer before we went to college, we tried to hang out as much as possible. I told him that I wanted him to take me somewhere special to close the day. He took me back to the park where everything had started. We were very silent that day and seldom made any eye contact. I thought at one point he was going to kiss me, and I turned away. To this day, I don't know why I did that. What if that was the moment we were supposed to share? What if that was the moment that would have made us end up together? Maybe if I had let it happen, I'd be the woman who now shares his bed. We had such a strange relationship; we were never a couple and remained only friends, although I went through my entire freshmen year feeling as though I had a boyfriend in school in Florida.

My freshmen year of college was hell. I missed him so terribly that we wrote via email every day and talked every week. As the time passed by, we drifted apart, and he had what seemed like girlfriend after girlfriend. Finally, he met her: there was something different about this one. He met her, and they got married and had a child together. I can tell that he loves her so much, and I am happy for him; but I am always curious thinking about what could have been.

It wasn't until 2001 that I was finally able to let him go (so I thought). I had loved him since 1996. It was a hard past-time to give up. I wrote him the following good bye letter, which I never mailed, right before he got married.

Constantine,

My life would be so much easier if I could just hate you. I feel as if I spend too much of my time convincing myself that I am not thinking about you. I don't understand this grip you have over my heart. We are so wrong for each other, but that does not make letting go of you any easier. You have had such a profound effect on my life, and I sometimes wonder if that is a good thing. I am not angry with you for not calling, or for not writing, but for not caring. I have spent so much time loving you that I don't know how to be different.

I want so desperately to not love you and to forget about you, but that is like forgetting to breathe. Loving you just felt natural; it was innate. Loving you does not make any sense. No matter how many other guys come into my life, you are always there in the back of mind and in that place in my heart that is reserved for you and only you. Maybe I can't let you go because you represent a time in my life when I was happy, and everything I have done since is an attempt to get back there, to those moments that seemed to mean so much to both of us.

Hearing you laugh at the things I said made me feel alive; laughing at the things you said made me happy to be alive. I told myself that the last letter was truly the last letter, so I pray this letter never finds its way to you. The thing that's the craziest is it does not hurt me to know that you don't care, but it kills me that you know I still do. What plagues my mind is how come I was so easy to forget? Why didn't losing me hurt you and cause you to stay up very late writing bad poetry? Why isn't my smile so engraved in your mind that you couldn't forget it even if you wanted to? Some songs I hear remind me so much of you that it feels unbearable.

In my youth, the feelings I had for you were beautiful, and now they are anchors pulling me in a direction that I can no longer go. I decided very young to let myself fall, and I have been trying to catch myself ever since.

Do you ever miss me? Are you ever doing some random tedious chore of life and all of a sudden you wonder what I'm doing or what I am thinking at that particular moment? Or better yet, do you ever wonder whether we are thinking about each other at the same time? If not, why not? Why was I so easy to forget? Did you ever love me? Could I have imagined the whole thing? Perhaps that is the reason nothing can compare to how I feel about you. Nothing is as good as we imagine it. It has been years, and I am still up late contemplating my feelings for you. Just for one day, I wish we could trade places; I will be the cavalier bastard and you the weepy romantic.

Maybe it is hard to let go because things ended so unfinished, and I was afraid to love you in high school. I keep thinking maybe if I had done something differently you'd be preparing to marry me right now. Why is the heartache lasting longer than the relationship? I hope one day, when you are sleeping comfortably in your bed – content, reflecting on your life with happiness because your life is exactly how you envisioned it – that in a weak moment your mind will flash to me (who you haven't considered in years), and you will awake in a cold sweat wondering, what if?

One thing I know is that no one will ever love you the way I have. I know that we were not meant to be; we both deserve better. I am stronger today than I was then, but I know that given the right speech and that look in your eyes I have grown to love, that I would try. You went from an unexpected blessing to an incurable disease. I have grown weary from serving as host to memories of you. I am very afraid that my biggest hurt will always also serve as my biggest joy. Sometimes, I wish that we could be together for just one day, so I would truly know that us being apart is for the best. We never made promises to each other, but for some reason I feel as if you have broken promises to me. I feel betrayed by you, but there is no rational reason for this. There is no rational reason for any of this.

I needed to thank you for serving as the muse for my adolescent poetry and for being my story to share with the girls – and for being my reason for smiling for no apparent reason. I thank you most of all for allowing me to know what it is that I want in a friend, soul mate, lover, and spouse. Now that I know what I want, I will not take anything less, not even from you, my teacher. I cannot continue to tell myself you care when everything you do says you don't. I think all I ever really wanted from you was to know that I mattered to you. I wanted to know that if I ever truly needed you, you would be just a phone call away. I wanted a friend in you; I wanted to find my best friend in you. I foolishly believed that you were my soul mate. I held on so tightly when everything told me to let go. I just wanted then what I want now: to be with someone who understands. I was looking for something deeper than friendship and less common than infatuation and not as overrated as being in love.

What kills me is that you still like me. You want to be my friend. I don't want to be friends. I am trying my level best to hate you. I have not been successful, but the last thing in the world I want is to be friends. Maybe it's immature, but friendship cannot occur between us. I need to forget about you. I don't like who I am when it comes to you. With you, I suddenly become all that I hate. I become weak, naive, and poetic, not to mention pathetic. I want to know what life is like not carrying you so deeply in my heart. I sometimes wonder who I would have been had I not met you. I wish I could change history and erase ours the way you have, with such ease and little grace.

Mary

That piece of paper I burned so many years ago at the retreat had the following written on it: "I hope Constantine changes my life." That he did, that he did.

...

Constantine is now married with four children. He has been married with children for several years now. For a while we had a great relationship, and then I ruined it, which is what I do when I get my feelings hurt. He was very generous to me during a time when I wasn't working and his wife had a problem with the terms of endearment I used for him. I'm southern, and I call everyone "honey" - to me it is nothing.

I didn't like the way Constantine talked to me about the issue, and I will admit I might have overreacted some by insinuating his wife was a hag and that he was weak and needed to grow some balls. I wasn't really all that upset with his wife because she doesn't know me, but he sure does. He didn't deserve my wrath; after all, he was doing me the favor, right? But I just couldn't help myself. What an ego???? Of course, I meant everything the way he took it, but he didn't know that – and to take it that way was a bit conceited, right? For the longest time I couldn't admit it, but now I sort of feel that our relationship – although, we were young – should matter for something. I'm not his wife. I'm not the mother of his children. We won't grow old together. But I did love him first, and that feels like it should mean something, even if only to me.

I can't believe how much resentment I still feel towards him because he found love. He was able to get it right, and I wasn't. Why wasn't I? I couldn't make it right with him. We had something complicated and special, but it wasn't something I could name or pinpoint. It wasn't simple. One would think I would have learned something from this experience and put it into practice with Paul and Alistair.

Denial, Anger, Bargaining, Depression, And Finally ... Acceptance

She wrote,

Hey Paul,

Last night I had this weird dream that I want to share with you. I dreamed that we saw each other a lot, I guess because we lived in the same area. In my dream, you told me that you had an English girlfriend and that you stayed the night at her house and slept on the sofa. I know this sounds weird, but it's true. I was very mad at you in my dream, because apparently I had been doing the dorky stuff I do in real life in the dream. I was angry, because she had been your girlfriend for years and you had never said anything. I felt like you should have told me earlier on, so I could have stopped being a dumbass.

When I woke up, I was so glad it was a dream. Then I thought about it and realized it wasn't so far off. Inevitably, one day, this *will* happen. You are a nice person and will meet someone that you like. I have got to get myself in a better place, because I am wasting a lot of time hoping for something that is never going to happen. The dream was very sobering.

In my dream, I was destroyed, and I don't want that to happen for real. Life is so weird. I was talking to my cousin about this the other night. It's as if a single man always has at least two hundred desperate women that he could date if he wanted to, and he'd have no trouble finding a woman to marry. Women, on the other hand, seem to have trouble finding a man. Maybe there are more women than men. Anyway, after we talked, I realized that I don't want to be one of the desperate two hundred. Well, this stuff was on my mind, so I wrote about it.

With much affection,
Mary

He wrote,

Mary,
Well, let's get some stuff out in the open since you seem to be digging. I do go on dates, and right now I'm talking to this girl (Agnes) I work with at TV Depot. We've been friends for a long time (since I started there last year), and we go out with friends. She was in a relationship for a long time and is interested in companionship, and that's cool. That's about all there is to tell there. You made a paranoid remark one day about her, back when I mentioned I was watching her dog while she was on vacation with her mom, and I GUESS you weren't far off. I tell you this because it seems like you were asking, "Is there someone, anyone at all?" and even though this isn't something I've hidden (we aren't dating, and I don't like to jump to conclusions), I think this will come across like something completely out of the blue to you, perhaps.

Anyway, I guess I'll write more later ... I need to get some laundry done and get off to work.
Paul

And with that, a three-year fantasy ended. I actually think I heard my heart break when I read his email.
She wrote,

Paul,

I have this tendency of giving people tests unbeknownst to them. I kept telling myself that if we were truly friends, you would write me back. Then I thought about how long you can go without writing and that I would explode by then. So I guess I am willing to have that question unanswered. I have had a very full weekend. I did manage to do a little thinking. When I first got your email, I was shocked and then LIVID at myself. I felt stupid and regretful. I tried to be angry with you, but the sane part of myself couldn't allow me to do that. Surprisingly, I haven't discussed any of this with anyone. I have sort of been dealing with things on my own. Honestly, I was humiliated enough not to write you, but I had this epiphany this evening that was stronger than my embarrassment.

I am a very open person. That is my greatest and worst trait. Nothing happens in my life that I don't share with someone. You are not at all as open as I am about things. This isn't a new revelation for me, but it has suddenly taken on a new meaning. I tell you everything that happens in my life, and I know this is my choice, but I was just blown away to find I was so off-base in terms of knowing what is going on in yours. Right now, I don't know how I feel. I have felt angry, humiliated, and now nothing. Actually, I think I am regretful at this particular moment. There are so many things I should not have said, done, felt, desired, and prayed for. Suddenly, this three-year fantasy has ended, and I don't know how to act. I just don't know who to be right now.

I keep trying to reassure myself by saying there is never anything wrong with being honest. That brings me little comfort. I know that I have said things in the past that were "paranoid" and pathetic in regards to you and your love life. I thought I had tried really hard to be your friend, but now I know that isn't the truth. I had tried really hard to carve out a little place in your heart for me. A friend would have had a relationship with you that made you feel comfortable enough to discuss your personal life with me. I have certainly taken some wrong turns throughout this journey. I admit that, and I am trying to forgive myself for those mistakes.

I had this image of you being this emotionally constipated person who would have problems with intimacy with anyone. I guess in some ways I accepted this about you. I didn't care, as long as that was how you were with other people. I needed to believe that in my own way, I had this intimacy with you. Maybe that's why I felt so compelled to share things with you. I needed to believe that on some level I meant something to you and that you had contact with me because you wanted to and not because you pity me.

I also realize that I clung to you so tightly because you were safe. I have more than my fair share of drama weighing down on me and this is something that I just won't carry. I can't do it. It is ridiculous to be so upset over something so _____ (I don't know what to put there, so just pick a word and fill it in). I have spent more time thinking about all of this than I will ever admit. I don't understand my feelings. On some levels, I feel sad. Maybe it's because I enjoyed this ride, and I am sorry that it's over; or maybe it's because I feel as if something is wrong with me.

There's this book called *LOVE LANGUAGES*, and it's basically about the different ways people express their love. I'm so confused right now. I think maybe we aren't friends, and then I think that's stupid and quickly move on to something new. I am a talker. I tell people things, and I have a hard time relating to people who express emotions through actions and other means. Maybe it's stupidity that makes me need things to be laid out in black and white. I think one of the things that bothers me the most is that I don't really know that we are friends. I write you, so you write me back; I make you a CD, so you make me one; or I call you, and

_____. I know this will probably piss you off but this is how I feel, so I hope it doesn't.

A person might think that there is no such thing as loving a person too much or admiring someone so much, but there are some things wrong with that. I have made you a little too important to me. I can't for the life of me figure out why. I did it to fill some kind of void. I must have needed someone to play that role and I elected you. On a lot of levels, that wasn't fair. I made you who I wanted you to be. I wanted to believe that I have a deep and personal relationship with you. I needed to believe that. I needed to think that you cared about me in some form or fashion that wasn't as common as being email pals. You are a very nice person, and for whatever reason you maintained some kind of relationship with me; and I don't want to undermine any of that.

I'd be lying if I wrote that I wasn't hurt. I'd be lying if I wrote that I wasn't disappointed. What is so disappointing and what hurts so badly is that I have to wake up now. I have no choice, and that's what kills. I can't live in this reality if the only time I feel really alive is in fantasies and dreams. I have done myself such a disservice. I feel compelled to write here that I am over the romantic fantasies and I am really on the friendship page, but I don't know if that's the truth. I don't know if the humiliation will ever allow me to be so open anymore or ever be able to see you or talk to you without wanting to disappear or pretend to be someone else.

I don't know what tomorrow will bring. Maybe I'll wake up and things will be all better and I will be able to send you my stupid daily emails, or maybe I won't be able to for awhile – or ever. I just don't know. My feelings change with each breath. I said earlier that I was regretful about a lot and that is the truth, but I can't discount the whole experience. I have been genuinely happy to receive your emails, your surprises in the mail, and the blue-moon phone calls. I have genuinely been glad that I met you. I have learned so much about myself the last few years, and for that I am grateful. I think I am on my way to becoming a better writer because of the last few years.

I wish I knew the perfect thing to write to end this email. I wish I knew the right way to feel right now. I wish I were smarter, more realistic, more honest with myself, and – most of I all – I wish I didn't think I loved you. I'm sorry if all of this was ridiculous and hopeless to you. Just be glad that you only had to read it and not feel it. All this isn't just because of your last email. This has been coming for a long time. I have been trying to wake up for awhile now. I have felt dumb for a long time. I'm not mad at you and could never hate you, even in my most insane irrational moments. You know that, so to go on and list all the reasons why I could never hate you would be a waste of time, because you know all of that shit; I have been telling you those things for three fucking years. Feelings haven't changed, just my perspective. So maybe I am growing, if only just a little bit.

    With Much Affection,
    Mary

He wrote,

Mary,
This is the most honest I think you've ever been with me. You say you talk a lot, and you say you share feelings, but I think you'll find that if you look over the last three years and compare it with this latest letter, it's written by a very different person than I've been reading. I don't say that out of anger, and I don't say it with any negative implications whatsoever. It's just a fact.

The last email I sent you, well, I knew it would cause something. I didn't know what, EXACTLY, but I guess I did. That said, I didn't do it to humiliate you, a word you used very often in your letter. I know you say you're not angry with me, but I'm pretty sure you are. I sent that email out of the most sincere and bold-faced honesty I could muster up, and you know what? – every word was true, and there was nothing hidden there. I am not, for instance, dating anyone.

My relationship with you has not changed, in my eyes, and you can't be serious if you want me really to believe that I've never gone out with a friend who happened to be a girl in the last three years.

The funny thing is, you were right about something that you think you are now wrong about. I'm very bottled up emotionally. I don't give myself to people easily. You know this, but you assume now, I think, that I'm just that way with you, which just isn't true. It's not true at all. People get along with me, but for years, people have wondered why I haven't either been DATING or flat-out married. It's something I can't answer either. For years, I genuinely had no interest in dating. For years, I had no interest in marriage. That has changed but slightly.

I'm not an easy person to get close to, and it frustrates the hell out of people. It's an insecurity thing with me, I think. If I stay far away, people get interested, and as long as people are interested, as long as I keep them guessing, there's no chance I've overstayed my welcome or bored them to death. It's when I get close to people that I feel like I will lose them.

I feel I've done you a great disservice over the years. My lack of communication (I've probably said more in the last three paragraphs than I have in a hundred emails) has left you in a whirl of doubt and self-examination and anxiety. I'm sorry. But I'm not sorry that I've been your friend. I was not your friend out of pity.

I'm not sure what I'm trying to say or if there's anything left to say at this point. You wrote your letter with such an air of finality that I'll be honest ... it took me aback. Don't be ashamed and don't be sad and don't regret it. But it really shook me.

I will say this. I feel like you've spent a long time thinking about me, and I'm not worthy. I'm not, Mary. You seem to have come to this conclusion on your own, of course, but I'm going to say it (even though I've basically said it in the past, especially in response to your writings). If you believe we are not friends, I understand. Maybe I'm even lying to myself and to you when I say we are. But I don't believe that.

Then again, maybe you're right. Maybe if I were your friend, I would have called more, I would have visited more (or ever), and I wouldn't merely have reciprocated when you did something for me (I don't believe I've done that, but you can think what you want). I'm sorry if I haven't lived up to your expectations as a friend or as what you wanted me to be.

I've long thought I was doing you a disservice, like I said, just by BEING your friend. You had heaped so much false imagery on top of the "real" me that I had become something that I wasn't. You probably wouldn't even recognize me if you met me today, and you've actually wondered about that in past emails. Or maybe it wasn't all false; it was just glorified, and you dwelled on the good as if it were the whole. I'm rambling here, and I think you're going to read some of this as being a lot more harsh than I intend it to be, but I'm sending it anyway. Just read it with care, and read it again if you have to.

Perhaps it really is time for you to take a breath, even though NOTHING has changed but your own perspective. Maybe you should just leave me waiting and waiting for an email that never seems to arrive and, when it does, it answers no questions and reveals nothing. That's how I feel I've treated you at this point, given what you've said, and that's being as blunt as I can be.

Paul

She wrote,

Hey,

I seem to have turned into such a crybaby lately. I cried Thursday and then Friday because I had a migraine. I cried Saturday because my dad got released from the hospital, and then again on Sunday when he returned to the hospital. I continued to cry as I wrote that email to you last night and then I cried this morning when I read yours. Maybe its hormones or God only knows what else could be wrong with me.

I am a wreck. I don't know how to fix anything. I don't even know that it's even possible. I wanted so desperately to give all of this some space and some time and figure out why I am behaving so irrationally. When I wrote you last night, I really wanted to be able to get some self-control and wait before I wrote you back. Obviously, I am still lacking the self-control that I am seeking. I sincerely and honestly don't want to stop being friends or being able to communicate with you. I know I don't want that. I just want it to not make me feel bad – that's what I want to end. I am far too weak to stop being your friend and break all communication with you. I learned that today. I just thought that maybe if I said it, or in this case wrote it, I would be able to. I can't stress enough that's not what I meant. I just feel like crap and I don't know what I hell I am saying or feeling most of the time.

I do feel as if you are worth all the adoration. I know that everything that I have ever said about you is how I honestly feel about you. I am just trying to get myself to a place where I understand that I can't focus all of my energy there. I don't even know if that made any damn sense. This whole thing isn't about living up to expectations. Or maybe it is, but if anything I haven't lived up to my own. I loathe being weak. That's not what I want for myself. The truth is that I think we are friends, but I think it's because I have demanded that you not forget about me or ignore me for very long. I don't mean that rudely, but it's true. I don't think that you'd never write me, but I know the reason we have communicated as much as we have is because I have been a woman possessed. I didn't want to come across as if I was saying, "I thought you were so great. Boy, I sure was wrong!" That's not it at all. I am not angry with you. I have no legitimate reason to be.

My favorite scene in the movie *AMERICAN BEAUTY* is when Kevin Spacey is talking to the neighbor boy. Spacey is having a hard time believing that the kid's parents don't know he is doing something shady to buy all this cool stuff he has, and the kid responds by saying, "Never underestimate the power of denial." I love that. That's me, and so when you say that I had to know that you were going on a date, that's not necessarily the truth. I didn't want to think that, so I didn't. I just kept thinking, "He'd mention it." I now realize that I have been a complete psycho for some time now and didn't act maturely when you mentioned females to me. Why in the hell would you mention it to me? I get this now.

I'm so sick to death of all the thinking and feeling that I do. I'm just tired. I am trying to figure things out and that's what I know right now. I meant a lot of what I said, and then maybe again I didn't. I just don't know. I am just sorry for a lot of stuff that I have done. I know that I just want to be your friend and don't want all of the other feelings that I have. I want to be OK with just being friends. I want to get to a point where you feel comfortable enough to mention things to me. I am not there yet, but I am trying so hard to get there.

I do know that dealing with stuff like this isn't something you like to do, so I do appreciate that you took the time to write me back and sort of deal with some emotional stuff with me. I don't have any more left to write on this subject so you don't have to worry about these LONG emails on this topic. I once asked if we could start over and forget all the stupid romantic stuff I said and thought about. You told me that was impossible because that stuff was an inextricable part of our friendship. I know that's true, but I am going to try anyway. I don't mean that I don't want you to write me back if you have more to say. I just want you to know that I've said everything. I'm just going to try and move on and leave the heavy stuff alone for awhile.

Write me back if you want to on this topic or anything. I am going to try to work through my emotions and feelings concerning you. I am sorry if I said or did anything that was offensive to you. And lastly, I do know that you are a hard person to be close to. I know that's not just with me. I just meant that going out on dates and that kind of stuff is you opening up a little. I was jealous. I think that's the real truth. Saying that I am jealous can just sum everything up. I am woman enough or foolish enough to admit that.

With much affection,
Mary

He wrote,

Mary,
And let me reiterate: I have been on one blind date (disaster) and a few "dates" with this girl I've mentioned. We're pals, and that's that. You can call them outings, or group gatherings, or whatever. I'm not big on the dating scene by any stretch of the imagination, but it wouldn't be unfair to say that you're right about my opening up a little. Things begin to unfold, one might say.

I think this email you've just sent me finds you still in a rough state emotionally, but I think there's already something good happening here. I really do. Maybe it's something you added to add positivism unconsciously, but I don't think so. I want you to feel better and be happy, and it makes me absolutely sick that I'm involved in your unhappiness. I'm so sorry for that, and you don't have to tell me it's not my fault.

Have you given real thought to moving back to your hometown lately? When you mentioned it, I got the feeling it was something you really wanted, and I daresay it's something that I think you might really need. At the very least, you need to take a break.

Keep in touch with me, write about whatever you want, don't try to calculate.

Talk to you soon.
P

Last Friday night, I was alone and feeling romantic. On the way home from work I heard *Abraham, Martin and John*. Immediately, I became fixated on my thoughts about Alistair. I decided to turn on some Etta James and began to write what must be the millionth letter I have written him over the last few years. The letter went something like this,

Alistair,

I had been doing well in terms of pestering you. I have actually been focused on things other than you. I was on the road to recovery, I swear it, and then the other afternoon I was having the worst day, so I turned on the radio to relax, and I heard *Abraham, Martin and John*, and I was fucked up again. I am hoping that rehabilitation is within my reach. I have this nerdy tendency of going to the bookstore and walking around for hours. Barnes and Noble is my favorite store, because I can get coffee and just look at books. I know I need help. I really do know this. Anyway, I was in B and N, and I was so tempted to buy Bill Clinton's book. I wanted to buy it, and then I saw this stationery. I picked this paper over my husband's book. I am glad that I made the purchase, but I know I will probably break down and buy his book; after all, he is my husband. It's only right.

I think I bought the stationery because I am this ridiculous romantic, and it's so alluring to me to write sappy letters on expensive paper. I write about you a lot more than I am willing to admit at this point. In many ways, I think writing has been cathartic for me. Maybe that's why I have been able to control myself A LITTLE MORE. I guess even a little control is better than nothing, so I guess this is progress for me.

I have about four pictures of you in my office. I know it's pathetic. In my defense, I also have pictures of Sal, Eric and a lot of you guys' crew from the Café. Anyway, I digress. Whenever I get really busy and I am totally focused on work, I will make the mistake of catching a glimpse of your face, and it takes my breath away. I am literally left breathless. I don't know why any of this is the way it is. I don't know why I can't stop myself from writing you or thinking about you. If I knew of some sort of elixir that I could drink and wake up from this intoxicating fantasy that I have created, I would so drink it. I make myself miserable. It's like, I like you, and so what? I won't do anything about it other than write you these juvenile letters. Can you imagine how frustrating this is for me? I have turned into some kind of masochist that gets some sort of erotic pleasure from torturing myself and testing my ability to resist temptation.

I have all of these scenarios playing out in my head as to what kind of a person you really are. The scenario I like best is thinking of you as this idiot savant with haunting, monstrously cruel demons. I don't think of you as retarded, but I used "idiot savant" for lack of a better explanation. I hope you forgive me for that.

Lately, I have been doing a lot of thinking about my life and where it's going and what I want out of it. I realized that I am really a very simple person and it's the little things that mean the most. A few moments of uninterrupted time with you sometimes feels like everything to me. I feel like every now and then I get these milliseconds of real intimacy with you, and that's ... well, that's just indescribable for me. Imagine that, I am at a loss for words.

I am embarrassingly addicted to television. I have to work on that, but it's because of this addiction that I had the following revelation: I become this human TiVo when it comes to you. It's like I record everything that happens with you or that I hear you say, or things I hear about you. It's scary or pathetic, I can't decide which, so I will let you decide. I still get weak in the knees thinking about moments with you that happened so long ago. Things I know you don't remember, because most of the time you were inexcusably inebriated.

One memory that stands out the most is listening to you talk about the movie, *Punch-Drunk Love.* I hated that movie, but after I listened to you I didn't hate it anymore. What stays with me most is hearing you talk about the piano. You said something about liking the fact that the piano was left in the street and Sandler's character had to go and get it. He wanted it, so he had to go and get it. If a person truly wants something, they have to want it bad enough to go and get it. I don't know why that has stayed with me for so long. Then you made this remarkably observant and brilliant comment about how most everything in life is about love. Everything

somehow always comes down to that. If I didn't love you before, then I certainly did from that moment on.

**With Much Affection,
Mary**

Whenever I write him, my life then revolves around delivering the letter to him. The next night, Sal I went to the movies. We have this way of only going to this one theater that happens to be about five miles from Alistair and Eric's house. We have this unspoken understanding that we will see all movies at this theater. It is very rare for us not to stop by their house after we've seen a movie. I knew this, so I made sure to bring Alistair's letter with me.

When we arrived at the house, Alistair was outside with friends, laughing and drinking in the doorway of his house. I attempted to walk past him and put the letter in his room so I wouldn't have to embarrass myself in front of his friends. He made some comment about me walking past him and trying to ignore him. I told him it wasn't my intention to ignore him. He followed me to his room, and I gave him the letter. He looked at it and asked, "Is this a good letter or a mean one?"

I told him that my letters to him were never mean. He nodded and agreed but said that sometimes they were "condescending" and made him feel as if he should change his life. I wanted to slide in a smart remark, but I refrained for some reason. His reference to some of my letters as condescending kept rolling around in my head. I knew I would obsess over that comment for awhile.

When we left his room, he asked if I knew how to play dominos. I told him I had never played. He then asked me to watch him and his friends play. I tried to pay attention but found the game to be quite boring. I quickly lost interest, but I would suffer any discomfort to be by his side. I sat there around his table with him and his friends as they smoked marijuana, got drunk off beer and made obnoxious statements. A large cloud of smoke was blown directly in my face, and I thought, "Why in the hell am I here right now?" At that moment, he asked me something, and I quickly remembered why I was there: he was there, and where he would go I would go.

Alistair's friend, Tony, asked where all the women were. Alistair looked at him and then at me and said, "I am only interested in one," and stroked my arm.

I looked directly in his face and said, "Shut up." When he says things like that, it makes me so angry. I knew he was lying, he knew he was lying and all his friends knew he was lying.

After a few games of dominos, one of his friends suggested that the already tipsy group should go to a bar downtown. I watched as each person stated why he or she could not be the person to drive. Some passed because they realized they were too far gone to drive, and others passed because they already had DUI charges on their records. It was at this moment that I volunteered to drive them all downtown.

At first, Alistair declined the offer, but a few moments later he recanted his refusal and asked me to drive them. The group seemed surprised that I would drive them to a bar at 2 AM. I kept thinking, don't they know that I would crawl on broken glass for that boy?

In the car, Alistair rode up front with me. It was obvious that Alistair was already drunk and that driving him to a bar was going to prove to be a bad idea. While in the car, an Aerosmith song came on. As soon as I heard the song, I thought I was going to be sick.

Alistair turned the radio up and began to sing the song as loudly as he could. He asked me why I wasn't singing, and I told him that the song always brought back a bad memory for me. He misunderstood what I said and thought I had told him that *this* night was going to be a bad memory for me. I corrected him, but he still seemed to be stuck on what he thought I had said. He went on and on about how much he cared about me and told me that he never wanted to be a bad memory for me, nor did he want me to have any regrets about him. I knew that he was drunk, but something about the way he looked at me when he said it made me believe him. He then took my hand and held it until we got downtown.

I knew that if we were alone, I would have given in and finally let myself make love to him that night. When we arrived at the bar, he grabbed my hand again and said, "Thank you so much for driving us. I know that I would have been stupid and would have attempted to drive."

He got out of the car and walked around to my window. I rolled it down to hear what he had to say. He leaned in and kissed me on the face and then grabbed my hand one more time.

Without thinking, I said, "I'll see you later."

He looked back, smiled and said, "Really?"

I didn't mean it literally; it had just come out. I looked at him and shrugged my shoulders.

On the way back to his house to pick up Sal, I started thinking about the night. Suddenly, it hit me that I would do anything for him. I would even have come back and picked him up from the bar, if he had asked me to. They had decided they would split a cab back to his house. I couldn't stop myself from smiling. I had this renewed feeling of love for him, and it felt good. It felt damn good. I rolled down all the windows and let the cold night air rush all over me and cranked up the radio. "Hey Jude" was playing. Somehow, that just felt right, so I sang as loudly as I could. I felt like it is playing just for me.

When I got back to the house, Sal was already asleep. I woke her up and told her that I loved Alistair. She looked at me rolled her eyes and tried to go back to sleep. I again nudged her and told her I was serious. "I really am in love with him," I told her.

Again, she looked at me, rolled her eyes and went back to sleep. In Sal's mind, Alistair is tantamount to a walking venereal disease. I was feeling so ardent that I didn't even try to convince her to get up and go home. I wanted to wait for Alistair.

I fell asleep next to Sal, and a few hours later Eric entered the room and told me that "my boy" was home. I moved to get up, but Eric went on to say that Alistair was very drunk and was falling down and knocking things over. I wanted to remember the car ride; I didn't want to lose that moment. He was drunk, and any idea that I had of any romance seemed ridiculous. I decided it would be best if I stayed put. I still don't know if that was a good or bad call.

Sometime during the night, I moved from Eric's room to a futon in their den. Early the next morning, I was awakened by the most maddening sound. It could be equated to nails on a chalkboard: the sound of a female giggling from his room. I frantically grabbed pieces of paper out of my purse and searched for gum wrappers to journal my emotions right that second. At the time, journaling seemed like the best therapy.

All I can do is focus on that damn giggle. I am infuriated by its sound. I feel like the character in Poe's *The Tell-Tale Heart*. Poe's protagonist was driven mad by the sound of a dead man's beating heart, and I by that giggle. I have no real reason to be upset, but I am dying inside. Why did I choose to stay? Why couldn't I just go back to sleep? I am so jealous that I can't even breathe. My teeth are grinding, my heart is pounding, and my stomach is in knots. Being angry and

heartbroken doesn't make any sense; it's ludicrous. Right now, all that is keeping me sane is writing. If only I could just write forever.

That giggle is driving me insane. I am straining trying to hear what is being said in there. What's killing me is that I have no right to be mad or hurt, but I'm both. Now it's quiet. Maybe they went back to sleep, or worse. I was wrong; the silence is worse than the giggle. What would happen if I made a scene? I feel like making a scene. It always seems to come down to this: me outside the bedroom, wishing I were inside. I feel as if my insides are melting. I want to rip out her larynx.

Maybe I need this to slap me in the face. I need reality to slap me in the face. I need to stop all of this. Why am I waiting around here? I'm waiting here so when she leaves, he can make this alright for me. I just want to be alright. I don't want to hurt like this anymore. I wish I didn't care that he is in there with HER. I can't be only his friend, caring this deeply. "You're not with him, Mary. Let's remember that. He's just being who he is, the person you have fallen in love with."

That damn giggling has started up again, only now it's softer and somehow gentler. I was right at first – the giggling is worse. I don't think I can endure much more of this. I hate myself right now. I just want to go back to sleep. I am running out of damn receipts to write on. What am I waiting for? I could so easily go in and wake Sal up and tell her I need to leave, but no, I am waiting for him. I am waiting for him. This is so sick. I am a sick and twisted person. I'd believe anything right now. I need this to stop, and I need the pain to stop. Maybe I should tell him what all of this is doing to me?

How did I get here? This is no longer fun for me. I used to only hurt when I was away from him, reflecting on the reality of this relationship; now I hurt when I'm with him. The girls don't matter. They're like the letter x in an algebra equation. It's what they stand for that kills me. He can't be different, so I have no choice but to be different. I am jealous of a bunch of unnamed, unidentified women, whom I don't have the courage to be like. I can't fuck him, but I sure can write about how much I'd like to. This is what I do: I write in lieu of living.

There's that damn giggle again. I've managed to ruin my whole week in one night. I've played out this scene many times. I will die if Sal learns of any of this after my declarations to her the night before. I wish I could go back to sleep. He's no altar boy, yet I put these unrealistic expectations on him. I am about to explode! Everything with him is an illusion. If I look close enough, I can see the smoke, trap doors, mirrors and strings.

I always push this too far. Why didn't I leave on the high last night? Had I left, I would have woke up singing an entirely different tune. It's like I have this insane plan to hurt myself so deeply. I thought we connected, but obviously that was not the case. Part of me wants to bang on his door and make a scene. How psycho is that? When did I turn into Glenn Close in *Fatal Attraction*? If I opt for the scene, maybe I'll humiliate myself to the point of no return. Maybe I will be too embarrassed to return to the scene of the crime. I don't think it's possible for me to feel any worse. OK, Mary, if you were assertive and bold, what would you do? I'm going to bang on that bastard's door! I'll think of something when the door opens. Why couldn't I just go back to sleep?

I banged on the door twice before he answered. He said, "Come in."

Slowly I opened the door. He and the X were lying on his bed, fully clothed but very close together. My heart went to my throat. All I could muster was a pitiful, "I'm leaving. Goodbye."

Would you believe the X had the audacity to smile and wave at me like we were friends? She had no idea how close she came to not making it out of bed that day. Why are women automatically mad at other women? I had little reason to be mad at him but even less of a reason to be mad at her, yet I was mad as HELL.

I woke Sal, and we left. I could not hold it any longer. As soon as I made it in, I cried until I was numb. I hated myself that day.

Later, I marveled that I was able to leave before he could make things better for me. I was surprised, but I knew that was the smartest thing I have ever done in regards to him. I needed to make me better. For most of the morning, I cursed him in my head. By the afternoon, I had made peace with everything. I told myself that a person should never regret loving someone. Sex was not a part of our relationship. Sex was not what made our relationship special and unique. I didn't want him to destroy me, and inevitably sex with him would obliterate me. I think it would murder my soul. Loving him now, without anything physical, has already weakened me. In some weird way, us not sleeping together made our relationship that much more unique and – in a way only I could appreciate – more romantic.

The next day, I did the most logical (Mary) thing I could think of: I went back to his house to talk. So much for not returning to the scene of the crime. I knew that Eric was with Sal, so I gambled that he would be alone. I drove up to his house slowly. I had already told myself that if I saw a strange car, I would keep on driving.

When I got there, the only car I saw was his. I noticed that I had this Michael Moore book I had been meaning to loan to him in my car, so I decided to use that as my excuse for dropping by. I would use the old "I was in the neighborhood" routine.

I knocked on the door several times and heard no reply. Just as I was leaving, he came to the door. It was obvious that I had awakened him from a nap. I apologized, and he told me he was glad I had come by because otherwise he would have slept way too long.

He invited me in, and I quickly presented the book. We talked about it for awhile, and then there was dead silence. I wondered if he knew I had left the previous morning brokenhearted. I decided not to ask. I told him that I had some things I wanted to talk to him about. He asked me if this was going to be an intervention of some sort. We both laughed and I said no.

I asked if he had read my letter. He gave me this blank look, and I knew he had put the letter up that night and had been so drunk he didn't remember receiving it. I told him that was OK. I was just curious about whether he found it condescending. I wanted to tell him that being his friend was too painful and I couldn't do it any longer, but instead I told him how much I cared about him and how there wasn't much that I wouldn't do for him. I wanted to tell him that I was crazy jealous knowing and seeing another girl in his bed, but instead I told him how special he was to me. I hated my weakness at that moment.

I can't just think of him as a friend, and I can't let myself be free enough to love him the way I want to. I feel trapped. Somehow, looking at him made all the anger dissipate and the pain dull. He captivates me. It's as if I am in a trance around him. I have tried so hard to break free, but I always get pulled back in. He looked so enticing that night. All I could focus on was him. I couldn't remember the pain of Sunday morning, or the hurt I have felt over the last three years. When it's just the two of us, it feels right. We make this parallel universe when we are alone. This is the only place where we make sense. I know this all too well, and yet I act as if that magic can be recaptured in the real world. All that experimentation does is devastate me. We don't make sense in the real world, just in the world that I have created for us.

We ended up going to Wendy's because he was hungry. When we got back to his house, the talking seemed to evaporate and we were just there together, watching the Simpsons. Sometimes, just being with him is everything. That night, he told me he was aware that I had trouble falling asleep when we lay next to each other. I asked him how he knew this, and he told me that he just feels it when we are close together. For some reason, this observation made me feel wonderful. He noticed something about me that I did not tell him. Somehow, this meant the world to me. The skeptic in me wonders if maybe, in one of the letters or emails, I had mentioned this to him. I am choosing to believe that it is just as he said: he felt it. Maybe I was elated because he felt something, something that had to do with me. Whenever I am close to him, my heart starts to race and about a hundred different things run through my mind. I always want to take things further, but I feel paralyzed. I want to touch him, but I feel as if my arms are welded to the bed. Being close to him and not being able to touch him is excruciating for me.

We discussed marriage and family. Alistair stated that he had no interest in marriage. I had heard this several times, and it came as no surprise; but what he went on to say did come as a surprise. He told me that he could see himself with one girl, "and do all of things that wouldn't fuck it up." I had wanted to hear that for so long, I thought. I only wanted to know if the girl could be me. I knew this revelation would consume me. There was some safety in believing that he could not commit to anyone. Somehow, this belief made me feel less defective. Apparently, there is someone out there special enough to be with him. It was OK as long as no one could be with him and get in the way of my dreams. The night ended with a hug. I floated all the way home.

It is my fashion to ruin great moments, and that night's magic was no exception. A day later, Sal asked me to come out to hear Alistair's brother perform. I agreed to go because I love watching his brother and I am just not strong enough to decline an invitation to somewhere I will run into Alistair. Since I was still feeling high from a few nights ago, I agreed. It was as if Sunday morning never happened; it was as if nothing painful had ever happened.

Sal and I headed downtown at around 10 PM. As soon as I caught a glimpse of his face, I knew I had made a huge mistake. I saw him, and I felt as if someone had knocked the air out of me. I was used to feeling breathless around him, but this was different. This hurt. We were outside of our world. We don't work anywhere else. He looked delicious that night.

He was all decked out in his 70s' regalia, paying homage to the late pimps of the decade with his outfit made complete by the Tito Jackson hat that adorned his head.

Suddenly, he began the Salinger swing. The Salinger swing is the name Sal and I coined for Alistair's signature dance move. All the move consists of is his placing his right hand above his chest and repeatedly leaning back and forth. The funniest part of the dance is that it can be done to any type of music, because he will speed it up or slow it down depending on the music.

I saw several of the X's. They swarmed around him like flies on trash. By every standard, they were beautiful, vivacious, young, free, and aggressive. I stood out like a sore thumb. In that sea of beautiful people, I wished I were invisible. People looked as if they wondered why I was there. Maybe they thought I was lost. In many ways, I was lost. I didn't know why I was there. That night did was serve as a reminder to me that I don't belong in his world.

I don't think any of Alistair's X's know that I have any sort of a relationship with him and that we actually talk to each other. I know they don't know I'm in love with him. I listened to them talk about what a stud he is. They made comments about his voracious sexual appetite. I listened to story after story about Alistair and the X's. I wanted to get up and move, but I couldn't. I just sat there feeling dejected and foolish. Some acted as if they hated him and some as if they lusted after him, and I just sat there, loving him. One thing I noticed was that all of us had that same spark in our eyes whenever someone uttered his name. I know it wasn't for the same reasons, but it was definitely there. He hadn't touched anyone's life without leaving some sort of ineradicable impression. A couple of times, I considered telling my story, but I knew that it somehow wasn't the same. I don't know if that's something to be proud of or to feel regretful about. I was definitely out of my league that night. I began to worry if maybe something was wrong with me, because we had been playing this cat and mouse game for years and we hadn't slept together – at least, not in the way he had with the X's.

I think I want Alistair to settle down and be with one woman – this woman – but not at any cost. I don't just want him in the form of a title, like a boyfriend, or in the shape of a commitment such as marriage. I want his heart, I want his devotion, I want all of him; and I don't want to ever share that with anyone.

When we arrived downtown, and inside the club, Alistair made some innocuous comment to Sal and me as we entered the bar. After that, he never acknowledged me again. I caught a glimpse of myself in the mirror and wondered why I was there. Why didn't I just leave? Suddenly, Sunday morning came back to me, like bad memories of Alistair often did. I was doing it again. I was waiting for him to acknowledge me and make everything all right for me. Finally, I decided to stop waiting and left. This time I didn't even bother to say goodbye; but then again, maybe leaving was goodbye, and maybe I thought then that it wasn't just for that that night.

I tried unbelievably hard to not think about him. Obviously, I failed. All the drama with Alistair managed to distract me from noticing that Paul has not responded to my email in about two weeks. I was afraid that all the honesty between Paul and me might have cost us our friendship. I am in no way over my devastation regarding him, but he is important enough to me for me to pretend that I am. Everything is always about everybody else.

In that moment, I felt as if I could put some distance between Alistair and me. I guess I will have to attempt to let go of the fantasy of Alistair serenading me with the lyrics to John Lennon's "Woman." I know I have to be crazy by somebody's standards.

I was not sure how long I could do this. I felt damned if I do and damned if I don't. It's going to sting either way. I am so confused as to what to think. I don't know if life is keeping Paul from communicating with me or whether is it a conscious decision on his part. I mean, he has gone a lot longer than this without writing me. In light of our past correspondence however, I feel as if this gap of time might be intentional. I hope he at least has the decency to tell me that he doesn't want to communicate with me. Not knowing is almost unbearable. He takes his time writing me back, he never returns my phone calls. I just don't know what to do. I want to believe I am above begging, but that's what pursuing this would entail. For the sake of my dignity, I have to wait.

At some point, there has to be some sort of real resolution. I cannot do this forever. The answer is simple; all I have to do is let go. The tricky part is figuring out how to do that. How does a person suddenly make one of the most important things in their life a tertiary thought? How does number one suddenly become number ten? It seems unfair that I have to let them both go at the same time. Maybe I should consult them, because they seem to be unaffected by my presence or absence in their lives; that's painfully clear. I seem to be pretty forgettable. Constantine had no problems forgetting me. Alistair only seems to think about me when I'm in his face, and Paul only when I bombard him with thousands of emails. Is there someone out there for me? Is there something wrong with me? Am I doing something wrong? Why am I alone?

All I want is for someone to miss me when I've gone away. I want someone to want to kiss me goodnight and hold me as I sleep. I want to be important to someone. I want to leave a man breathless. I want the very thought of me to bring a smile to someone's face. I want to be pursued. I want someone to walk me to my car when it's dark. I want someone to call me just to hear my voice. I want to be noticed the minute I enter a room. I want to be someone's whole world. I want someone to write me a sappy love letter, or bad poetry, or maybe sing me a song out of key. I want to make a lasting impression on someone's heart. I want to hear someone say, "I love you," first. Is this asking too much?

Things with Alistair are not improving. I am still going back and forth. One day I hate him, then the next I love him. When is this going to end? This situation is not going to improve on its own. I have to make a decision and stick with it. I just want to love him and not hurt me so badly. He is so easy to love. This is all making me so very crazy. Letting him go is proving to be impossible. At this very moment, I am yearning to call him or send him some pathetic email. When it comes to him, I am a burnt-out junkie. These feelings control me. Loving him is so out of control.

Another friend just called to say that they're engaged. When will the madness end? I can't even feign enthusiasm at this point. Every time I think about all the wasted time, it makes me want to vomit. Alistair is never going to be with me, and neither is Paul. I have got to internalize this and move on. I am going to wake up one day and be old and alone. I have got to start living my life now and not wait to be made complete by another. That is so sad. A person shouldn't need another person to feel whole.

I'm angry and I don't exactly know whom I am mad at. I am sad, and I can't pinpoint what is making me so melancholy. I just want to be in love with someone who loves me back. I wish that Paul and Alistair hated me, because then maybe letting go would be easier. They are both so kind and gentle with me. Alistair hurts me to my core at times, but it's unintentional, and I know this. He can't stop being who he is because sometimes it hurts my feelings. Where does the strength come from to overcome an addiction? Is there a twelve-step program for what I've got?

I feel as if there isn't a single person that understands what this is doing to me. I know how pathetic this looks. I feel as though I am watching myself through an impenetrable shield. I see myself making all these grave errors in judgment, and all I can do is watch and prepare myself to pick up the pieces. Trying to ingratiate myself into Alistair's world will do nothing other than lead me down a path I do not want to go down.

I see all of this so clearly yet blindly; I walk deeper and deeper into this fog. My love for him is so much greater than all the pain or self-doubt or life's cruel realities. I have to tell myself that I am stronger than all of this misguided affection. If I believe this attraction is bigger than I am, then there is no way I will have the confidence to overcome it. I am making myself miserable, and there is no reason for it. I always have to make situations more complicated than they need to be. I thrive on drama. My favorite pastime is watching soap operas – ABC soap operas. Why can't a complicated man like Sonny Corinthos on *General Hospital* love me? That's a man worth all of this trouble.

Some months ago, Alistair accompanied me to a work function. This may not sound like a huge deal, but it was. I knew about this event several months in advance. My boss decided to host an event for everyone in our team plus their significant others. I had no real significant other and felt immense anxiety right away. Days later, I spoke with Alistair and mentioned the event to him. I asked him if maybe he'd be interested in going as my friend. He told me that he most likely would but to mention it to him again closer to the date.

The weeks rolled by and finally the week of the cookout arrived. I tried for a few days to get him on the phone but that was to no avail. When I got frustrated, I started emailing him daily. One random Friday night, I ran into him, and he told me that he had just gotten my emails the day before. He told me that he might have to do something with his nephew but he'd let me know. I waited all day Saturday and no word.

Saturday night, I decided to stop waiting and make other plans. I called my good friend, Claire, and asked her if she wanted to go with me to the cookout. Claire also works at my office, but in a different program. She agreed and we planned to meet Sunday afternoon and ride together to the cookout.

I went to church on Sunday morning and decided to take a nap before the function. Just as I was falling asleep, Alistair called and asked if we were still going to the event. I was in utter shock that he had called me wanting to go. I told him that I planned on going but had been under the impression that he was busy. He told me that his plans changed and he was going.

So, Alistair, Claire, and I rode to my bosses together. In the car, we listened to a CD of John Lennon's greatest hits. I was in heaven listening to him sing along with the CD and get so excited when one of his favorite songs was played. Listening to him singing *Mind games* stands out the most, I don't know why.

When we arrived, everyone was in shock to see him. One of my co-workers, Carmen, has sort of become my sponsor in my attempt to overcome my Alistair addiction. Carmen could not hide the look of shock and disgust when we walked through the door.

Every time he'd leave the room, someone would make some comment to me about how cute and nice Alistair seemed. Everyone wanted to know our status. It hurt like hell, but I told the truth. I told them we were just friends. Everyone except Claire and Carmen were disappointed to hear there was nothing going on between us.

My boss, Elizabeth, is goofy and insisted that we all go around the room and tell some story from our childhood. I didn't know what to expect from Alistair, so I was a little nervous. I figured he'd pass on the storytelling. He shocked me once again that afternoon when he shared a childhood memory with the group. His story was funny and engaging. He seemed to genuinely enjoy himself that afternoon. I was so charged sitting next to him, watching him interact with my work friends. I can't explain what his presence meant to me. Most times it is me who has to visit his world in order to spend time with him. I know that he wasn't dying to meet my co-workers. He went because he knew how much it meant to me.

These are the things that I can't forget. He was there with me, and he was wonderful. He made a dream come true for me. It was a simple dream but it meant so much, more than he will ever fully understand. On some level, he does care about me. I need these little reminders every now and again. He was in my world for a little while and, well, that was everything to me. I knew it couldn't last forever, but I let myself forget that for a little while – and I was just happy.

Another Sunday afternoon – Sunday seems to be my day with him; I call it his "drying-out day", drying out from a weekend of fast living and even faster women – anyway, on this day we went to the museum to see a Renoir exhibit. We had been talking about going for months and it had gotten to the point where I began to think it was just talk. The last day of the exhibit rolled around and, as was his fashion, he called and asked if I wanted to go.

I tried to stay calm and act cool because I had called him several times in the past about it. Well, we finally made it to the exhibit, and we genuinely had a nice time. He wasn't in a hurry. We just took our time. I feel so often as though I have to travel to his world just to spend any time with him, it's nice when we meet somewhere we both fit. He does things in his own time, and that's maddening; but when things really matter to me and he knows it, he comes through. And that's what no one else seems to get. These are the moments I will cherish forever. I remember that the night air had this chill about it that somehow made me want to freeze the moment.

Running On Empty

You drive me insane. I swear crazy is what I crave.
Proving my existence to you has become my existence.
Longing to occupy places in you, dead or non-existent, consume me.
Searching for truth in your humor has proven futile.
Hoping the next conversation will be *the* conversation has proven
pathetic.
Sadly, my deepest wish remains hearing that all was not in vain.

I swear crazy is what I crave.

Convinced that patience shall be my salvation.
Feeling on the cusp of something, so sought after,
then awakened just before climax, a wet dream deferred.

I swear crazy is what I crave.

Believing tonight's lunacy is moon driven,
I find comfort in what is felt but remains unknown.
Made wild wondering if all is known and I have just refused
to recognize what has been clear from the start.
Needing affection so desperately from you, that I convince myself
you desire the same.

I Swear Crazy is What I Crave.

Words have the power to sting. Words can strike a chord like a sword. There is all this pain that is not discussed. So much frustration and longing in an attempt to find that inner peace that eludes so many. Taking time as time, I try to let it pass without remorse. I race in an attempt to outrun time, trying to capture my life before it gets too far ahead of me. It's been so long that I have forgotten why I started this race in the first place. What will happen when I finally capture myself? Will this race ever really end? If so, will I end right along with it?

There have been so many flowers that I have passed by while I was too occupied to ask their names. I have sped by thousands of blank faces, never having enough time to say hello or unearth what lies behind those vacant stares. Perhaps it is too late to go back and retrieve what has been lost. Maybe there is time to slow down a bit and, at the very least, wave and learn a name or two.

I wonder if this journey is a search for self-discovery or an excuse for self-destruction? All this has done is leave me empty handed, broken hearted and without hope. My body encompasses a heavy heart. This heart has been weighed down by sorrow, anger, loneliness – a soul that longs for one that understands and a need for freedom from those trials that test the spirit and weaken it.

Detested and always a bit dejected, I have managed to learn that I know nothing about living life to the fullest. I have just been content being a rat in this race. Anger and disappointment have fueled my desire to finish this race.

I long for the day when I learn to shed this heavy load and become immune to the venom that it has injected into me. When I finally catch up with myself, I know I will probably be under the shade of some large tree, enjoying the rest and time off. I know that I will question myself as to what took me so long to get there. Together, whole, I will walk the rest of this journey. This time I will be sure to question the flowers I pass. I will take time to learn more than a name or two, a task that has proven impossible when I was too busy finding myself.

Somehow, I believed that being with Alistair or Paul would make my life start to make sense. I have believed that being loved by one or both of them would be the catalyst that would start my life. I've actually used them as an excuse not to leave Alabama and return home to Georgia to be closer to my family. I thought I wouldn't be able to bear being so far away from them. Right now, I am three hours away from Paul, and that seems unbearable. Alistair is now only about twenty minutes away from me, and at times that feels far away. I keep feeling as if there is no end to this drama. I don't know how to make it end. I am tired of thinking so much and feeling so much. I am alone, and I have to face that. This situation is not going to be rectified by either Alistair or Paul.

Paul has sort of started to fade over the last few months. I have tried really hard not to lose touch with him but that seems to be what he desires. I can only do what I can do. I can't make him care. My feelings are still the same, but that feeling of urgency has somehow left me. I knew that our last real correspondence would change things, but I didn't realize how immediate this change would be. I guess I somehow believed that the change would be on my part and not on his. I am the person that gets left; I never leave first. I miss Paul terribly but the pain isn't as unbearable as I would have expected. Maybe drifting away from Alistair might not be the agonizing, rip-your-heart-out cry-fest that I have anticipated. I never thought I would be able to let Paul go, but now it seems possible. Maybe three years is the mark. Perhaps, in another year, I will be able to let Alistair go. I am the queen of wasted time and energy. I could teach a seminar on how not to get the most out of your life. Is this all there truly is to life? If so, I'd like a refund. I keep telling myself that things are going to get better and they never seem to.

I saw something unbelievable the other night. I met Alistair's match. There is this woman: she is elevated from the X-status girls that Alistair has been involved with off and on for awhile. She is strong and independent, and she sort of treats Alistair the way he treats women. I saw her in action, and I felt inspired. She has still managed to keep that mystery that intrigues the opposite sex. It's obvious that she has yet to reveal all of her secrets to him.

I think the problem with the X's and me is that there is no mystery left to us. We couldn't wait to unveil all that we are to him. Strangely enough, I didn't feel threatened by this woman. I felt hopeful about the possibility of what I can still become. This woman knows him, and I am sure she loves him in some form or fashion, but she doesn't wear it on her sleeve. She can go through long periods of time without speaking to him. She doesn't spend her free time wondering what he is doing or with whom for that matter. I want my life back. I want to love him but be free from all the crap, the way she is.

I truly do love him, and I hope some years down the road I can still say that. I don't ever want to hate him, and I am terrified that this might happen. I keep focusing on that thin line between love and hate. Emotions are so funny and delicate, yet they seem to be so carelessly strewn all over the place. I fell for both Alistair and Paul so fast that I don't recall the progression. It is as if I woke up one morning and decided that I was in love. I know I did something wrong, but I'm not sure exactly sure when and where I made a wrong turn. I keep hoping that someone could help me determine where I went awry because I am at an utter and total loss. Sometimes I feel as if growth and maturity are all I need. Does it even really matter if I ever figure these things out? What if I just lived?

Maybe the problem has been that I have been trying to answer unanswerable questions. Truly living might just be going through the experience. Some of the best things in life don't make sense. Is there an explanation as to why kissing in the rain is romantic? Or why unspoken words mean the most? I need to let the good feel good and let the bad hurt. Understanding the reasons behind all of my emotions won't make the good times any better or the hard times hurt any less. All I am doing is wasting the energy I could be using to really live my life. *I'm in love with Alistair, and I am in love with Paul. Why does that have to have some deep meaning? Why can't it just be love? Could I have solved this conundrum? Instead of there not being any answers, maybe there aren't any real questions. Could truly living just be evolving in the unknown?*

I've tried through countless letters to try and capture my feelings for Alistair in words. I think I send letter after letter because it's not something that can be captured by words. It's something that I have to show him. He has to be able to feel it. I find strength and bravery through my writing. I have trouble having action without words. I don't want to tell him any longer that I love him; I want to show him. The million-dollar question is, how do I show him? What's love to him? I'm not even sure I know what it is to me. There's another question for me to ponder.

Each new epiphany I have in regards to Alistair brings me that much further from getting him out of my system. The truth is that I don't want Alistair out of my life. I just can't find a way to keep him in it and not hurt because things are not the way I think they should be. I sit here in my office, and I stare at his picture, and in flashes the realization that we aren't meant to be comes to me. How do I know this yet pray that all of this will work out for me?

Yesterday, I was talking to my friend, Rachel, and we got onto the subject of love. I was so burnt out on the subject that I just listened to her rant. To be honest, I really wasn't paying too much attention to what she was saying. Close to the conversation's end, she said something that really struck a chord with me. She told me that she was ready for a man to pursue her instead of her doing all the chasing. She went on to say that even if the chase appears successful, she is constantly feeling insecure about the relationship.

I thought about this for awhile. If Alistair or Paul came around and were all that I wished for, would I trust that they were sincere? No, I wouldn't! I know that I wouldn't. I'm too insecure to believe that someone would want to be with me and only me. So why am I waiting for them? If one of them did try to be with me, I'd screw the whole thing up anyway. I'm so much more messed up than I ever would have believed.

I am back to playing the same cat and mouse game with Paul. It is as if his revelation about the woman in his life never happened. I am back to sending him romantic emails with sexual innuendoes. He is back to ignoring them, and sometimes me, entirely. For a while, I thought my feelings were waning, but obviously I was mistaken. I have not even talked to Paul in months and I haven't seen him in years. He goes through days, weeks, months, without thinking about me. I can't even go through one lousy damn day without the thought of him crossing my mind. Why am I such a fool?

On Saturday night, I decided to once again venture into Alistair's world. I have lost a little weight, and I am feeling better about myself. Sal and I went out and bought new outfits to go to this bar and listen to his brother sing. By the time we left Sal's, I was pretty pleased with how I looked that night.

As soon as we got to the bar, I was stricken by one of my hellish migraines. Right then, I should have told Sal I was in pain. We should have gone to the ER. I have never experienced any pain that remotely resembles the agony I feel when I have a migraine. Only one thing in the world is strong enough to motivate me when I am in that kind of pain ... and his name is Alistair.

I couldn't hide my pain for very long because I kept going back and forth to the bathroom. I knew I was going to throw up. On my way back from one of my many trips to the restroom, an older gentleman stopped me and asked where I had been all of his life? I was in shock. A man was actually paying attention to me. Of course, this *would* happen when I feel like I am dying. The man offered to buy me a drink when I declined he offered to give me a ride home. I thanked him but told him I had a way home.

Later, another fellow motioned to me to come to him. I slowly walked towards him. He asked if I was having a good time, because I looked like I was having a miserable time. I told him that I had a migraine. He quickly stood up right in front of me and took off my glasses and began to put pressure on the back of my head and massaged my neck. Instantly my migraine left, and stayed away for about twenty minutes. I thanked the guy. Later, I told Sal that I needed to marry that man or at least get his number.

I finally got to the point where I couldn't hold on any longer and I told Sal that I needed to go to the ER. I tried to find Alistair, but he was nowhere in sight. I hugged Eric and asked him to tell Alistair that I said goodbye.

Eric said, "Wait right here, and I will find him."

He was off before I could say that I was feeling too bad to wait. What felt like an eternity later, Alistair appeared and gave me this look I had never seen before. He said, "Baby, haven't we gotten to a place in our relationship where you can find me and say goodbye without having to send someone to find me?"

I thought, *We have a relationship?* I said, "I tried to find you, and I couldn't. I didn't ask Eric to go and get you; he volunteered." Then I asked him to walk me to the car. I told him I was sick and on my way to the ER.

He gave me hug, and I just wanted to melt right there in his arms and chest. I could feel his heartbeat. There is no better place than close to him. He looked and smelled so good that night. He is my walking, talking, breathing fantasy.

I got into the passenger side of the car, and he got into the driver's side because he hadn't seen Sal's new car. When we were in the car alone together, he said, "You're a beautiful writer."

I looked at him perplexed. I hadn't written him in months. I was trying to fight back tears because my head was killing me. Then I remembered that I had sent him some of my writings via email. He told me that they were very good and beautiful and made him think about a lot of stuff. I wondered what it made him think about, but I was hurting too badly to press him for information.

Soon after we finished chatting, Sal arrived and drove me to the ER. As we left the bar parking lot, I laid my forehead against the cold glass. Somehow the coolness seemed to alleviate some of the pulsating pain. Through the window, I watched Alistair get smaller and smaller as we drove further and further away. For some unknown reason, the lyrics to a

Steve Miller Band song started going through my head as I watched him disappear. I was crying uncontrollably by the time we got to the hospital. Honestly, I don't know if it was because of the pain in my head or the pain in my heart. Whatever the cause, I was miserable.

Immediately, the doctor ordered a cat scan. I was terrified. I just knew that I was going to have a tumor.

The results of the cat scan didn't find anything wrong with my brain. I threw up a few times, and the doctor asked if I should be admitted. I told him that I wanted to go home. He made me lie down for a while and gave me two shots of Demerol. When I started to feel a little better, I looked at Sal and weakly said, "Alistair told me that I was a beautiful writer."

Sal looked at me and rolled her eyes. At this point, we had been at the ER for five hours. I lay there, sedated and sleepy, as visions of Alistair frolicked around in my now dully throbbing head. I actually think what he meant was that I wrote beautifully, but I'll take the compliment just the same. The rest of the night the Steve Miller Band song continued to go through my head.

"I'm a joker,
I'm a smoker,
I'm a midnight toker,
I sure don't want to hurt no one."

One thing that Alistair and I definitely have in common is politics. We are both die-hard democrats. We were both enthralled by the 2004 Kerry/ Bush election. We were both supporters of John Kerry in '04 and Barack Obama in '08. This particular story occurred with the '04 campaign. Anyway, some months ago I went to Belmont University to hear John Kerry speak. While I was there, I got a sign for Alistair to put in his yard. He was very excited when I presented him with it.

Carmen, one of my co-workers at the time, who also happens to be one of my good friends, is married to a republican – not just a republican, but a Bush-supporter republican. He would leave notes in my office that read, "Four more years." He was relentless in his support of GOP. For revenge, a friend of mine, Claire, and I decided to get all the John Kerry signs we could find and just litter their yard with support for Senator Kerry. We had a hard time finding signs that were not in people's yards and were too chicken to steal signs out of them. If only I could have seen into the future and just told myself to hold on, because we (the American people) would finally get it right in 2008, I would have been a much calmer person.

I called Alistair and asked him if I could have the sign back. Claire and I quickly realized that we didn't have enough signs to really make our point. I talked Claire into calling Alistair back on three-way so she could ask him to steal us some signs from around his neighborhood.

She called him, but when she asked he laughed and refused. Just as the conversation died down, Claire said, "And I thought you loved, Mary."

I wanted to die; I wanted to die, but not before I killed Claire. My heart stopped, and it felt as if the world had done the same. About six million things went through my mind at once. What if he thinks I told her that he loves me? What if he says he doesn't? What if hell has frozen over, and he *does*? What if this freaks him out and he never talks to me again?

After what felt like an eternity, he responded by saying, "I do, but not enough to steal for her."

I couldn't believe he had said that he loved me. I don't know if he said it to save face or to spare my feelings, or if he truly does. I still can't believe that he said it. Moments like those make me remember why I have wasted years of my life on him.

Things with Alistair have been so intense lately that I have almost managed to put Paul in the back of my mind. In all honesty, I think Paul has been with me a little more than normal. It hurts too badly right now to put too much energy into calling and emailing him. He is going through a horrible time in his life right now. He is in a lot of pain, and I hate that I am not a person who he cleaves to for support and love. That hurts me like hell.

In an email a couple of weeks ago, Paul told me that his grandmother has been diagnosed with terminal cancer and wouldn't live much longer. I could feel his pain through his words. I desperately wanted to write something back or call him with something that would somehow help him. As if this wasn't enough, my last email from him informed me that his mother had had a heart attack. I think mine stopped when I read that.

His mother is everything to him. It would devastate me for him to lose her. I can't imagine what it would do to him. He derives a lot of strength and wisdom from his mother, I believe. In some ways, I do understand, because of the pain I have in regards to my father's declining health. I immediately said a prayer for his mother's speedy recovery, and I also begged God to not take his mother from him. I don't want him to endure that. His mom has got to be the most important thing in his life. I know that it would be near impossible for him to survive without her. I read his words describing him crying after receiving the news about his mother, and I found myself crying. Paul's hurting hurts me. I almost wish I hadn't told him that I loved him so much and so often, because maybe saying it now would mean more. I love him from the deepest and most sincere part of myself.

Just a few minutes ago, I mustered up enough intestinal fortitude to call Paul. I called and got his voicemail, so I left a message. I was somewhat relieved that he didn't answer. I hadn't planned out anything to say. I just wanted him to know that I was thinking about him and calling seemed a bit more sincere than emailing him, again. He never called back, but I find comfort in knowing that he at least received the message. I desperately needed to give him some space and let him sort some things out. He most definitely doesn't need all of the drama that seems to accompany being friends with me.

I was on pins and needles waiting for Tuesday evening. I had never in my life been that engrossed in a presidential election (that was, up until 08). I prayed that John Kerry would win.

I found out this week that I am being laid off from my job in a month. Honestly, I was planning to put my notice in anyway, but I wanted to see if I got into graduate school. If I don't, I have no idea what to do. I hate that I have told so many people I was attempting to get into school. Now if I don't get in, I'll be devastated plus humiliated. My GRE scores were pitiful.

Worrying about a job, GRE scores, graduate school, being laid off in a month, love, life, and lupus – I am pretty much on the edge. If one more thing happens I think I'll need to be put in a padded room. Paul has basically dropped off of the face of the earth. He was always bad at emailing, but this has been bad even for him. I've called and left messages, and I've emailed, but he has made no attempts to respond, aside from the occasional token email. I have no clue what's happening in his life and that scares the living hell out of me. What if he and that girl are more serious? What if he loves her? What if I finally have to let him go? I don't feel ready as of yet. When I think about the situation, it's humorous. I'm here, he's there, my only connection to him is email (that he doesn't respond to), yet I think these emails will make a connection with him and he'll choose me, he'll love me. He's there in his hometown, having a real life and interacting with real people, and yet I think this might work out. There has to be something clinically wrong with me. There has to be! Normal people don't live life the way I do.

It's another Saturday night, and I am typing away on my little manifesto wishing that I were with Alistair or Paul. They are probably both out living life while I am contemplating a way to figure out how. Is this my destiny? How do I control my life? I don't like the direction that it seems to be going, and I don't know how to turn it around. I have these gigantic emotions, and they are suffocating me. I don't know how to channel all that I feel in a positive direction. I love Paul and Alistair, and so what. What does that mean? Is that anything profound or even noteworthy?

I managed to get into graduate school in the English department. I applied for unemployment and got on state-assisted health insurance. I no longer have to pay for meds. Hallelujah! I also have no co-pays. It appears as if life might be going in the right direction. I had to move out of my beautiful two-bedroom apartment and into a one-bedroom in a cheaper complex. That was a little depressing, but you do what you have do, right?

I'll Follow the Sun

"God, please let him return safely. Even if he is with another girl and if that is the way it will always be, just keep him safe. There are so many things that I don't understand and that I question daily, but I know without question that he needs to be loved. I know that you wouldn't have filled my heart with so much love for him had you not wanted me to love him so much. I just wish it did not have to hurt so badly."

I don't even remember what he was saying that night. I just remember looking up at him through the open car window and wanting to stroke his face. The urge to touch him was incredible. I don't know how I was able to resist. I am going crazy with hormonal desire. I have so much contained sexual energy that I am afraid I may implode. What does he spend his time doing? I spend mine trying not to implode. I am writing a tell-all about being a virgin in her late twenties. How do I make him feel? How does he classify our relationship? How does he feel about me? That's the question! What do I have to lose by asking him? This relationship can't get anymore fucked up than it already is. He knows that I love him and would do anything for him, and yet he does nothing. That answers the damn question right there. There's my damn answer!

He's considerate, and then he's not considerate. He cares, and then he doesn't care. I never know what I am doing, and I don't know what I want. I just love him. I don't know ANYTHING about real physical intimacy. What I do know is love and emotional intimacy. There are some moments when we catch glimpses into each other's eyes, and I see something in the way he looks at me that makes me think that there is something between us.

My New Year's resolution was to lose weight (of course) and break all ties with Alistair or truly view our relationship as a friendship, and to do the same with Paul – but the emphasis was on Alistair because that relationship is the most toxic.

The last time I saw Alistair, I told him about my resolution. He asked me how that was supposed to make him feel. I shrugged my shoulders like a shy child, and he told me that comment hurt him. I apologized but wondered if it really had any real affect on him at all. Did anything truly move him? I realized at that moment that everything I did, thought, ate, drank, and dreamed about was for his benefit. I only told him about the resolution to get his attention and evoke some sort of response. I don't mind hurting him, because I'll take anything as long as he feels something.

I can't help but wish somehow that I were a better person. Maybe if I were better he'd want me. Maybe he'd love me if I were thinner. Maybe he'd love me if I were more aggressive. I feel so undeserving in his presence. When I am with him, I hate myself. When he touches me, I feel disgusting. He makes me hate my body. I cannot even bear to look at myself naked. He needs to be with someone beautiful and thin – not someone unnoticeable, untouchable and fat. He deserves better than me, and what hurts is that we both know it.

I would pay any price to not love him anymore. I pray every night that God will help me to stop loving him. I wake up every morning disappointed because of how much I still do. It is as if my love grows stronger each and every day. I even went as far as to tell Alistair that I prayed for all of my love for him to dissipate. He told me that God knew how desperately he needed me to love him and that's why I still did. The comment infuriated me at first, but then later, in my sick fashion, I found a way to make it romantic and swooned over the misery of it.

I have all these things I want to say and all these feelings raging inside of me. I see him (Alistair), and I want to scream at him, I want to shout at him, "Choose me! Love me! I'm worth it." I want the physical with him, but more than that I want his heart. I want his love. I want that more than I have ever wanted anything in my whole life. I'd do anything for it. He does not know that he deserves to be loved. I just want to show him what he deserves. He stumbles from tryst to tryst, one meaningless encounter after another. I wonder if he ever finds any meaning in anything. Many an afternoon, I have found him in a cloud of purple haze, being enchanted by the sounds of Simon and Garfunkel, The Beatles, Hendrix, Otis Redding, and the Stones. Maybe he finds his solace in those artists the way I find mine in those quiet moments with him. He loves music the way I love him.

I can't understand how I have allowed myself to become so consumed by my feelings for Paul and Alistair. It is as if there is nothing else. It is as if they are gone, and I am left with nothing. When did I let them become everything? This was not their doing, admittedly; it is my own. I feel imprisoned. I am going insane. The truth of the matter is that I am terrified. I am scared that I am destined to feel this lonely forever. What if I am never loved the way I desire to be loved? I am scared of longing after the impossible for the rest of my life. I am scared of being so ashamed of my body that I never experience making love to a man. What if right now is my entire life? Holding on to Alistair and Paul is like holding on to my hope. Without hope, I have nothing. They are what's left of my belief in true love, soul mates and destiny. Letting go of them is letting go of living for me. What would be the point of going on for me?

I'm sitting on my couch, watching an old episode of Friends, eating sushi, trying desperately to resist the urge to write or call Alistair. I emailed Paul hours ago, so that battle has already been lost. My mind's so scattered, I sometimes wonder what my thought processes would be like if they were altered by some foreign substance. It has been my position in the past to leave all drugs to Alistair, but my curiosity has been piqued. One day, I may ask him about his experience with drugs. I wonder what they do for him, what feelings they dull or what experiences they enhance for him. I wonder if he'd take that trip with me. I wonder if he'd be my guide through that part of his world.

I can't imagine being anywhere really close inside him, where he'd allow me to hang out for very long. I'm greedy - no part of himself that he is ever willing to reveal is ever really enough. I always want just a little more. I want to understand not just the man but the soul of the man. Sometimes, I wonder if I'm in love with my idea of the man as opposed to the actual man. Am I even in love with a real person? I have the questions and none of the answers. What, if anything, keeps his ass up at night? Does anything about our relationship concern him? I wonder. Here's the million-dollar question everyone is dying to know but scared to ask: does he love me?

I haven't seen Paul in years. I have to take a minute to say that aloud. As I suspected, it sounds just as ridiculous aloud as it does in my head. I have begged him to come to Alabama to see me, and he has more excuses than Al Sharpton has combs. The last time we saw each other, I drove to Alansville, Mississippi, with my cousin, and we all spent the afternoon together. He treated us to a movie; we had lunch and spent hours at a local Starbucks just talking. The talking was the best part of the trip. I could have sat there all night listening to him.

On the way back to Alabama, my cousin turned to me and told me just before I fell asleep (she was driving), "I get it now. I know why you like him and, for what it's worth, I hope it works out and he appreciates how wonderful you are as well." My cousin and I have our moments – as a matter of fact, we aren't speaking now – but I never loved her more than I did that night. Not because she wished us well or because she had accompanied me to Alansville or because she approved, but because she got it. She felt the magic; she got that *je ne sais quoi* that encompasses him.

I know him in pieces. It is an odd love that I feel for him. It's not something that makes sense. Sometimes, the reality of it is frightening to me. How can I love this person? How can I love him and Alistair so much at the same time? I want to marry Paul. I need to see Paul again. I need to spend some real time with him. I need closure with him. I need something with him. I have grown weary with the blue-moon phone calls and with the daily emails on my part and whenever-emails on his part. It's about time to take the Band-Aid approach to this situation. I am closer to being thirty than twenty – THIRTY – I can't continue living in fairy tales. Crushes don't equal fulfilling adult relationships.

Paul responded to my request for a meeting. He acknowledged that it was indeed I who initiated our last meeting and that it is his turn to come to Alabama and see me. I don't know what is to come from this admission, but it's a start, and with Paul a start is no small feat. I, of course, accepted this response from him but let him know that sooner is definitely better than later. I want to know if that magic from that night at the coffee shop three years ago is still there. I just need to see the actual man. I need to touch him, smell him, and just be in his presence. I want to make sure that the Paul I love actually exists and isn't some person I have invented. I sometimes fear that I have created Alistair and Paul as a means to get through the lonely nights. Does his willingness to come down after all this time say anything at all about how he feels about me?

Earlier I wrote about how I felt as if maybe I held on to Alistair and Paul because they were my hope. What if they are holding on to me for the same reason? Alistair is not in love with me and nor is Paul, but maybe they are kind to me because it's comforting to them or safe for them to have someone who loves them. They know if the chips were down and it really comes down to it, they have at least one person that loves them unconditionally. On the surface that might not mean a whole lot, but underneath it all it means a whole hell of a lot, more than some of us care to admit at times. As sad as it is to acknowledge, there isn't much I wouldn't do for either of them —and what's worse is that both of them are very aware of this.

In September, I started working on Alistair's present For Christmas this year. For the last couple of years, I have been renewing his subscription to *Rolling Stone Magazine,* which I got him one year as a Christmas gift. In September's issue, they ran famous photos of rockers from past and present. I purchased a huge 40 x 60 foam board from Michaels and posted all the pictures on it. I had a piece of Plexiglas cut from Alabama Glass Company and then delivered to Michaels so they could frame it. I had to enlist Sal to help, because it was so huge I needed the extra hands and her truck.

The whole project cost me around three hundred dollars. This doesn't include the other trinkets I purchased for him. This item meant the most, because it was sort of a labor of love. I wrapped it in that huge Christmas plastic wrap they sell for wrapping large items such as bicycles. I stuck a homemade Christmas card on it that read, **"In lieu of a thousand words."** I actually think he got how much went into the gift. He seemed blown away by it and appreciative. I wanted to give him something that I had put a little bit of my heart and soul into and I think I accomplished my goal.

I ran into Eric today and we got onto the subject of the collage. I asked if Alistair had hung it up. Eric told me Alistair had had to go to the hardware store to get the right kind of fixture thingies to hang it. Eric went on to say that Alistair wanted to hang it in his room over his bed. For some reason, that touched me deeply. I don't know why, but it did. I'm a lunatic, I know. It just made me feel as if it might be something special to him. I so desperately want to be something special in his life and if, in some small way, something that I created could be, then it makes all this seem a little less futile and painful.

When I saw a preview for Zach Braff's *Garden State,* I knew it was going to be brilliant. Alistair studied film in college – actually, that was his major. It's interesting how that was his major and Paul wants to be a film critic. What's with me and these film types? But I digress yet again. Anyway, I told Alistair that we had to see it. He kept blowing smoke up my ass about us going to see it. Finally, I got fed up with him and went to see the movie with Sal.

Just as I had suspected, the movie was phenomenal, and this fact sent me into a tailspin. I asked him why I always had to join his world. I wanted to know why things that were important to me were, for the most part, ignored or became missed opportunities. After awhile, you can have so many conversations with a person that you assume the person isn't even listening to you anymore. It tore me up that we didn't see this movie together. I didn't even communicate to him how upset I was that we never made it to that movie.

For Christmas this year, he bought me *Garden State* on DVD and agreed to come over to MY apartment and watch it. I was absolutely blown away by his gift. I was in complete shock that he even remembered the movie. He actually remembered something that mattered to me, something that was important to me. These were those moments with him that no one else saw, those moments in the dark where there was just the two of us.

On Thursday evening, Alistair and I made plans to get together tonight to watch *Garden State.* He is the one who picked tonight as the night we would get together. I told him on Thursday that I would not be calling him to remind him about Monday. I would be leaving the remembering up to him. He looked me in my eyes with those beautiful eyes of his and told me he'd remember. I nodded, knowing that I would be sitting here alone tonight writing about the exchange. It is 6:30 and, to be fair, I will give him another hour and a half before I consider the evening a wash. Sal told me yesterday that she would consider herself on call tonight in the event he showed and we had sex; she'd come over after he left for all the details. And if he stood me up, she'd come over so that we could talk trash about him and watch a season of *Sex and the City.*

So here I sit, and I wait for him. This is the story of my life. No matter how horribly this hurts, I am resolved to not call him. I told him in no uncertain terms that I would not be reminding him, and he agreed. If this meant anything to him, if this was something he truly wanted to do, if I meant anything to him, he would remember. I remembered.

Will he call? Will I have my romantic night with him? Does he care?

He called at 7:00. When he called, he asked me if I thought he had forgotten. I told him honestly that I did. He asked why I had so little faith in him. No sooner did he say that than I heard that familiar sound of an X in the background. They've made their return! Vermin! It was stunts like double-booking that were the reason I had such little faith in him. He went on to say that he had dinner plans but we were still on for the movie, if I still wanted to watch it.

So he had called, but at what price? What was he thinking? Does he think? Does he even consider that I might possibly have feelings? I told him that we were definitely still on for that night. I sensed that he wanted me to say we could reschedule, but I wasn't about to give him a damn thing that he wanted. Do I even have grounds to be upset? I don't even know anymore. What a strange trip it has been. I not even angry at this point, just disappointed – and not even in him but in myself. The adage definitely holds true that "only fools fall in love." I love him, and I swear that makes me insane. I just want to stop loving him and God, help me, I don't know how. What comes of spending time with him? Another letter? Lascivious thoughts? Hurt Feelings? I can't even tell him what the hell I want from him.

This whole experience is probably all too familiar for him and maybe a little boring at times. I fool myself into thinking that our relationship is unique and maybe sometimes even go as far as to say it is special, but I am sure that having a woman fawn all over him is common place for a lothario such as he. There's this intoxicating blend of romanticism and masochism that has captivated me. Here I am once again, back to this sick idea of deriving pleasure from pain.

"Goodnight, Baby doll"

I once overheard a conversation where someone asked him if he was an alcoholic, and without missing a beat he retorted, "No, I'm a drunk; alcoholics go to meetings." He's the sort of person who refers to an alcohol-warning label on a pill bottle as a serving suggestion. This is the man I can't forget – the man who, at twenty-six years of age, I think I am in love with.

Alistair did make it over to my apartment that night and we watched the movie and had dinner. The evening felt very natural. I felt at ease with him. I felt as if we had spent many evenings alone together, eating and watching primetime television. I savored every moment of our time together. I kept taking moments to close my eyes and inhale deeply to fill myself with him. His scent is so strong and intoxicating.

Once, without thinking, I let myself reach out and grab his hand to get his attention. His skin was so soft, warm, and sensual. I wanted so desperately to explore more of him, but I quickly relinquished my hold on his arm. There were so many things that I wanted to say to him and so many things that I wanted to ask him, but I didn't. I wanted to tell him how desperately I wanted to make love to him and how I had planned it all out the night before. I was desperate to let him know that this hold he had on me was crippling me in other areas of my life. I just sat there in awe of him.

When he got ready to leave, he hugged me, and I just wanted to stay right there buried in his chest and remain in his arms forever. He told me that I smelled good, and I wanted to tell him that he felt good, but of course I said nothing. Later that evening, I called him right before I fell asleep to make sure he made it home. We chatted about unimportant things, and I just let him know I wanted to know he was home. We have these sorts of anti-climatic conversations all the time. I told him goodnight and just as I was about to hang up he says, "Goodnight, baby doll." I don't know why this felt different. He had never said that to me before. Something about it, or maybe how he said it, made me feel safe and somehow cradled. I don't know if I needed that from him because of our relationship or in light of all that I am going through in terms of my parent's relationship right now.

I've let him have total control of my emotions. He controls my highs and my lows. And to be fair whenever Paul decides to pay me some attention that always brightens my day. Alistair's brother is playing tonight. Initially, I thought it might get my mind off of things to go downtown and listen. Now, I just don't know if I can deal with seeing all those X's all over him – not tonight when I am feeling so undesirable and fat.

Rachel, the Dr. Phil fan, told me to make the night about me and not about him. She told me to focus on having as much fun as I can. She told me to ignore Alistair. Is that possible? I thought. I just don't want to feel any worse. I don't want to focus on the negative, but sometimes I feel like that's all I have. There are so many people out there who give a damn about me, and I focus on the one or two who don't. Why is that? Maybe I just have to put one foot in front of the other and just make myself move past the insecurities, the infatuation, and finally the man … I keep saying I can't help myself. Maybe I just need to pretend I can, until suddenly it just happens and I'm not faking it any longer. As you probably guessed, I stayed home that night.

Now that I have gotten Paul to somewhat commit to coming to Alabama to see me, I can't seem to get him to communicate with me. I don't know what is going on with him, and I don't have the energy to push. I have tried on at least five different occasions to write Alistair a letter but I can't. I can't commit to writing Paul an email with any emotion attached to it. I am tired and resentful. I am tired of giving so much of my heart and soul to them with such little return, and so I guess I put it all here. All the feelings are still here; I just keep them with me. They know how I feel about them; they have always known it. If they cared, it is so past time for them to do something, anything, about it. In some sick way, I think me writing letter after letter or email after email is my way of trying to convince them to love me. It's just not worth all the hard work anymore, so maybe that's something.

My friend, Rachel, is a die-hard Dr. Phil fan and quotes him the way some people can quote the Bible. I used to laugh whenever she would use a Dr. Philism to solve my current life problem. Recently, I watched a bit of a show about overweight soon-to-be brides desperate to lose weight before their weddings. What caught my attention was a story about this one woman who was about my size and seriously depressed about her weight. I was intrigued, because I couldn't believe that someone my size would have a fiancé. The woman went on and on about how she couldn't understand how her fiancé could be attracted to her. I understood this woman's pain, because in many ways I am her. I sat there listening to her pain as she described how much she hated her body, and I just cried right along with her. And then Dr. Phil said to her, "We believe what we tell ourselves..." and just that little bit of what he said took me into another realm.

At my current size, I have convinced myself that I am undesirable, that no man will ever want to make love to a fat woman, and that nobody falls in love with fat women. Everything I tell myself about me physically is negative. I believe that the reason I am alone is because I am unattractive and overweight. I truly believe this. This is the message I tell myself daily.

On New Year's Eve 2005, I resolved to not leave my twenties overweight. I joined a gym a week later. Many thoughts roamed through my mind that morning while I was there. I thought about how I seem to have a problem dealing with reality. In all honesty, I am hoping that at the end of this tale, I end up with either Alistair or Paul – even though logically I know that can't and won't happen. As I was temporarily blinded by my own perspiration, I thought, "This is real: me here, working my fat ass out, trying to lose weight." I had been so pissed off about being fat because I've felt like it isn't my fault that I am overweight. I gained eighty pounds when I was in high school as a result of taking steroids for my lupus. Recently, I have been taken off of the pills, so there is no reason now that I can't lose the weight. I worked out for three days and quit.

Grieving

I had believed up until now that in order to grieve, a physical death has to occur. As of late, I have realized grieving is about loss more so than it is about death. A person can grieve the loss of just about anything. One can grieve the loss of love, the end of an era, the dissolution of a dream, disappointments in life, the betrayal of a lover, or quite possibly even the awakening from a beautiful dream.

In some ways, the grief that goes along with a physical death is easier than grief over the loss of a lover or the relinquishing of a dream, because death is finite. When death occurs, the survivors have no choice but to accept. The tendency with lost lovers and dreams is to start second-guessing and hoping for second chances. When does the cycle end? And when does healing begin? Maybe I just need to cry this out – not just for a night or a weekend but for as long as it takes. My problem is that I'll be in the worst pain of my life one night and be resolved to move on, and then the next morning I'll be singing an entirely new song of love. I mourn the loss of my romanticism. I mourn the loss of a love I never possessed. I mourn the loss of a dream.

All through Friday's American literature class, I wanted to add something profound to the discussion. I sat there watching the time escape me. It was as if the ability to think rationally had left me. The ideas that would come to me somehow sounded so ludicrous in my head, I wouldn't allow myself to verbalize them aloud. I allowed my thought processes to be carried away. I don't even recall what I was daydreaming about. The works of Emerson were not enough to keep my attention until the very end of class. I had let myself drift so far away.

Just as my mind landed back on this planet, I heard the professor paraphrasing a statement of Emerson that went something like "the years know what the days cannot." I am ashamed to admit that I don't know what work this was from because soon after I heard this, my mind wandered yet again. I wondered what secrets the years would reveal to me.

Things seem so uncertain and frightening at this moment in my life. At every moment, I feel like I am at the brink of tears or a breakdown or total meltdown of some kind. The days feel cruel and unforgiving – more foe than friend.

Will she ever learn? I am afraid not. Instead of singing the same ole song again, let's offer the following synopsis,

Scene: Our heroine sees her hero at a function with a female that our heroine perceives as his girlfriend. This perception sends our heroine into a tailspin.

Heroine: (inner monologue) Why didn't he just tell me he had a girlfriend? Why in the hell has he let me embarrass the hell out of myself for months when all the while he has had a GIRLFRIEND? I'm not even jealous. I'm not! I am angry with myself for giving a damn. I don't want to care anymore. I don't want to be wrapped up in what he does, or whom with for that matter. We are friends. I hate that I even noticed he is with her. I hate that I fucking noticed that – I hate it. If he fucking loses an eyelash, I'd notice. I am the dumbest person in this room. Hey, anybody want to shake hands with the nerd that writes Alistair love letters? What a joke I am. I am some fucking charity case that he entertains when time permits. I bet hanging out with me makes him feel good about himself. It's like using a Saturday to play sports with retarded kids (she sobs).

She unloads on neutral third party...

Neutral third party: She's not his girlfriend. He is just doing it with her, but you knew that. She just likes him a lot, just like all the others ... *just like all the others, just like all the others, just like all the others.*

The End

The phrase "*just like all the others*" left a horrific taste in my mouth. It loomed over me like a haunting presence. The comment made me feel nauseated, common, one of the masses, and – my personal favorite – stupid. Just like all the others, with me being the exception because he isn't doing it with me.

I've been advised repeatedly to just let him go. I don't know exactly how to do that since I don't have him. I say that, but I understand the meaning behind the suggestion. My worry is that his absence will leave a greater presence than his actual presence. What a gaping hole his absence would leave! Sadly there is nothing that would remotely come close to filling the gigantic void he'd leave.

I sit here in front of my computer almost too embarrassed to admit that I cried myself to sleep last night. I don't know if it all had to do with Alistair. My dad's health is on a steady decline and each day he drifts further and further away from me, and that breaks my heart a little each day.

Last night was the first night in months that I attempted to sleep unaided by sleeping pills. I had one of those nights when you aren't quite sure that you ever actually fell asleep. Ironically, the only other time I have nights like these are when I sleep with Alistair. The only evidence that I actually got some shuteye last night is that I had a dream. Usually, my dreams are weird and very sexual/science fiction in nature. I find them very disturbing, but last night was different.

I dreamed in black in white last night. Is that not the strangest thing?

In my dream, I was in what I can only explain as a Jimmy Stewart movie. I was married to him, pregnant and exceedingly happy. I was so tickled by his humor and voice in my dream. Is that not the wildest dream? I found myself somewhat disappointed this morning when I awoke. All day today, I keep remembering that five-second feeling of happiness I had before I realized it had all been a dream. I wanted to get those five seconds back. I couldn't believe that after all the pain I was in before I fell asleep, I actually got a beautiful dream and awoke with a smile on my face. What kind of normal twenty-six-year-old woman dreams of marrying Jimmy Stewart in 2005?

When I think of all the lies I have told myself, I feel so ashamed. I don't believe I actually realized that I was being dishonest at the time. I actually convinced myself that I could have sex with Alistair, and it would just be sex. I thought that I could separate the act from my emotions at one point in our relationship. I wanted him so much that I thought I could just slake my lust and it would not have any impact on me emotionally. I honestly convinced myself of this. I let myself believe that I had this understanding or – better yet – this connection with Alistair that was unique between the two of us. The best part is that I actually thought he felt this too.

In November of 2004, I was laid off from my job. This did not come as a great shock to me. My program needed to make cutbacks and I was ready to try something new. I applied and was accepted to grad school here in Alabama and was planning to start in January of 2005. I was feeling a little stressed out about all the changes going on in my life, but I felt that I could handle it. I went home to Georgia for a month and spent time with my family for the holidays. When January rolled around, I was ready for a new beginning. I was living in a new (cheaper) apartment across the street from Sal; she and I had stopped living together about a year prior to all of this.

January came, and I got hit with massive anxiety attacks. The university I was attending was huge, unlike where I had been attending undergrad. Everyone in the class was so much more advanced than me, and I was too intimidated to even open my mouth. My silence did not go unnoticed. The English classes were held in small conference rooms and there were no more than ten people in my class. After one of my classes was adjourning for the day, the professor asked if anyone had any questions, and this middle-aged man spoke up and said, "Yeah, I was wondering if Mary had any vocal cords."

I just tried to smile and breathe. I packed up my stuff as fast as I could and ran to my car and cried all the way home.

I wasn't working. My only job was to go to class three days a week. I started skipping class because I just couldn't make myself leave the apartment. Every time I thought about leaving, I would have an anxiety attack. My mom would call me and it seemed as if every time she called it was to tell me that my dad's health was deteriorating. I found myself crying all the time. I started having insane thoughts about death. I kept wondering what would happen if I accidentally took too much of my medication? Or what would happen if I turned too deeply into a curve while driving? I was beginning to scare myself.

Against my better judgment, I talked Sal into going to see Alistair's brother perform one night, and afterwards we ended up going back to Alistair and Eric's. I was at my lowest point that night and, for some unknown reason, I thought that seeing him would help. It never had before, but at this point I was at the very definition of insanity.

When we got to the house, Alistair was so drunk I don't think he even knew that I was there. I just sat there on the couch, watching him stumble around and wondering why I had let this particular person become so very important to me.

While I was sitting there, this girl sat down next to me who was almost as drunk as Alistair. I recognized her immediately because at that particular time she was his flavor of the month. To this day, I don't know if she just randomly started to talk to me or if she knew that I loved him. She said to me in this slurred voice, "You know, I really like him."

I nodded.

She continued, "He is so cute. Look at him over there. Oh, I just really like him."

Then I said, "Have you told him?"

She said, "Yeah, and supposedly he really cares for me as well."

I took a deep breath and tried so hard not to let a tear fall. Then I said, "It sounds like you're all set then."

At that point, she got up and stumbled over to where he was standing. I kept looking at her and then at him, and then considered myself. I thought, why am I here? I'm never going to be where she's standing. I thought about this girl, and I saw her as a person – not as an X – and I thought, what if he could truly love this one? This sent me into a tailspin.

All these years, I kept letting myself use Alistair as a place of refuge. I took all of my problems to him. I believed that he cared a little more than

115

he actually did. I misunderstood his politeness for a place of solace. And then it happened: the night his indifference scolded me when I needed him most. That night, I felt so alone and at a loss as to what to do next. I was hurt that night, but by morning I realized that his callousness sent me into a place that in reality that I hadn't visited in quite awhile. He is not my therapist, and I got to thinking about other things in my life that maybe I had gotten wrong. Alistair may or may not be my soul mate, but so what? That doesn't mean we are destined to be together. Soul mates may or may not even exist. Who was I kidding? Sex is an extension of love for me, I can't even pretend that isn't so.

Alistair and I cannot be together; that is a fact. Even if he were willing, I'd never trust him or accept that he really loved me. I have to find a way to reconcile this knowledge with the intense feelings of love I have for him. I never dreamed that I could love anyone as much as I love him. He lives his life so recklessly. I am constantly worried about him. Sometimes I just wish that I could keep him safe. I pray for his safety every night, right after I pray that maybe I could love him a little less.

I wonder what past love of his hurt him and turned him into the person that attracts and repels me at the same time. I know he has been in love before; I can see it in him. I feel certain he'd deny it if I asked, but I know he has. It is something I see in his eyes. I do believe the eyes are the gateway to the soul. I see glimmers of this in the way that he looks at a certain woman he has known for awhile. I don't know if he loves her, but I see his softer side when he sees her, and some days I see it when he looks at me. He is so much deeper than he lets on. He escapes to those places within him through the music that he listens to and in the quiet places he finds inside all the loudness that he lives in. It would be interesting to unearth the secrets of his past and to understand why he makes the decisions that he does and why he is so unforgettable to me.

I kept wanting to find a place to fit somewhere in his world, somewhere in his heart. Thinking that would make everything all right. I thought if I could just get into graduate school, everything would be fine; but that wasn't the case. I am unhappy, and I don't know who is to blame for that. If it's my fault, I have no clue how to change anything. I have this profound sense of loneliness. No one knows how I feel. I sometimes feel as if I am the only person in the world to ever get down or be depressed.

I am tired of the pep talks and the suggestions of counseling. How about a little validation? I want someone to say that it's OK to cry and maybe say, "I know you love him, and it's OK to love someone who doesn't love you back. I know this hurts." I want someone to say that it's OK to be weak sometimes but remind me that there are times when I am strong and do hold things together. Sometimes a hug is all that is required. Why does it seem as though things always have to be rationalized? I'm just asking for some time to regain my breath and mourn these losses. It just seems like I should be allowed that.

My mom called the other night and told me that she has been racking her brain trying to remember where she and my father had gone wrong in rearing me. I asked her what she meant. She told me she wanted to know the root of my low self-esteem and went on to say that no matter how many compliments I received or accomplishments I made, it didn't matter; I never seemed to have any faith in myself. She then turned the question to me and asked where she had gone wrong. I felt so bad. No child wants to make their parent feel as if they have somehow failed them. I assured her that she and my dad always made me feel good about myself and that I always knew that they were proud of me.

I don't know when the low self-esteem crept in. I do know it is something I have done to myself, or something I have allowed to be done to me. Somehow the negative is just so much easier to believe. When I look into the mirror, I see the flaws. I don't see beauty. While engaging in conversations on politics instead focusing on what I do know, I am obsessed and feel intimidated by all that I don't know. It's hard to believe that someone else can see beauty or intelligence in you when you can't see it in yourself. Whenever a person is nice to me or wants to be my friend, I am constantly wondering, *Why is this person being nice to me? Why would they want to be friends with me?* People who believe in themselves don't have these sorts of thoughts. I don't want to question people's motives when they are nice to me, but I can't help it.

Things finally got to the point where the pain was greater than my desire to live. It had been so bleak in my world that I didn't think I would ever see my way out. I'd be driving in my car and wish that I'd lose control of the vehicle and be out of pain, or I'd hope that maybe my lupus would take a turn for the worse and kill me. There was one day in particular that I remember where I hurt so badly I literally couldn't even pick myself up of the floor. I spent an entire day of my life on my bedroom floor in tears. I cried mostly because of how much I hated myself. A few days following that, I finally found a therapist and got onto antidepressants. I needed to find out why I disliked myself so much, because my self-loathing was destroying me, and I didn't want to spend another twenty-six years feeling this way.

I had always told myself that I would never take medication for depression. There was such a stigma that went along with it in my mind. After several weeks of taking the meds, it was apparent how desperately I needed the pills. I had been obsessed with Alistair. I couldn't stop thinking about him and thinking about him hurting me. I would replay hurtful encounters over and over again; I couldn't help myself. I thought how much I had confessed to him and why. I thought about the confessions I had heard from other women. Why I wasn't good enough for him? How I could fall in love with someone so incapable of loving me back? I cried all the time without any real reason. I was on the edge, a time bomb. Things had gotten so bad that I was without a job and I had dropped out of graduate school. My life consisted of food, tears, and daytime-TV drama. I just lost all motivation for living. I had no initiative and didn't want anything out of life other than to leave it.

Things were so scary for me during this time that I decided to pack up and go home to Georgia for a few weeks, just to get away from things. I was carrying a lot of guilt from being away from my dad, so I thought this would be the perfect time to just be there with him.

The first couple of weeks were excruciatingly painful. Every time I saw a car the remotely resembled Alistair's, I wanted to cry. Forcing up the intestinal fortitude to go to the nursing home and see my father – so small, so frail, and so sick – was agonizing for me. It was hard to go, but even harder to leave. As the days passed and more and more medicine got into my system, my head became clearer and I became stronger.

When I go to Georgia, I stay with my cousin, Patrice, and her family. One day, Patrice, her four kids, and I went to Target, just to get out and walk around and – for no particular reason – I just felt happy. There wasn't anything spectacular that happened. I wasn't anticipating something massive, I still didn't have a job, and I was a grad-school dropout; but it was as if in an instant I felt that things were going to get better. I didn't know how, but I felt like there was a way out. I was happy right then, and I wanted to live again. I hadn't felt like that in months.

After that realization, I realized that Alistair hadn't crossed my mind in at least a few days, and for me that was monumental. I didn't know it was possible to go a single second without thinking about him, and here I had gone for days. I was amazed.

During my low moments in Alabama, I had learned that Paul had moved out of his parents' home. Apparently, his grandfather moved to California and gave Paul his house. Paul and I were emailing back and forth one night when he casually mentioned the joys of living alone. I reread the statement a couple of times and then whipped out my cell phone. When he answered, I said, "What? You live alone?"

He started laughing and said, "Surely, I mentioned that to you?"

He hadn't, but he has a habit of not mentioning things. I was in shock that he had moved out of his parents' house and was on his own, even if it was next door or down the road, and he hadn't told me. Later, this would bother more than I realized at the time.

The conversation that night sparked many others, and our relationship started to pick up a little again. I was happy to be talking to Paul again. We can talk on the phone forever about a wide array of topics. He makes me laugh, and he's the only person in the world that makes me feel as if I can breathe without Alistair.

One night, I was at my cousins and we were just sitting around laughing and goofing off. Out of the blue, Paul called. I was in shock and excited. Patrice stared at me as I stared at my cell phone. I couldn't believe he was calling me. He wasn't returning a call. I hadn't emailed him and asked him to call me; he was actually calling me.

I finally answered the phone and he told me he was on his way home from work and had just been thinking about me and had decided to call. *Could this night get any better?* I thought. I couldn't fathom that he had thought about me without any sort of prompting from me. That was the best conversation of my life. Sure, he had called before, but only to thank me for a gift, respond to an email, or return my call; never just to call. It made me feel special. I didn't even feel like myself.

The Man behind the Voice

The jubilation of late-night phone calls with Paul was sweet but short-lived not the rate at which we spoke but the magic that seemed to accompany our conversations. At first, Paul seemed to honestly enjoy talking to me – to the point where he encouraged me to "call anytime." However, I believe my tendency to become obsessed with any sort of male attention ruined any excitement on his part to talk to me. I'd call, and he wouldn't answer, or I'd call and the conversations would become shorter and shorter. I became this junkie who needed his voice. I have always been in love with the sound of his voice, and it has always been that the more he gave the more I would want. It seems nothing he ever gives is good enough. It makes sense that a person would get tired of never measuring up to a person's expectations.

Paul doesn't ever try to hurt me intentionally. He is just himself. I get frustrated being a now twenty-six-year-old woman tangled up in a fourth-grade relationship with a grown man. We are friends, and I try to accept that; but on days when I am honest with myself I can admit that statement is totally false. I keep hoping that being there will count for something. That one-day it will matter that I have these unexplainable feelings for him that don't make any sense. I keep hoping that even though he'd never admit it, maybe it does mean something poignant to him that I love him and maybe that's not always such a creepy thing – just possibly there is something romantic and poetic about loving someone you don't know entirely, where what you know is based solely on observation, instinct, and the tidbits they decide to share. It doesn't make sense, but what I have been trying to figure out is, does it have to?

The other night, I got an email from Paul and my reaction to it was completely unbalanced. In a previous email, Paul had nonchalantly mentioned that he had taken his mother and brother's fiancée shopping. My initial reaction was one of shock because he had never even mentioned his brother having a girlfriend, much less him being engaged. I am embarrassed to admit that it hurt my feelings a little that he didn't mention it to me. I expressed these feelings to Sal, and she gave me the whole "women and men think differently" talk and said it probably wasn't a big deal to him. This was something in his brother's life, not his; it's not like Paul got engaged and didn't tell me.

Sal's usually my voice of reason, so I let this soothe me a little. I realized it was irrational to be upset. In an overly dramatized, comedic way, I let him know I was surprised he hadn't mentioned it. Paul responded really well and basically stated, in his guy way, what Sal had said. Then he went on to describe what a great and beautiful woman his brother had in his life. It was obvious that Paul was genuinely happy for his brother. He went on to discuss what a fine girlfriend his younger brother was dating and said that he'd probably be engaged soon as well. Apparently, she is also someone that Paul holds in very high esteem. I felt very warm and tingly inside (at first), I genuinely did, while reading his endearing email about his brothers. I thought about how he was such a sincere person.

I read further into the email. Paul went on to describe how he ordered and received a typewriter off of the Internet. The typewriter was from the 1800s, and he described its intricacies with the same warmth and excitement he had used to describe the women in his brothers' lives. He went so far as to describe himself as being in love with it. I am not so far gone now or then not to know that he was exaggerating, but something about him writing that caused me to go temporarily insane. I snapped.

I got up from my computer ran around my room, jumped onto my bed repeatedly, and screamed until my pillow until I felt flushed. I got myself together enough to email him back a quick message back that read, "I am glad you are in love with something." I wanted to add "capable," but I thought that was a little bitchier than our relationship could handle. Sometimes, I throw in a quick jab here and there to vent some of my frustrations. I tell myself that he doesn't get it, but he probably does and just ignores me. He is good at that.

I don't know what happened to me that night. I just got frustrated. I thought, "Why the hell am I still hoping I will get some kind of relationship with this man? He gets more excited over inanimate objects than I have ever heard him get over anything remotely intimate or romantic with a woman. He could be a Don Juan for all I know but the point is that he isn't with me and is never going to be.

I think, on the night of my meltdown, I just needed to actually feel the pain that comes from beating your head against a brick wall. This isn't a new realization. Every couple of months I will have what I call a "lifetime moment." I will pull back from the calls and emails and trick myself into believing I am strong enough to just email and call as a friend. Soon after, I get sucked back into wanting him in a way that he is totally incapable of being in my life. I keep getting ripped apart, and the worst part is that it's my fault. I get mad at him and sometimes lash out to make myself feel better, but I know it isn't his fault.

I live in a fantasy world. I've never even dealt with the whole race issue. I spend so much time on "I'm not good a enough …" and on finding various reasons that I've never even considered whether being with a person of color would bother him or his family. I have been so convinced that love and romance would be enough and all else would work out. But the truth of the matter is that I could have wasted three years of my life in love with a person that could never love me back or be attracted to me because of my race. I put myself down because of my weight, my intelligence, and my tendency to have minor breakdowns over the tiniest of issues – but maybe there was never a chance. Maybe, from the moment he met me, there wasn't a chance. How humiliating would that be? See, this race issue gets to the crux of my problem; I don't deal with reality. In my world, issues such as that don't factor in, but that's not how this world works.

Whoever coined the phrase "when it rains it pours" must have had a window into my life. My state decided that the health problems of the poor were not issues that concerned them, and I lost my health insurance. The notice came in the form of a letter. At first, there was this mad dash to return all this paperwork, as if there was some hope I might be able to keep my healthcare. Finally, I got a second notice that stated I would lose my insurance in August. At this point, I was unemployed, a graduate school drop-out, and uninsurable because of my lupus. The pressure was now on to find a job. Also at this time, my unemployment had just run out. In retrospect, I see that I should have been using the six months I was on unemployment to find another job, but I was too preoccupied with my nervous breakdown and, to add insult to injury, I was also flat broke.

I sent out resume after resume and filled out one application after another. I didn't get one response in two months. My self-esteem was taking a beating it couldn't handle. I felt myself slipping back down that dark road of depression. It was time to run away again. The bad thoughts were back, and this time I was more terrified than ever before. I forwarded my home phone to my cell phone and headed back to Georgia. I knew when I left that things would be different when I returned; I just didn't know how so.

I spent week after week in Georgia trying to get the strength to return to my life in Alabama. At the close of each day, I would get more and more depressed that I had failed to receive a call from an interested employer. I had Sal checking my mail to see if I received any notices by mail, but of course nothing ever came. I began to feel more and more worthless.

Then came the decision to live in denial. I just put all of my problems out of my head for awhile. This actually worked, until I started running out of medication and did not have the money to refill them. This is when the borrowing began. Having to borrow from my friends put me into a level of despair I cannot fully explain.

My friend, Lily, who was in law school at Howard loaned me about $1,150. She was in law school, working hard, and here I was bumming money from her. She didn't loan it to me all at once; it was a little here and there. The thing about Lily is that she never made me feel as if it was favor. She never even hesitated; she just wrote me checks and wished me well. She gave the money knowing that I had no clue when I'd ever be able to pay it back. Every time I'd try to express my gratitude, she'd say she knew I'd do the same thing for her. I felt so ashamed for having to ask her, but she kept saying that we were friends and that's what friends do.

At one point, the last time, I begged for money. I thought she was upset with me because she hadn't responded right away. Because I am me, I had assumed the worse. A couple days later she called me and said law school had her running like crazy but of course she'd help. She was upset that I could ever think she'd let something like money come between us. She said we have been friends too long. What felt good about this was that she meant it.

I took a brief break from Georgia to attend Sal and Eric's wedding in Louisiana. Their wedding was the weekend before Hurricane Katrina struck. Right after the wedding, I returned to Campbellton, Georgia. One random day, without thinking, I said to my cousin, "We should get a house here, and I should move back." Surprisingly, my cousin agreed, and so did her husband; and before I could exhale we were moving into our dream house near Tara Boulevard.

I couldn't believe that a decision that had proven so difficult in the past was just made on a whim. There were so many things that I'd miss in my previous state: Sal, Carmen, Claire, my doctors, my life; but nothing cut to the bone like leaving Alistair. Paul didn't really enter my mind since we were apart all of the time anyway. I figured that if he could come to Alabama, he could come to Campbellton, Georgia; they were about the same distance.

I think Sal was in a state of shock when I told her. I don't blame her, because even as I was telling her I couldn't believe it. My mom was ecstatic about me moving back and it seemed to please my father, and that gave me some peace about the decision. All the signs seemed to be directing me back home. My apartment complex was very understanding, which is highly irregular for apartment complexes. They let my out of my lease free of charge. They understood my situation with healthcare and not being able to afford my meds. In Georgia, I was eligible for assistance.

Moving was not a cheap, so I was forced once again to start panhandling among my friends. I had exhausted all of my friends to the point that my friends, Lori and Mark, went to their church and asked for money for me. The move, meds, bills, and food was piling on me, and my poor mother was doing her very best to keep us afloat; but I was drowning us. I promised myself that I would never ask Alistair or Paul for money, but things got so bad that I had to break that promise to myself.

I was too much of a coward to ask Paul via phone, so I sent him an email that went something like this. "You wouldn't happen to have a spare three hundred dollars lying under your floor boards that you could loan me until I got a job?"

His response: "I'll send you a check tomorrow."

I was in shock when I later checked my email and saw his response. I was embarrassed, thankful, and relieved. I called him and left a thank you message and asked him if this meant I was his girlfriend, since he'd loaned me this money without even thinking about it. Paul being Paul just ignored me and told me I was silly. I was too love-struck to be insulted.

One of my biggest fears is that Paul will find someone to love that's not me. I actually cry myself to sleep over that very thought. I know that he considers me someone near to him, because you don't just Willie Nillie loan some jerk off of the street three hundred dollars. I just want to be someone other than his friend, Mary. I have this strong desire to be someone's girlfriend before I die. I don't think that's unreasonable or unusual for most people; it just seems to be impossible for me for some unknown reason.

After the loaning of the money, I again started with the calling and he again started with the ignoring. It is as if the more he pulls away, the more I chase. I am so scared of being forgotten. Deep down inside, I know I have made myself so available to him that he couldn't forget if he wanted to, but that's not really comforting or all that positive. I keep thinking, "Why doesn't he love me?"

I sit here and wish that somehow Paul would realize that he does want me and that will be it, but I have no real clue as to what is going on in his life. What if there is already someone? I keep thinking he'd tell me. After what we went through before, and because he knows I am into him, he'll tell me; but I'm scared. I want to ask him, but once I do there's no going back. I'm not sure my heart recovered from the last blow. I know I am somewhat on the move because things with that last girl ended horribly. Things were so bad that he still to this day won't tell me what happened. I know I shouldn't derive happiness from a bad relationship experience that he had, but I can't help myself. I don't think I can be happy for him being with anyone that's not me.

I am as over Constantine as I can possibly be, but I still have no desire to meet his wife. I have no doubt that she is intelligent, pretty, warm, and giving; but I can't bring myself to be around the woman he could make it work with. I know that's selfish, but it's honest, and if I can't at least be honest with myself, what's the point of any of this?

It's been months since Paul has called or emailed or anything without my prompting. I try to remind myself of this whenever the impulse to call him or email him strikes, but the impulse is always stronger than I am. Just recently, I spent two weeks leaving messages and text messages and emailing. I received no response. Undaunted, I wrote him a letter and made him a CD with a few of my favorites. Everything would have been fine if I had been able to control myself from turning a simple track listing into a love letter. I know he received it because he told me so in a text message, which I prompted, but he hasn't responded. In his defense, he's been in Mississippi visiting and taking care of his grandmother. I know that chemo can be pretty rough, so of course his mind is there and not with some silly girl that's in love with him. Plus, nothing in the letter was a new revelation. He probably read it and was like "and ... so what?" Why am I so stupid?

I am so tempted to take a weekend and drive to his town to see him. I need to see him, if for no other reason to end this story on paper and in my life. He obviously has no intention of getting down here anytime soon. My urgency is definitely not his emergency. His friend Matt lives here. I almost wish Matt and I were close enough for me to enlist his help in getting Paul down here. I wish Paul realized how important all of this is to me or, better yet, gave a damn.

A Drunken Man's Words are a Sober Man's Thoughts

Over the last few months, it has become clear to me that the great love of Alistair's life is Alistair, but last night I realized that I was mistaken. Much to my surprise, Alistair loves Eric – not in a romantic way, of course, but in the way you do a great true friend, the way I love Sal. He and Eric were drunk last night, and it all came pouring out. Sadly, I can't help but be a little jealous. Alistair is really torn up about losing his connection with Eric when he marries Sal next month and moves out. I know that this does not sound like much, but just to see him capable of real emotion and real pain made mine somehow seem more justified in some unexplainable way.

I also realized that Alistair and I would be linked together through Eric and Sal forever. Alistair is not about to lose Eric anytime soon, and I am for damn sure not going to lose Sal or Eric, who I've come to love as a brother. As I've known for awhile, Alistair is never going to change and therefore the course of our relationship will never change, unless I change it. We have the same fights, flirtatious moments, close encounters, missed opportunities, unsaid words, and times were we've said way too much every time we see each other.

Whenever I see him, my mouth says one thing while my heart is screaming something else. I just want to convince him to change and to want to be with me and settle down. Instead, I say something that I hope passes for clever or maybe even seductive, and then we begin the dance that we do. Sometimes I wonder if he sees this in the same way I do. He gets frustrated with me because he says that I act as if we aren't friends when we're in public. How does he want me to act? I wonder. I see women from his harem who follow him around from room to room, salivating for a pat on the head from their master. When I'm around him, I do the best I can. It rips my heart out to see him with other women, but I have mastered pretending to not notice. I can hold four different conversations at once and still be zeroed in on wherever the hell he is in the room. Being in love with him is a full-time job and sometimes it feels like a mental illness.

I still worry that he will get one of his X's pregnant. Sadly, I am still not worried about the ramifications for him, the child, or the mother; I am fixated on the intense jealousy that I will feel. I can't even comprehend the insane jealousy that will take over my body. Sex is one thing, because let's face it he sleeps with a lot of women. Sex is an act for him; it isn't love. But a baby … that's real. I can't make that ugly or mean nothing – a baby could be nothing other than beautiful. I act so nonchalant about having babies. I say things like, "Maybe I'll have children," or "I don't know if I want children," but the truth is that I do want children, and I worry every day that it isn't going to happen. I'm wasting time holding out for him.

Alistair came over one night for dinner, and we had a really good talk. This night was different because I really listened to him. Usually he talks and I am looking at his hair or his arms, or I get lost in his eyes; but this night I stayed focused. He told me with no hesitation whatsoever that he did not want to have children. Secretly, I wanted to tell him how desperately I want the whole picture. I wanted to tell him how I want the husband, the solid marriage, the children, the family; I want all of it. God help me, I want it with him, even knowing that it would never work and he isn't the kind of man that needs to be a father – at least, not at this point in his life. He has made a clear choice about who he wants to be, and that person is irresponsible and at times a selfish dickhead.

A couple of months ago, Alistair and I were talking on the phone and he was a little sedate. I didn't mention it, but I noticed. He made some random comment, and I didn't get the reference. He then went on to explain to me that Hunter S. Thompson had committed suicide. I took a respectful moment of silence and then I asked, "Who's Hunter S. Thompson?"

He then took a moment, surprised that the aspiring writer who had majored in English was ignorant on this particular subject. Alistair explained to me about Gonzo journalism and Thompson's writing. I felt a little better when I could say I had heard of *Fear and Loathing in Las Vegas*. I was moved that this had impacted him. He always turned me on when he was soulful. I felt kind of honored that he even mentioned it to me. After we finished talking, I did a Google search on Thompson and read up on him. I saw a web site for a DVD all about Thompson and starring Thompson. I whipped out my plastic and purchased the DVD and waited anxiously for it to arrive. The next day, I purchased two of his books. After investigating Thompson, it became obvious to me why Alistair would be an admirer of his. I was willing to do just about anything to get inside Alistair's head. I wanted to know what made him tick. I wanted to know what he cared about.

After a few days, the DVD, *Breakfast with Hunter*, arrived, and I packed it up and delivered it to Alistair. When I gave it to him, he was really surprised, I think. I wrote him some sort of dorky note to go along with the DVD. I can't remember what the note said, but it basically said that I was sort of moved by his passion or feelings for a fallen idol and that I cared and was listening, or something like that. It seemed as if he was genuinely happy to receive the gift, and that made my heart soar. For some reason, making him happy just sometimes makes me feel as if I have purpose. I know that can't be good. I just love making him happy. I just wish someone loved me that way. I feel like I deserve a little bit of that. I just want to know what that feels like before I leave this earth.

I had told him that if ever I had a son, I would name him Atticus after the character in *To Kill A Mockingbird*, but after our conversations about Hunter Thompson I daydreamed about having son with him that I'd name Atticus Hunter Salinger. If I truly wanted Alistair out of my life, confessing this fantasy to him would surely rid him from my life. He probably thinks I'm crazy already but this tidbit of information would certainly remove all doubt.

Things had gotten so bad at home prior to moving to Georgia that I was unable to pick myself up off of the floor. There was a day where I fell to the ground and remained there for the entire day, crying, because Alistair had another X – an X who was my polar opposite and who made me acutely aware of everything hideous and grotesque about me. During that time, I felt so ashamed of myself and who I was, and I hated everything about me. I wanted to die. This time, it wasn't for dramatic effect; I just wanted the pain to stop. Hating oneself is a pain that is crippling and felt throughout one's whole self. I allowed myself to want to die, and I couldn't help myself.

I cried so much that my face swelled and my head ached. I made myself ill with the depression. Finally, I got scared, and somehow I managed to pick myself up from the floor and contact a lifeline. I made the decision to return home to Campbellton, Georgia. I felt I needed to escape the madness in Alabama, and somehow thought the voices in my head would cease if I ran. I didn't give myself time to think the move through.

Uncharacteristically, I didn't consult Sal. I didn't give anyone a chance to convince me to stay in Alabama. I just ran. The first couple of weeks I was there, the tears continually fell and I felt hollow, as if I was gasping for air. Before I left Alabama, I started anti-depressants. They hadn't worked in Alabama, but I hoped Georgia would be a different story, even though in my heart I didn't believe they would or could do me any good.

Though I was doubtful, I robotically took the pills each day. I felt as if I was living in a fog. The world seemed out of focus and surreal to me. Everything reminded me of what I had left behind in Alabama. I couldn't even hear the name of Alistair's latest X without breaking down and completely falling apart. This was problematic, because the cousin I lived with has a daughter with the exact same name as the X. The name was frequently called, and I'd cry. Hall and Oates sing a song about her smile, and I'd die a little each time I heard them croon about her. I'd smell something, and it would remind me of him in some form of fashion, and I would become unglued. I was constantly thinking about him and wondering whether he was thinking about me. My love of all things Beatles was in jeopardy, for everything I saw or heard just broke me. Life in general reminded me of him.

At that time, I felt that I'd never be free. I obsessed over him. I'd call and I'd call and I'd call. When he didn't answer, I was convinced that he was there, looking at the caller id and not answering because it was me again. Each time I'd swear I wouldn't call again, and then I did time after time. I'd call until I got him on the line. Once I had him, I'd act like all was well and that I was just casually calling to say hello. He didn't know I needed those little mundane conversations so my mind could focus on something else for a while. I needed that semblance of normalcy, however briefly it lasted. I hated myself every time we talked. I was desperate and pathetic each and every time I talked to him. I kept thinking there was something I could say that would matter and he'd love me they way I loved him and we could be together.

Throughout my whole life, I have been delusional, and I realize this and wonder if somehow the realization of this makes me less crazy, despite the delusions. In my mind, I'd imagine him as lovesick and as torn up as me. I envisioned him tormented by his demons, different than mine but still these obstacles that prevented us from getting together. Some days, I convinced myself that he loved me too, despite the fact that he never called, never initiated any interaction between the two of us, and was never intimate with me on an emotional level. I know now that I needed these delusions to keep going and to justify my feelings for him. I had to believe there was something in this for me, even though time and time again I was given nothing and not promised anything. I am nothing, to him.

I tell myself that my rational self made the decision to leave because the other part of me would never have been able to leave. The main part of me, the irrational, would have remained in Alabama, waiting for Alistair or Paul to suddenly become what I thought I needed at the time. The hope of this was too much for my larger self. What was truly terrifying was the idea that I could delude myself for a lifetime. That's all I knew. If I had tuned into this channel in anyone else's life, I would have seen the futility, but since it was my show I couldn't break free from it and be better. I knew that we – me and Paul, me and Alistair – wouldn't be together; I knew this, but I couldn't believe it and nor could I feel it. Neither fellow has given me any reason to think differently, but still my whole heart and soul are invested in this obsession, praying and lusting for them – for what?

I'm scared, because I don't know how to let go. I love with all that I have in me. I've never learned how to let go. At this point, I am twenty-eight years old, and I still love Constantine. There are dark days when I can go back there. That was the one time in my life where I felt love from the person who had currently captured my heart. What does this say about me? Is it possible that I am in anyway sane?

Now it has been about two years since I left Alabama, and after being away and taking time to reflect, I realize that sadly I'm no better off than when I left. My head is a little clearer, thanks to the meds that finally started to work months after I had started them. I realize that perhaps they had worked some before Georgia, because I believe they could possibly be the reason I got up off that floor that day and decided to move.

Since I've been in Georgia, I have tried so hard to focus on getting a job and remaining healthy, but much to my dismay Alistair is always there in the back of my mind. He's there and I hate it.

A few Friday's ago, Patrice and I had some of the family over to celebrate big Samuel's birthday. Patrice's little sis, my little cousin, Michele, has been dying to get me to open a MySpace account. Michele had mentioned it no less than a hundred times, but I never had the time to commit to setting it up. That sounds like such the lie, coming from the woman who seemed to have nothing but time. Finally, I made time to sit down with her to set the account up. What really motivated me was that there was this song on *General Hospital* that I was desperate to possess, and the artist was subscribed to MySpace, so I figured I could catch up with her that way.

Once Michele and I got started, I realized how much fun this could be to work on the site. Long after I left Michele, I continued to work on MySpace account. I even figured out a way to search University Alum to see who members were. I was psyched when I ran across three old friends.

The night before last, I got released from the hospital. My lupus managed to get the best of me and I had no choice but to be taken to the ER. I was horrified when I learned I was being admitted. I let my lupus get way out of control because I couldn't afford my meds or afford to go to appointments without health insurance. Now that I am feeling better, I don't know what I am going to do to ensure that I stay feeling this way. While I was in the hospital, the social worker helped me apply for disability. Disability will take at least four months to answer. I can't wait that long to have money rolling in, but anyway, as usual I digress.

Since I have been back home, I have just been resting and taking it easy, so nothing different to any other day. I decided to get on MySpace and mess around. I didn't have any new messages, so I decided to cruise the University Alum's again. After about thirty minutes of thinking, *Well, he looks familiar*, or, *I took Bible with her*, or, *He was strange*, I decided to call it a day. As I started to sign off, it hit me. The idea of ideas hit me. I decided to cruise a list of current students and see if I could locate Alistair's last flavor of the month.

I knew it was a crazy idea, but I had to do it. The whole MySpace thing seemed so up her alley. I knew she'd have a profile. I sat there searching picture after picture until finally, EUREKA! I found her. I stared at her picture so long and hard, and I hated her all over again, and then I thought how he had hurt her and I just felt numb. I wanted to cry when I thought about all the times he had made love to her or all the times their lips had touched. I felt ill at the very thought of it. All finding her did was remind me of all the things that were wrong with me. Everything that was wrong about me was right about her, and yet he couldn't love her either – at least, not in a committed till-death-do-us-part kind of way.

Without even thinking, I started emailing her. I reintroduced myself to her and I told her that we should talk and that I had a lot I needed to say to her and probably apologize for. I told her that I had a complicated and challenging relationship with Alistair, and that she had entered the picture at one of the most difficult times in my life. I asked her to write me back or call me, and I left my cell phone number.

I don't know if she'll write or call, but I had to do it. I had to. I don't know why, but I did. Maybe it was some strange way of keeping enemies closer, or maybe it's working towards letting some of the pain go. She never called. We became MySpace friends but we never spoke to each other about him or about anything for that matter. I'm guessing that's what he advised.

The last time Alistair and I spent real time with each other before I moved back to Georgia was the trip to and from Louisiana for Sal and Eric's wedding. I was in shock that things actually worked out where the two of us rode together – us, alone. These things never worked out like this, but this time it did. We got to spend a total of sixteen hours together in the car, all cozy, just the two of us. I was a little worried about the trip at first because he was tired from the jump. He got into the car with shades on and went to sleep. I was a bit heartbroken but I trudged on. I had made several mixed CD's and I think my eclectic taste grabbed his attention. Before I knew it, we were singing to the Beatles and burning tracks down the highway. Slowly, conversation brewed, and then laughter, and then into our little world, population two.

He has this way of telling tales from his childhood that engage me and make me laugh. I never laugh the way I laugh with him. We played car games, and I lost every time; but I enjoyed every minute of it. Usually on car trips, I'm thinking I can't wait to get there, but on this trip I kept hoping for traffic or misdirection. More time with him is everything. I kept thinking, is he enjoying this half as much as I am? I know that he probably didn't, not even a fourth as much; but denial is my main thing so I'll imagine it was a special time for us both.

I knew several months before the wedding that Sal's families' homes in Louisiana were all going to be inundated with other family, so I made reservations at a local hotel. By the time we made it to Louisiana, Alistair had gotten hold of Eric, who was already drunk, and found out that Eric and the other guys were headed to a club. I gleaned from Alistair's part of the conversation that Eric wanted him to meet them at the club.

Alistair was hesitant but not for any reason that would make me happy. Alistair is the vainest man I have ever met, and he was not in going-out attire, so he didn't want to go to a club until he could at least change if not shower as well.

Eric convinced Alistair to come out with very little effort. Alistair explained that we were still an hour and a half away if we were lucky and asked whether Eric was sure that they would still be at the club by the time we got there and wouldn't be so drunk it would be pointless for him to come. Eric promised that all would be cool an hour and a half from then. After the conversation (on my phone, I should say) was finished, Alistair said, "Baby, you don't mind dropping me off at the club before you go to your hotel, do you?"

I mind a whole lot, you selfish piece of trash – but of course I only thought that and didn't say it. I said something like "Of course I don't." I was peeved that after all that time that had seemed so perfect, he didn't want to spend the rest of the evening with me. He didn't even ask me if I wanted to go to the club with him. He just wanted to be dropped off.

As usual it took little to no time for me to turn my frown upside down and get back to "Alistair and Mary" land. It was less than two hours before the clock struck twelve and I would turn back into a pathetic world-record virgin and he would turn back into a big ole jack ass. Why waste the spell on something as insignificant as my feelings or reality? We went back to car games and the Beatles.

When we were about twenty minutes from meeting the fellas, Eric calls Alistair again, on my phone, to say that all the guys were drunker than Alistair had been on Tuesday and were heading back in for the night. Alistair was pissed, because he had known that would happen. Then Alistair realized he had no where to stay because he could no longer get in contact with the person he was staying with. I sat there thinking, how do I play this? Here is my chance. He needs a room; I have a room: there's an obvious solution to this problem.

I wanted to make the offer, but not in a way that he would know how desperately I wanted him in my room. I didn't want to seem hurt or honestly devastated by him declining my offer, so I didn't mention my room right away. We went back to our talks and listening to music. When there seemed to be a lull, I said, "I don't want this to come out like a lame come on, but if you want to stay in my room that would be cool with me, because I have an extra bed. Please don't take this as a booty call." Inside, I was thinking, *That is exactly what this is, my friend.*

He smiled his Alistair-smile that said nothing while his face said everything. I wasn't his plan for the evening. He seemed to be thinking,

How do I get out of this without being an even huger dick than she already believes me to be? Before either of us could calculate our next move, my phone rang again. Would you believe that it was his MIA friend from earlier, the one he was supposed to be staying with for his stay in Louisiana? By this time, Alistair was driving and I was riding. Alistair ended his call quickly and told me that he was going to turn around and go back a few miles and meet his friend.

"You don't mind driving in by yourself the rest of the way, do you?"

"No, that is totally fine," I said as I bit my lip and grabbed onto the door handle for support.

We meet his friend at a gas station. I said a quick hello and got a nice sideways hug from Alistair and a rather endearing hug from his friend before I left them both at the gas station. I got in the car as if I had no cares in the world. As I pulled out of the gas station parking lot, I saw them leave through the rearview mirror. As we turned in opposite directions, I began to cry, silently, carefully, painfully and with familiarity. That night truly marked the end of whatever we had. I didn't know it at the time, but that was definitely the end.

I finally arrived at the hotel after midnight checked in went straight to my room and put on my PJs. I then called Sal, who told me that she was at her bachelorette party and gave me directions. I told her I was too tired to come out and I ached. Thankfully, she didn't ask where.

Awhile later, Sal arrived at my hotel room decorated and beaming. I tried my best to appear tired and worn out from the trip and not devastated and heartbroken. She shouldn't have known during one of the best moments of her life that I was having one of the worst of mine. That always seemed to happen to me after I spent any time with Alistair. Maybe I should be learning something from these encounters? I convinced Sal that I was too tired to do anything other than rest, and so she left, but not before I promised that I would be up to par the next day and ready to help out with wedding stuff.

After Sal had left, I got a cup of water, thanked God for Ambien and anti-depressants, and drifted off to sleep. I woke the next morning aching and tired as if I hadn't slept at all the night before. I rolled over, looked at the clock, and knew that Sal would be calling me soon to take me up on my offer to help with wedding preparations. I thought about telling her that I felt bad and needed to stay in bed so I'd be up to snuff for the wedding the next day, but I said nothing. I ended up at Sal's grandmother's house, folding and printing wedding programs and stuffing them with bookmarks that had Eric and Sal's picture on them. The job was easy and for awhile I forgot that I was sad and that Alistair had rejected me.

When we finished the programs I was taken to the church to help decorate. As soon as I got to the church, I knew I was not going to make it. I ached so terribly and felt this huge hole inside that seemed to make breathing hard and painful. I cursed myself for letting Alistair make me so miserable for my best friend's wedding. I hung flowers, made party favors, mingled with friends and family, and tried desperately to fight back the tears that felt inevitable.

After what seemed like years, I made it back to my room and tried to wash off whatever was bringing me down and get ready for Sal's wedding the next day. While I was in the shower, it finally hit me as to why Alistair's usual antics had devastated me so greatly. He had done nothing out of character or unexpected. He was there, being himself, and I was convenient to him – and that hadn't changed. Suddenly, that hole inside seemed to be growing larger and larger, and slowly I realized that it wasn't Alistair who had gotten a hold of me; it was a green-eyed monster that I fooled myself into thinking I was immune to. I was jealous.

I realized that even my spit tasted sour and bitter. Sal was marrying Eric. I chased love with all that I had, and it eluded me; and here I am watching Sal get everything that I have dreamed of. I wanted someone to love me and be willing to confess that aloud and make promises to me in front of God, and for once in my life I wanted to be chased and caught instead of pursuing and trying to hold onto water.

This realization made me feel so small and hateful and even more undeserving of love. Alistair was never going to marry me, and neither was Paul for that matter.

The wedding came and the wedding went. My pain became physical and that, coupled with the Louisiana heat, caused me to nearly pass out while I was standing with the other bridesmaids. I became dizzy and sweat poured from me as I tried to focus on the event and not on myself. The dizziness got to the point where I whispered to Sal's cousin who was next to me that I was feeling lightheaded and asked if I could lean on her. She very sweetly said, "Of course," and I did. This caused the other bridesmaids to look at me and encourage me to sit down on a front pew. I tried to wave them off and say that I was fine, but I wasn't and apparently it showed. Finally, one of the bridesmaids told me that if I didn't go and sit down she was going to get out of the line and grab my arm and drag me to a seat.

At this point my vision was dark, so I accepted my fate and sat down.

I was humiliated and felt terrible. As if I hadn't brought enough drama to the ceremony, Sal's sweet silver-haired grandmother stood up behind me and began to fan me. I wanted to die right there.

Five million hours later, the wedding ended and the groomsman began to line up for the walk down the aisle. After they were in place, the bridesmaids began to line up with their escorts. My escort, a friend of Eric's who I did not know, gave me a look and said, "Are you going to be able to walk back?"

I shook my head pathetically to indicate that I would not be able to do that.

He gave a me look of complete understanding and sympathy, but before I could really embrace how comforting that was, everyone else said to me as if to say, "You can't *at least* walk back with him?" The painful, jagged way the words hit me jerked me out of the moment I was having with my unknown escort: experiencing a stranger's serene kindness. Everything happened so fast that I couldn't process my response fast enough. Usually, I think through my responses and don't come across as ruffled, even though I may be completely put off – no such luck at that moment. I snapped my head around to where I couldn't see anyone and let out this huge, exasperated sigh.

I couldn't believe I had done that, and the adrenaline quickly took over. I flew off the pew and into my escort. As if we had practiced my recovery, he grabbed my arm and steered me to the right position, and we were off down the aisle.

I was so humiliated and felt so terrible that I didn't make it to the reception. Eric's sister and her husband drove me back to the hotel, and then they went on the reception. I just hurt so emotionally and physically that I knew I couldn't get through a reception. I didn't feel like being the wallflower and watching Alistair do his thing with women he preferred over me, but who were more whore than lady. I told myself this so I wouldn't have to face how pervasive my jealousy had become. Not only did I envy Sal's day but I also envied the women who owned their sexuality and used their imperfections as garnishment as opposed to shackles. I envied his women as much as I hated them.

As soon as I got into my room, I stripped my dress off, put on my pajamas and ordered a pizza and a liter of soda. It took several acts of congress before my pizza was delivered. I quickly wolfed down four or five slices in record time, washed them down with half the soda, and crawled into bed once again to sing the praises of sleeping medication and happy pills. I just wanted to sleep and wake up to a new day.

Before I could have another thought, I woke up to that new day. As soon as I woke up, I threw my stuff into my suitcase and got ready to get the hell out of dodge. Alistair and I hadn't spoken the day before, and I had no idea whether or not he was riding back with me. I tried not to invest in the idea of us going back together, but it was no use. As I was loading up, I saw Sal drive into the hotel parking lot. She was there to clean out the room she had spent several nights in. Apparently, the night before, she and Eric had stayed in a nicer hotel for the evening.

Sal and I conversed briefly. She asked me how I was feeling, and I asked her about the reception. As we stood outside talking, we realized how ominous the sky looked. Sal told me a storm was coming that was supposed to hit New Orleans pretty hard. That is where she and Eric had originally planned to go for their honeymoon, but they changed their plans when they heard about the storm. I hate rain, thunderstorms, lightning, and anything to do with rain. This made me all the more anxious to have Alistair head back to Alabama with me.

I waited around for him to notice me and address the elephant in the room. Finally he says, exasperated, as if he was waiting on me, "Are we headed back?"

I tried not to look relieved and said, "Ready when you are."

We headed out, away from the room where so many of my hopes, dreams and desires had been quelled by his non-interest in me. He drove most of the way, and the trip home was lot more quiet than the trip there had been. I felt sad inside, because I knew that the ride home was somehow the last bit of real time I'd ever have with him.

After eight awkward hours, we made it to Alistair's house. I didn't even go inside; I just waited for him to get out and collect his stuff. We said our goodbyes, which consisted of *see ya*'s. He walked away, and I took off.

The next day, I drove to Campbellton, Georgia, where I'd remain for the next two years. The day after that, Hurricane Katrina struck.

Scarlett Wasn't the Last Broad to Lose Her Mind in Tara

*I*n Georgia, I tried to put Paul behind me. I thought it was a new beginning for me and so I should leave Alistair and Paul back where I had come from. As was my pattern, I slowly let Alistair go, but then I started obsessing over Paul again.

Finally, I found a job working at an in-patient women's drug rehabilitation center, as a resident assistant. This was not a dream job, but it was something. It was an uncomfortable job for me, but I learned a lot about myself, human nature, addiction, redemption and the power of rehabilitation. These women were from all walks of life and were every color of the rainbow. The center was a place where women could heal from past and present addiction and live with their children.

Narcotics Anonymous was an enormous part of these women's recovery and of all of our growth. I learned so much from these women. My experience there was immeasurable. Life had been hard for me at times, but nothing compared to the degradation, self loathing and powerlessness these women had faced. More times than I can count, women so close to the end would relapse and return to the streets. Some of the women would return to the program to begin again, but others wouldn't make it back.

With time, I was able to see that my troubles with Alistair and Paul were my addiction. In every way that these women felt powerless when it came to crack, cocaine, heroin and methamphetamines, I felt the same in regards to my feelings regarding Mutt and Jeff.

As a resident assistant, I frequently had to transport the women to different places, and many times it would be to NA meetings or retreats. Being privy to these meetings and hearing different stories of such despair, and then hearing the hope and the turnaround, really gave me strength at a time I really needed it. I feel I did the best while I was there, but then I got a job that paid more and so I left.

The new job was terrible, and the people who worked there were horrible to me, and that made me weak; and that's when I let them creep back in.

Paul was gracious at first when the emails started rolling in again, and soon they were followed by regular calls. The more I put in, the more I wanted him to put in; and – sadly – the more I expected him to put in. After my pleading and hurt feelings waned, I began to get pissed.

My premonition that my friendship with Paul was on borrowed time became stronger than ever. My email contact with him became an obsession. It was bigger than me. I could not help myself. I left him with no choice …

Mary: Please call me. I am sorry, OK. Don't make me beg. Be my friend enough not to make me beg.

Paul: Mary, I'll call you in the morning. Just got home a bit ago. I would say something like, "This had better be a big deal," but since it probably IS a big deal, I won't. Sorry I missed your calls. You always call and leave messages that make it sound like there's some kind of conspiracy going on … haha.

I hope you're OK and this important message that you couldn't tell me about in message form is just a message you wanted to tell me about in person, just because.

P

Mary: Don't call me back. I don't think what I have to say will meet your criteria of importance and hearing your annoyance at this fact will only make me feel bad. Sorry, I was annoyingly persistent. I just wanted to apologize for my email. I don't know why I say such things. I just get frustrated sometimes when I think about how much time I've wasted hoping you'd change your mind about me.

Mary

Paul: Cards-on-table-honesty-time (and I know you'll be mad about how I always choose the worst things to respond to): I don't know what to say to any of this. This kind of thing has been going on for years now; you realize that, don't you? You're my friend, but sometimes I have no idea what you're talking about or why, overnight, you go into all this about "changing my mind" about you and such. You're going to have to tell me what you want me to say, because I'm pretty lost at this point. Try re-reading your recent emails or the phone messages you've left. When I get home and I've got voicemails and emails about Spastically calling my cell, my home, my mom's house, I figure the earth might've cracked open, you know? Today, the email you sent tells me that's not really the case. What are you looking for from me at this point, exactly?

It's Sunday, and you've just gotten over a nasty bout in the ER and are probably still sick, but I just doubt any of this has anything to do with any delirium brought on by sickness. This sort of thing is bubbling under the surface all the time with you, I think, and if you don't do something about it, it's going to hurt you for the long-term in a big way; you've let it go on for far too long. Hopefully you see some truth in what I'm saying here, even if I've somehow missed the mark. I'm not trying to upset you, but I want to get this out in the open. 2/26/06

Mary: I can't remember everything that I tell you because I tell you so much. For the last couple of years, my favorite song has been "A Case of You" by Joni Mitchell. I love that song so much. I like the version where it is her just playing a guitar and singing. I was going through something at the time when I heard it, and I really connected with the song. I absolutely adore the whole song, but the part that gives me chills and moves me the most is the part of the song that says:

"Oh I am a lonely painter,
I live in a box of paints,
I'm frightened by the devil,
And I'm drawn to those ones that ain't afraid.
I remember that time that you told me,
you said, 'Love is touching souls,'
Surely you touched mine,
Cause part of you pours out of me,

In these lines from time to time."

Well, I think the whole song is wonderful, but that is my favorite part. The other day, I was downloading some music and I was having a PRINCE moment (don't ask me why) I love Prince. Anyway, I noticed that he has a version of the song. It said it was a tribute to Joni Mitchell. His version starts with those lines. Basically, the whole song is those lines. I thought, *See, it's not just me who thinks that is great.* But, it was nice to see someone who is "cool" digging Joni Mitchell – and not just her, but that song. 2/28/06

Mary: If I were white do you think we'd relate to each other better? 2/28/06

Paul: I'm not even going to respond to that in any way. Sorry, but I'm not biting. 2/28/06

Mary: It was an honest question but as always it is your choice to respond or not to respond. 2/28/06

Paul: This is such bull. I'm finished here. 2/28/06

Mary: Whatever, Paul. I'm sure that's easier for you. 2/28/06

Paul: You know what? I don't know what's gotten in to you that makes you believe I've wronged you or owe you something, but it pisses me off. Just now, I realized it. I've now written three or four emails that I've, thank God, deleted. I want you to understand something. Somewhere around five years ago, I met you. You were a nice person. I think you still are. Somewhere around five years ago, you expressed interest by telling me so. I remember; it was in your car. I made it pretty clear that I wasn't interested in a relationship, and damn it that wasn't a lie. You understood me. I understood you. I graduated. So did you. Years went by. You, as you say, "pined." You, as you say, "got your feelings hurt." You, as you say, grew to "love" me.

I say, you fell in love with someone who doesn't and maybe even can't exist. You made me feel guilty with every email where you basically blamed me for not "loving you" in return, the way you wanted me to, and therefore you felt like you could take your dissatisfaction with certain aspects of your life (as you said) and pin them on me. I took it, because I'm a pretty strong guy emotionally, and I wanted to be there for you in SOME capacity, even if it didn't come close to meeting your standards.

Now this. You treat me like I've led you on. You talk to me like I promised you everything and never delivered. That's your delusion, Mary. I was a friend, and I might even still be, but I'm sure it doesn't matter to you because that's not enough anyway.

You think I'm defending myself? No. I didn't do anything wrong. We never dated. We never even met more than once since 2001 or 2002. But I often talked about you, worried about you, tried to encourage you. And I began to feel that you just weren't going to make progress emotionally unless you got rid of me, or at least the "me" you had created in your own mind. You think I'm so naive and clueless. Nothing could be further from the truth. I've been onto you for years, and I've watched the cycle, this game you are so addicted to, as you said – the game I told you a while ago that I wasn't going to play into; and it pisses you off. Well, it's about time it happened. I hope it helps, because I'm done.

So, you're bringing race into this? Thanks for insulting me. You know what?--maybe instead of race it was just the fact that I was honest with you a long time ago and you couldn't take it. If you've put your stock in someone far away and lived in a dream world, you did it to yourself. Don't send me any more of these emails detailing how I've been a crappy friend. I don't need it, and I don't deserve it.

I'm pretty sure you're just going to respond to all this with some kind of rage or shocked hurt or whatever, but if you're really in control of your life (and how did you ever get it into your head that I was in control of it???), as you say, how about making the last email you sent just that, unless you think I've missed something here. I think it's clear that your cycle of self-pity is never going to end as long as I stay in the picture. You've made that abundantly clear.

You are a special woman, indeed. And you could even be strong and happy one day. I hope and pray that day comes.

How's that for honesty? 2/28/06

Mary: I guess time is the thing. I've started to write you and call you many times, but I wouldn't allow myself to do so until I got a little clarity. Every time I felt a little weak or missed you, I'd reread your last email and that helped the feeling pass. I don't know where we are. I don't know if we are friends. I don't know if that's what you want or if that's what I need. I wanted to just let your email be it and let it all go. I decided to break my silence only because I am feeling a lot better about some things, and if we never communicate again after this point I need for you to know a few things.

I need you to know that I never considered you a bad friend. In that capacity, you were always incredible to me, and I am not so crazy and far gone that I don't realize that. You just sucked as a boyfriend, and that's because you weren't! I still think despite all of this that you are a fantastic person and that's why all of this has been so hard. It is excruciating to know this person that you consider to be so special and wonderful in your life, and you see yourself doing everything to destroy that person's presence in your life; but you can't stop it because you are this train wreck. My initial email that started this situation was not written out of anger at you but out of intense anger at me, myself. I know that from your perspective it didn't feel that way. I hate that you felt attacked by that.

So many times I kept wanting to make this right with you, BUT then I'd have to question my motives. I hate not talking to you. I hate it, but I didn't want this to be resolved while things had not changed in my mind and heart. I didn't want to be able to call you again, email you again and be friends again, and still be hoping that we could be together. And I knew/know that would have been the case.

I also hesitated making any moves because I had to get to a point where I was saying what I needed to say, for me, no matter your response. I have to say I felt ridiculed by your email and so I guess I sort of needed to get my nerve to write you. Also, I guess I just wanted to see if our friendship, if that relationship, meant anything to you. I guess I was gauging that by the days. I hated that I missed you, because that reminded me how alone in that I was – and have been for a long time. Every day it got a little easier not to write or wonder whether you even thought about the fact we weren't communicating. Then I'd remind myself that it didn't/doesn't really matter.

I finally realized that waiting on you to write me to see if you cared or missed me was proof that I have a lot more work to do. I must say that I have made some HUGE steps in the right direction BUT I still have miles to go.

I just wrote because I needed you to know these things, whether we are friends are not. Some of these things were burning in me, and

I needed to say them to you. This might have been the wrong decision. Perhaps, I should have stayed silent and just let go. All I can do is learn from my mistakes. I am trying not to have expectations when it comes to you, so I am not expecting anything. I just needed you to know that the genuineness of your friendship with me was never in question in my mind.

I can't really explain how I felt after I read your email. It was sort of out of body for me. I look back on it, and I am surprised that it didn't completely destroy me. You seemed to think I would feel angry and hurt, and that's sort of how I would have guessed I would feel. I just sort of felt numb when I read it, maybe because I wasn't surprised by what you wrote. It's one thing when *I* say I'm crazy but to have someone else say it :) Wow, that's something. I am not going to lie to you and say that I have everything under control, but I am not the same person I was three or four weeks ago. A lot of my illusions about a boy who lived far away have faded, and I see what's here and I know what I have and what I don't. It's funny because I didn't cry ONCE during this whole period, until I was writing you now.

Mary 3/21/06

Paul: I'm going to keep this as brief as I can.

I want you to know that my letter was not written out of anger, and it went against every instinct I had to write it. My instincts tell me to always build people up, to always be polite, to always be positive, and the entire thing smacked of righteous indignation and egotism and cruelty. But, something underneath all my worries over ornament and politeness and peace-making told me that what I had to say was not only necessary but long, long, long overdue. You can make of that what you want, but what I have to say is the most important part, I think:

Writing it was one of the most difficult things I've done in regards to my relationship with someone. It was not written with any facility, I can assure you, and if you could talk to a few my friends who heard me say it time and again, I agonized over that letter. I worried over it for weeks. And I still worry over it, but I still know it was the right thing, and I think it contained the right things, even when most of me was objecting entirely.

So, for what it's worth, yes, we're friends. I've always thought so, and I stand by my belief that I had to take that friendship away some distance because it wasn't good for you. You can call that egotism or pretention or whatever, and you might even be right, but I don't think I was doing you any good, and that should've been made clear a long, long time ago. Heck, you said it yourself on many occasions.

This isn't going to build back any bridges or patch up any gaping holes, but I wanted to respond to your email in an attempt to help to continue to set your mind at ease. I've always thought of you as my friend and wished you well and kept you in my thoughts during your most difficult times, and that hasn't changed.

P 3/22/06

Mary: Hey,
I think I am finally tired of getting my face smashed. I think what was most devastating to me was losing you as a friend, not the fantasy that this would somehow work out and we would end up in love, but the friendship. I know, I know, I did my part to wreck that, but I also worked like hell to maintain it and keep it going; but obviously I can't do that if I'm the only one interested in maintaining it. I am finally – FINALLY – at a point where I realize that I could email or call you every day and it wouldn't make a damn difference. Anyway, peace and love. I hope you have a great life, and I am sorry that we couldn't continue to be friends. Please don't insult me by attempting to email now, but this is you we are talking about, so maybe I flatter myself in even thinking you care just a little bit.

Peace 10/23/06

Paul: Not sure what to say, as usual. Time sure gets away, doesn't it?

You do what you need to do.

All the best,

-Paul 10/23/06

Mary: Yeah, I am probably just overreacting like I always do in these situations. This is just me throwing a temper tantrum, because you didn't call me back. You know how silly we women can be. But I'll take your advice and do what I need to so I won't be so sensitive. Forget I mentioned it. It's not like every time I call, you don't answer and then don't call me back; or like every time I email, you don't email me back. I was just trying to get your attention with my melodrama. Well, Babe, thanks for getting back to me; and like I said, I hope your well. Glad to know I still leave you speechless. Even more elated to know that you are alive and well.

All the best to you,
--Mary 10/23/06

Paul: Mary,
Your sarcasm and/or sincerity is kind of lost on me by now. I'm not really sure what you're talking about sometimes (often). However, your main point is that I didn't/don't call/e-mail back. I can say with some confidence that this has happened for two reasons: 1) I thought it was the right thing to do: to limit my contact with you, a person I consider a friend of mine, for obvious reasons; and 2) I honestly lost track of time and the goings-on of life got the better of me. You probably have a hard time believing me, but I have a pile of issues on my own plate, and I have lost a great many things, sometimes even my own friends, sadly.

I meant what I said at #1, though, and I don't say that cruelly. I say it because it's for the best, and perhaps subconsciously just knowing that "helped" me do a poor job of keeping in touch with you as I should have (or at least how you think I should have). It's all very confusing to me and has been for, well, years. For a long time, I just assumed we had an understanding, and then suddenly I get these vitriolic e-mails, and I'm at a loss. Sometimes, I think you send these assuming they are going out into the ether never to be seen by human eyes. Sometimes, I think you're fully aware of them, too. Who knows.

I'm not a heartless jerk, contrary to the many evidences on hand, apparently; and I do think of you very often, wonder about you, worry about you (I think I'm experiencing déjà vu), but I admit that I have had to let a lot of that go, if only for your sake (but the truth is, for mine as well). Among many things, something deeply unhealthy happened between us, something I had absolutely no power over given my own ingratiating and dodge-ridden personality, and I regret that. However, I don't regret knowing you, and I wish you well. I say that knowing full well that it sounds false and overly formal. Still true.

Take out your anger at me, whether I deserve it or not (and, hey, maybe I do); and yes, you should take it personally. But that wasn't really my intention even if you have every right to be angry.

This is not a pity-inducing e-mail or me attempting to make you feel bad or let myself off the hook or vice-versa, so I don't expect or WANT any reciprocity, further anger, reversals, or added confusion. I simply want this charade to stop if that's what's necessary. 10/23/06

Mary: One day when I grow up I hope to be the sort of person who lets my silence speak volumes. I want to be able to say "FUCK YOU" without actually having to say it. Clearly, today, I am not that woman. You're right: I've wasted a lot of time on you. And I'm sure that often you are unsure about most everything I have to say. I'm glad you got to make all the decisions regarding our relationship, because obviously I am too unstable to have any say in the matter. I guess this where I thank you for the favor. I agree that this has gotten ridiculous, and I fully intend on letting go of this "friendship," but not before I say a few last things that I should be big enough to let go but I guess we can both agree that I am not only unstable but immature.

It fucking drives me crazy when you blame your lack of effort on time and forgetfulness. That's lame now, and it has always been lame. I was just too afraid to say that for fear of upsetting you. I don't know what I feared; it wasn't like you were going to get mad and stop calling or stop coming to visit. I understand being busy and having shit on one's plate, but when a friendship matters to someone they occasionally manage to return a damn call, a text message, or something. Throughout the entire time we've known each other, it was always me begging you – begging you to call, begging you to visit, begging you for something. I should have known that was fucked up. Who has to beg their friends to be friends with them. That is so pathetic, and I played the hell out of that role.

You keep mentioning all this anger that you think I have, and I guess I am a little pissed but not at you, because you never fucking changed. I am livid with myself for being so ridiculous and clueless. I am tired of carrying this and worrying about this, so I am so done pushing myself on you so let all the things that make you so busy take you where they might. The charade has ended. I won't let months pass and then try again. I am sold. I am convinced now that I was some charity project for you. I don't care what in the hell you say, but I will – even if I die trying or have to borrow it from someone else – be sending you back your money. I hate that I asked you for it.

"This is not a pity-inducing e-mail or me attempting to make you feel bad or let myself off the hook or vice-versa, so I don't expect or WANT any reciprocity, further anger, reversals, or added confusion. I simply want this charade to stop if that's what's necessary" 10/24/06

Mary: I never could keep my word. That's something I just can't do, no matter how hard I try. Honestly, I have done really well in terms of letting you go and moving on BUT – there is always a but – I am having to face several things that I have runaway from, and you are one of those things. I guess this is sort of my making amends in an attempt to refocus my life in a positive direction. This is really hard for me to do, but I think that means this is the right thing. I am not angry anymore, but my enormous PRIDE would not allow me to really think about this situation or even try to apologize. I owe you an apology. I don't take back 100% of what I said, because I think some of it was right, honest and accurate; but I was wrong in my approach. I know that now, and to be truthful I knew it then. I was just really angry about so many things, and I needed a focal point, and so I unleashed on you.

As of late, the dissemination of our friendship has troubled me. I am not interested in going back to whatever it was we did before I had my breakdown. I just felt as if I needed to address this, because it was sort of looming over me. I have let go of so much and dealt with many of the things that were weighing on me and causing me to be so angry. I guess I sort of feel that I need to handle this so I can say that I have dealt with my issues and tried to rectify wrongs that I am responsible for.

I was just so tired of pining after you, and I couldn't help myself, and it drove me crazy and angered me; and that got misdirected, and I blamed you because it was too hard to face that I was ultimately in control of my actions and emotions. I convinced myself that you had wronged me, and I told myself to hate you. I don't really understand why, but I needed you to be angry with me or hate me. Who knows why I do the things I do or say the things I say. I'm dramatic, and perhaps starting something with you was my way of evoking some kind of emotion from you. Attacking you in a manner I knew would piss you off was my way of ensuring that I wouldn't call you or write you and would for once and all stop my insane "crush/fixation" with you.

What I can honestly say is that I am feeling much better now and, in the wake of my realizations, I realize I owed you this apology – not in an attempt to rekindle something between us but because it's the decent thing to do. As I type this I am unsure whether I will send it, because as far as my pride goes this is so hard but it is supposed to be, I guess. Also, I know now that I had been angry and hurt for a long time and I didn't deal with it; I let it eat me up from the inside and then I spewed out my own special venom.

I didn't really deal with my hurt feelings and anger towards you because of this email you wrote me some time ago. I kept telling myself that I wasn't upset about it, and I kept trying to not be, but I WAS. I was incredibly hurt by it, but I didn't deal with it. I just tried to move on and act as if it didn't happen. That was stupid, because things really did change between us at that point, and it wasn't something we could just bounce back from. I think that ripped me so terribly because I really understood how you saw me and what you thought of me, and it wasn't pretty; it wasn't what I wanted you to see and definitely not how I wanted you to feel.

Anyway, I am sorry for the way I handled things with you. I was wrong to attack you. I am sincerely sorry for that and, as humiliated as I am in writing this, I also feel incredibly good and sort of liberated. I am NOT expecting any sort of acknowledgment from you on this. I don't even know that you'd read this, but I needed to do it because I think it is the right thing to do. I tried to hate you and it didn't work because it wasn't right. I still think the world of you and wish you good things. Most of all, I hope you are happy. I really am now, and I know that's the only way to live. Life is too short to sweat the small stuff.

Mary 2/4/07

Mary: Happy B'day

--

Wishing You a Lifetime of Learning
        Mary 05/30/07

Mary: How long are you going to punish me for being emotionally disturbed??? Isn't everyone entitled to mental breakdown at least once, twice, as many as it takes to get it right? Anyway, I am better in terms of thinking I am in love with you. Hell has frozen over, and I'm over it. I just miss my friend (nothing else).

It's funny, but you are still in my dreams. You ignore me in my dreams as well. It would be funny if it wasn't so sad and tragic. Usually, we are somewhere like university, and I see you and get this sick feeling in my stomach because we are not talking, and then I am stabbed when you talk to someone I am close to but don't talk to me. It's strange, because it's a recurring dream of mine. I don't have it often, but I do have it.

For the most part, I have made peace with us not communicating or being friends but then you creep into my sub-conscience (subconscious) – pick the one that is correct – and I think about you and our demolished friendship. Well, every now and then I will whisper a little something in your ear, and maybe one day you'll see fit to talk to me again. Perhaps not, but there is no harm in trying. Well, if this finds you, I hope it finds you well and happy.

Mary 8/05/07

Paul: Mary,

Your letter does find me well, overall, I guess. I'm working with my siblings in my dad's printing business (I know, it's farcical) while I look for a new path. Oddly enough, that new path may have been opened after only a month of work with my sibs. Hugh Chandler, the father of one of my friends, Greg, found out I was working in the printing business (he owns a large printing company) and called me basically to say: "I wish I had known you were thinking of printing, because I want you to be my project manager." I was fairly blown away, especially since I'm a true novice. So, I'm going to meet him tomorrow. I talked to his wife, Tina. She said, "So, are you coming to work?" "Well, I don't know. I would like to talk to Hugh, and he can decide whether or not I'm qualified for something like that," to which she responded, laughing: "He wouldn't have asked you if he didn't know that." Who knows? I might make more than $20,000 a year for the first time. *sigh*

Nothing is new anywhere else. So, other than the fact that I now have a steady 40-hour job, in at 7 AM, off at 3:30 PM, weekends off forever, I'm much the same. No marriage. No love interest (just can't seem to be bothered with all that). Very little personal satisfaction since I'm an undisciplined wastrel ... haha. But heck, people say life is short; I feel like there's still time to sort all those goals out. If it's naiveté, oh well.

About us as friends. If we're to communicate in some way, I hope you will be at peace with the fact that I truly think everything that can be said about the past has been said, twice. Or three times. I'd like to leave it that way, regrets and should've and all that. Passed by to the past. Good riddance.

With a nod to the aforementioned past, I would like to add that you've always hovered in that part of my mind that remembers and considers and wonders about and hopes for. All things said and done, that's the plain truth.

I still hope and think these things. Apologies if that wasn't clear. 8/06/07

Mary: Well are you now gainfully employed as a project manager? 8/08/07

Paul: No. I met with Hugh for three hours last night, and basically I told him I want to take some time to think it over, do some research, etc. He said, "I'd rather you took two months only to say 'No,' rather than to too hastily say 'Yes' and not know what you were getting into." It was a very good conversation, and I'm fairly certain I'm going to take it. It's just a big, BIG decision because I found out last night he wants me to eventually take his position. In ten years. I don't know if I'm prepared to devote myself to one thing like that. We'll see.

Also: Amy Winehouse's new CD is unbelievable. 8/08/07

Mary: I know, I have it (Amy Winehouse CD). Also, that is a lot to think about but so flattering even if you decide that it is not for you. It is always good to have options and for someone to have that kind of faith in you. Do you have a favorite song on the CD? 8/8/07

Paul: "You Know I'm No Good" is the one I'm really hung up on, but the ENTIRE album is basically brilliant (if MAYBE a little overly retro, not that I care). Sure, "Rehab" is so overplayed, but that's not her fault. Still a crackin' tune. "Back to Black" is pretty great, too. Also: didn't know she was British for a while. Also: didn't know she was Jewish. From the cover, I just assumed she was a fair-skinned

African American, but now I've seen other pictures and she's Jewish. Maybe I'm an idiot.

I picked up her actual debut ("Salk") the other day, and it's good, too. Haven't given it as much time as "Back to Black" though. I fear she's going to burn up and burn out, though. By all accounts, she's an alcoholic and belligerent towards her audience at shows. Now, I'm seeing the cliché news stories about her where she's canceling shows due to "exhaustion," which is, according to the Lindsay Lohan School of Maturing Badly, a euphemism for "strung out on crack."

Oh well. 8/08/07

Mary: I know "Rehab" is overplayed BUT I do love it. That's funny to me that you thought she was black. She looks like Fran Dresher to me so right away I thought Jewish. I'm at work waiting on the phone to ring, so I am emailing. It is not that busy tonight. I am curious about this: I have just discovered Ray Lamontagne. Have you heard of him? If so, do you like him? I just found out about him like two months ago, and whenever I ask people they are like you are so LATE. 8/08/07

Paul: One more for tonight.

I like "Rehab," too. The song, that is. I'm always defending Winehouse because all anyone can say when you tell them they should listen to her is, "Oh, that 'Rehab' song???" which they follow with a bad rendition of the "Nooo, nooo, no" part. Oh well. Once I actually SAW her, it was pretty clear I was wrong about her ethnicity. I guess I'm racist because her voice ... her voice ... umm .... umm .... yeah. Fran Drescher's a bit much, though ... haha.

Ray Lamontagne. Yeah, he's old news, but I've yet to hear much from him. My pal Nathan recommended him a couple years ago I guess, but I never did look into him. Meant to.

I'm totally going to sleep. Sleep well. 08/08/07

Mary: Hey,

You should look up Lamontagne and listen to "Trouble," "Hold You In My Arms" and "Until the Sun Turns Black." That is some good stuff. YOU MUST LISTEN TO THOSE SONGS TODAY, RIGHT NOW. There is something about his voice that is sooooooooo nice to me As for Winehouse, I am in love with tracks 5,6,7. I like the whole CD but those are my faves.

Do you have big plans for the weekend? I had planned to sleep and then try to fit three movies in this weekend. I want to see *Becoming Jane, Rush Hour 3* (don't laugh), and *Harry Potter*. I think that might be a little much. Tomorrow morning is Sal's graduation and so I have that, but then I am going to the movies.

I had planned to go to Sal's graduation, but now I am going to her house tonight and spending the night and then going with her. This week has been pure DRAMA for her. She found out, well she told me that Eric, her husband, has been CHEATING on her!!!!!!!! It is horrible. When she told me, I CRIED. I didn't mean to, but I was soooo surprised and I felt hurt (weird). I really LOVED Eric; he was like my brother and I just can't believe it. PAUL, I wish you could see the cheap piece of trash he cheated with. She is disgusting. I hope that wasn't offensive to say "trash," but she is just that. What gets me is that he and all his friends talk about this girl and how slutty she is and how DUMB, and yet he sleeps with her. YUCK!!!!!!!!

When Sal told him that was it, she was getting a divorce, she said he cried and begged and got down on his knees crying and begging. I truly believe he is sorry and wishes he hadn't, but it is too late. I wonder why he didn't think of all of this before he decided to take a turn on the human door knob.

Anyway, Sal is on her way here to get me. It will be weird tonight because I haven't seen Eric since all this went down. They are still sharing their house; they are just sleeping in separate rooms. How do I get on these topics? I know my emailing is schizophrenic, but that is how I think, one thing to the next without warning. Well have a nice weekend.

Mary

P.S. I am listening to Lamontagne and I am even more convinced that you should listen to him some, a little bit. Let me know if you do and WHAT YOU TRULY THINK. Make sure you listen to "Trouble" or "Hold You in My Arms" first!!!!!! 08/07/07

Paul: Quick response: First listen of "Trouble": LOVE IT. I had no idea he sounded like this. Now I feel bad I didn't check him out a while back; but it honestly slipped my mind.

That's so, so sad to hear about Sal's situation. That's got to be devastating. How did she find out? He told her?

More soon. 08/12/07

Mary: Paul, Paul, Paul,

"He told her?" No, no, no, he did not tell her. Not to rip on your gender or anything, but typically cheaters are caught due to extreme stupidity, not because they suddenly grow a conscience and confess. This idiot had explicit text messages on his cell phone. He tried to claim that his friend and brother made the calls using his phone. Well, that's interesting because both his brother and friend have cell phones. Why would they (both single males) use a married man's cell phone to text the whore and ask her if they were on for that night and to tell her that he was after sex?

Anyway, he lied and lied, but in the end he admitted just enough, and Sal feels she has grounds to leave his ass. Also to be completely honest, Sal was feeling a bit trapped and wasn't happy and wanted out, but she felt that she had to stay and make it work. She told me she was almost relieved. Although she isn't happy that she has to now be tested for STD's, she is glad to be free. Apparently, he lies about a multitude of things. If you can't tell, I am a little hot about the situation. She was too good for him anyway.

Oh get this, her husband, Eric, is blaming me for his predicament. I am super pissed about that. We all three went to Disney World in July. One night, Eric and I decided we were too tired to return to Disney World, so we went out to eat, talk, do a little drinking (at least, I did). Eric drinks like a fish and when he gets drunk he tells you way too much information. Anyway, he told me that before he and Sal got married, he cheated on her twice. I decided that I was going to keep that knowledge to myself, because I thought they were happy. He was drunk when he told me, and it was none of my business. This is huge for me because I don't keep things from Samantha, but I figured this one would cause big problems.

Anyway, AFTER he was busted and she told me she was filing for divorce, I told her about his confession. I did it to ease her mind, because she felt like maybe she was making him guilty so she could walk. I told her so she'd know that he is capable of cheating and most likely would do it again.

Anyway that bastard is saying I told her and that is why she checked his cell phone. So now he calls himself mad at me. He is such a child. Instead of saying, "I fucked up royally," he tries to blame me. Well, even if I had told her earlier (which I didn't), there'd be nothing to tell if he had just kept it in his pants. I know you didn't want all of this info, I just get SO MAD when I think about everything.

As for the song "I Told You So," that is some good stuff. I am glad that you listened.

I am still trying to master brevity.

Mary 08/13/07

Mary: I'm at work and BORED. Do you know any good jokes or riddles? I'll even take an interesting anecdote.

--

Wishing You a Lifetime of Learning
                    -Mary 08/19/07

Mary: Yesterday was so busy at work, I couldn't catch my breath but the time flew by. On my way here today I kept thinking I hope we aren't as busy as we were last night. This just shows be careful what you ask for because we aren't as busy and time is moving painfully slow. It is funny how things work out. How are you? Are you doing alright? I had an interesting dream about you over the weekend and you've been on my mind ever since. I'll spare you the details because it was a weird dream that made no sense. I am sure that it means something but probably just that I am strange.

I had a nice girls weekend with Sal and Rhoda. Rhoda only hung Friday night but Sal and I hung out until Sunday. We rented a bunch of scary movies (I am paying for that now) and ate junk and laughed about dumb stuff. We had a lot of fun. I smile just thinking about it. How was your weekend?? 08/21/07

Mary: Did I offend you with my cussing? If so, I am sorry I am trying to work on that but when I start thinking about Eric I get mad and that's what comes out.

--

Wishing You a Lifetime of Learning
                    -Mary 08/22/07

Paul: I had a good weekend. I can't believe tomorrow's Friday, and I'm writing this now. To say the very least, it's been one hell of a week. Over the weekend, I saw *Superbad* and *Stardust*, both of which were at least pretty good. *Superbad*, I thought, was brilliantly hilarious. I laughed. A lot. I think *Knocked Up* is a better movie ..., but *Superbad* is all about the funny (and a dash of the heartfelt, of course). Judd Apatow and Seth Rogen are just making great, great comedies right now.

Monday, I worked from seven to three-thirty, showered, drove to Dawn Ridge, packed up half my friend Jeremy's stuff, and drove back to my town so we could stow it in my garage until he can get this house he's waiting on (why he moved out and away from his roommate is a long story, as usual). We finished around eleven thirty. PM. I was dead and back up at six the next morning. Then I did it all again. Done around 11:45 Tuesday. Back up at six. Worked. Got home, baked a cinnamon-raisin cake for my brother Jacob's birthday (34), had dinner up at mom's, stayed until nine or so, got home and finally fell asleep around eleven-thirty! Haha ... a decent night's rest at least. Needless to say, today is recuperation day. I'm doing laundry, playing videogames, reading, and, best of all, not leaving the house for the night. What a week!

Amy Winehouse's first record is so, SO good. You need it, if you don't have it. It may even be better than the new. Who knows about such things.

I'm well; thanks for asking. Hope you're well. And, it's nice to hear you and Sal and Rhoda still hang out. I know it's all been tumultuous over the years, eh? 08/23/07

Mary: I'm tired just reading your email. I do agree that the week has just flown by; it is unbelievable. I am so behind on movies these days that the only movie reference I had heard of before was *Knocked Up*, and that's just because Izzie is in it. I don't know why, but I think it is noteworthy that you bake. I don't hear that too much from guys. Sal and I didn't finish all of our movies, so we are having part II this weekend. I am so excited because at midnight tonight I am off; today is my Friday. I am not doing spit tomorrow. I am going to stay on the couch and watch television.

Oh, this is one of my schizophrenic moments; I have another subject. Anyway, one night I couldn't sleep (don't know if I told you this or not – I told someone) so I flipped on the TV and went to on-demand. I started cruising their list of old TV shows and came across the show *Soap*. Anyway, I sort of remembered that show, because I knew Benson was on there, Billy Crystal and Mona from *Who's the Boss*. I remembered that my dad wouldn't let me watch it because he said it was dirty. Of course, you know I started watching the show. There were nine or ten episodes on there, and I watched them all. Then ... it ended on a cliff hanger, and there were no more episodes. Do you know what I did? I went to Borders and BOUGHT THE FIRST SEASON!! It didn't stop there, because season one was so entertaining that I bought season two, and a week ago I ordered three and four from Amazon. I finished two today, and I so hope three is here tomorrow. It is the dumbest, craziest, most ridiculous thing, and I have thoroughly enjoyed watching the show. I love it!!

The show totally makes fun of soap operas, which isn't cool, but it still makes you connect with the family and really invest. Also, it is very funny, I think. One episode actually made me cry. It was horrible and I loved every minute of it. In the show, Billy Crystal is gay, sort of, and his boyfriend dumped him and that was so sad and heartbreaking. Also I like it because the same people who did *Golden Girls* and *Empty Nest* are the creators of this show and you can see the similarities and the same actors being used.

Boy, I can drag out anything, right? I am glad that you are well. I am jealous that you are home relaxing while I am here at work with really bad menstrual cramps ... TMI, right? Yesterday, Sal actually waited up for me, and we talked while I drove home, and then once I got home I just kept talking – you know how I can go on – and finally Sal was like, "I love you, but I can't listen anymore. Goodnight." I was so excited to have someone to talk to that I got a little too excited. Plus, I am always a little scared coming home thinking there is going to be someone in my apartment. I don't have an alarm right now so I'm a little paranoid. 08/23/07

Mary: Well, today my week officially starts. I am off Friday and Saturday's. Those days go so fast. Anyway, I am sounding like I am about to complain, but I shouldn't because I love my job here. It is the best job I've ever had (so far).

Another weekend went by and I didn't make it to the movies. Sal and I watched rentals all weekend. She spent the weekend again. I don't know why we have regressed. We bring my mattress into the den and just camp out. We had PJ's on all day yesterday. We were such bums. We got up EARLY yesterday morning and went to pancake pantry (in our PJ's) and after that the rest of the day was just a waste. We watched *I Think I Love My Wife*; it wasn't great, but we laughed and it was entertaining. I think it is a man movie. I mean, I think men are supposed to relate to it, because it definitely wasn't a movie any woman wants to relate to. We also watched *Vacancy,* and it SUCKED, but I still screamed and was afraid to the point of tears (I know, that was pathetic). Sal was laughing, but I was so scared and jumpy. I made her go to the bathroom with me; it was bad. While we watching, we kept hearing this noise and couldn't figure out what is was, and so that just sent me over the edge. Last night, we figured out the noise, but I will spare you that detail. Oh, and we watched *Number* 23 or something like that with Jim Carey. It was entertaining and of course a little scary to me, but at the beginning I said, "This will have a bootleg ending," and I took a guess at what would probably happen. I made a prediction about the movie, and I was spot on. I was not happy with the movie but Sal liked it.

Oh, and when we got back from church today, the last two seasons *of Soap* were waiting at my front door. I was so HAPPY. I am going to start season three when I get home. I loaned one and two to Sal and told her to watch them.

School starts back for me on Tuesday, so I had to buy a desk for my computer and all my junk that goes with it. I am going to attempt to assemble it after work tonight. I know I can do it because I have put things together before, but they always come out slightly remixed. I have a TV stand that leans and an entertainment center that … well, you just have to see it :)

--

Wishing You a Lifetime of Learning 08/26/07

Mary: I have overwhelmed you with so many emails already. I can't help it. I email the way I talk. Sal is good about telling me to shut up, but when people don't tell me I run on and on. ANYWAY, I am sorry for that. In my defense, I was stranded at home for a few days and that made me a little stir crazy. Well, in all honesty, I probably would have written as much under normal circumstances. It's like, I ask you so many questions in all these emails, and if I can't keep up then I know you can't. I am waiting up tonight for Sal. She was supposed to come over after we had dinner but then her soon-to-be-ex husband called, acting like the bastard that he is, and she had to go home first before coming here. Anyway, my questions: Do you watch *Big Love?* Will you send me some pictures? Have you ever heard of *Soap?* I guess for now that will have to do. As fun as this is, I am going to cut this short to watch some TV. Luckily for all my friends who I email constantly, I get the creeps being in this room – the room where the computer is – at night, and I can't stand being in here so long. This is why when I am home, I am always trying to get you to call me. I keep saying I am going to fix the lighting in here, but then I don't and then I am scared. I am such a wimp. Anyway, hope you are well and sorry if I have overwhelmed you with too much too soon.

Mary 8/31/07

Paul: Mary,

I don't watch *Big Love*. I've heard it's great, but I don't watch it. I used to watch *Soap* years ago, and my dad recently got it on DVD. I remember last year when he was watching them, he was choking with laughter practically the entire time. Funny show, as I recall. Need to watch it again.

Last week was madness and tiring. On Friday, I was supposed to take mom up to Mississippi for a couple days to visit my great aunt. That fell through when I had to call in sick to work on Friday; just stomach pains. I'm feeling fine today but for fatigue and some diarrhea. I have one of those really annoying, lame bugs. I was worried it might be stomach flu because two of the guys I work with have had daughters come down with it this last week. So, statistically and all that ...

Basically, I've been resting and watching *Jeeves and Wooster* episodes (I'm obsessed with Hugh Laurie and Stephen Fry; Hugh Laurie's book *The Gun Seller* is a really fun read and quick), playing some video games – this one called *BioShock* that has absolutely dazzled me with its storytelling and atmosphere. I'll bore you with the details now.

The game opens (in first person) with a fella sitting on an airplane. You see him smoking, opening a wallet, looking at a photo. He's narrating a bit saying, "My parents always told me I was born to do great things; they were right," and he holds up this gift with a note attached that reads, "Dear Jack, Would you kindly not open this until [some date]?" from his parents. Just as he says, "They were right," the lights go out, the plane crashes, and in the next scene you're desperately swimming to the surface of the ocean, baggage floating around, propellers shooting down through the water just missing you. You break the surface, gasping for air, fiery wreckage all around you. You look around and see a tower in the moonlight.

You swim towards it. The door closes behind you, the lights begin to kick on. Glazed staircases and a giant sculpture greet you, and under the sculpture is a huge red and yellow banner that reads, "No Gods or Kings, Only Man."

You've entered the underwater utopian city gone horribly, horribly wrong, Rapture, founded by Ayn Rand Objectivist Andrew Ryan (nice play on the name, eh?). Without going into too much more detail, what you're faced with is a city where people were juicing up on these things called Plasmids, which were basically these injections that genetically enhance you in some way. They can make you smarter, faster, telekinetic, pyrokinetic, etc. So, basically, the city is one big self-centered paradise where you can become anything you want, and thanks to their obsession with plastic surgery, you can look however you want.

Once you've arrived, the disaster has already struck; one final New Years Eve party in 1959 that saw the end of whatever dream Andrew Ryan dreamt. The submarine-like "bathyspheres" have been in lockdown, so no one can leave; there are bloody picket signs all over the place that say things like, "We Are Not Your Property!" and "Down With Andrew Ryan!" etc. The story of the game is slowly revealed as you find these audio tapes spread around Rapture, detailing everyone's final hours. It's an unbelievably well-acted, well-written game that also happens to be positively terrifying. All in all, a huge time-killer, but, for once, it actually feels somehow meaningful and even intellectual.

You think I'm a huge nerd, and you're right, but really, it's purdy sweet. Why haven't I e-mailed you back sooner? Hard to say. I intended to, actually, two days ago. It wasn't until today that I realized I hadn't. You seemed more and more anxious in your e-mails until the last couple where you kind of tapered off (haha), and I kept thinking, "Oh crap, she's going to get ticked at me again," and I just kept running into little diversions that made me forget I hadn't e-mailed. It's ridiculous, really. But, you're used to that.

I do hope you're well; I'll write again soon. Be good.
P 09/01/07

Paul: Oh, I went into all that "Would you kindly" stuff because it's directly related to this huge plot twist in the game towards the end. I won't bore you with that ... JUST NOW ... but I realized I hadn't explained why all that extra nerdy info was in there. I'm off. 09/01/07

Mary (inner monologue): Dude, have you even seen a vagina? Better question, do you even want to?

Mary: I am glad you wrote. So sorry you have been sick; that's not what I wanted to hear. The video game sounds interesting. I couldn't really follow any of that, but I am sure that you kind of have to be there. Sal's husband likes games and I have watched him play, and I just feel like I am going to have a seizure at times. I guess I am lame in gaming circles.

I am not the psycho that I once was, and I think/hope I can say that I would not go all dog-day afternoon on you if I don't hear from you right away. You're you, and I'm me, and if you can deal with the hundreds of emails that I send and not complain then I can be patient and hear from you when you write, right? So anyway, again I am sorry you have been ill; I know that sucks.

Sal and I saw *Rush Hour 3* today. It was so stupid, but we laughed the whole way through. I think Chris Tucker and Jackie Chan are so funny together. Their on-screen banter is hilarious and the way they feed off of each other reminds me of me and Sal (or Sal and I – I never get that straight. My mom hates when I get that wrong, and I hate when she corrects me when I am in the middle of a story). I still have seasons three and four of *Soap* to watch, so I think that is my plan for the evening. Lastly, I don't think I've ever seen a game like that. Eric's games are usually golf (Tiger Woods [not a big fan]), football games, and I think I have seen fighting games. He also has this headphone set so he can talk to other people who are playing the game. I think it is like some Internet hook up or something where somehow they are linked and playing against each other. Usually he is just doing a lot of trash talking.

OK, well I am off for real to watch my show. Have a good night and Sweet Dreams.
Mary 09/01/07

Mary: Paul,

I'm at work and just dog tired. I have no clue why. All I did was rest until I got here. I am such a slacker at times. I can't wait until I get off. I miss my couch. This is just a random thought, so if you do want to chase this rabbit with me, good; if not, I understand. You know I work at a call center, right? Well, if you don't, I do. Anyway, we take calls from the whole state. I get calls from places I have never heard of before. I am learning a lot about places in ALABAMA. Anyway, every now and again I get callers from your neck of the woods, and I wonder if you know the people. I won't ever know because it is confidential, but my real question is, how small is where you live?

Where Sal is from is itty bitty. I mean, everybody knows everybody, and I swear everyone is related some kind of way. Or take where my grandpa lives for an example: it is a small town called Bakers Grove, Alabama. He has probably lived there for like 45 years. HE KNOWS EVERYBODY. My grandfather drives SO SLOW – not because he is old but because he has to wave at everybody on the street like we are in a parade. I mean, everywhere we go people are like, "Brother August, Brother August, how are you? How about this and that?" My grandfather is a retired minister. There are two churches of Christ in Bakers Grove: the black one and the white one. When I was a kid and we went there for the summers, I seriously did not think white people lived there. The town is seriously segregated and separated by railroad tracks. It is so weird and fascinating. Everyone seems to get along really well, but they are separated.

Remember that girl who loved you and wanted to be your baby's mama (Kimberly Lucas)? She was from there. Her family was so sweet, and they knew my granddad and were like "He is such a good man" and this and that; and then I went to the white church with Kimberly, and when they found out who my granddad was I felt like royalty. Small towns are very interesting to me.

I couldn't resist making a crack about Kimberly; I am sorry. I think if we know each other for 50 years, I will still bring that up every so often. Sal and I still laugh at the Kimberly mishaps (nothing on Kimberly; I love her to death. I swear it is totally on me and the fact I am an idiot. I swear, I do love Kimberly).

Mary 09/02/07

Paul: My town, Alansville, Mississippi, is tiny. It's like a, I think, 6,000 population or something. Really.

I'm still feeling down in the dumps with this strange nasty I'm carrying around, but I do have to comment on Kimberly. I laugh every time you bring her up. We barely knew each other, and we had coffee one time. I never had any inkling that she was interested, and I still think you've made it up when you say she did. That's just me though; always doubtful of such things. I wonder if she and John are still doing OK, now that you bring her up.

Anyway, enjoy your last bit at work. I'll talk to you soon. 09/02/07

Mary: Like the heading said, DO NOT WRITE ME BACK; this is for your amusement. I am not expecting you to respond. I know you feel bad and I have time to write and this is sort of funny, so just read this laugh if you want, and move on.

OK, think back to 2000 or 2001. Anyway, Kimberly and I started hanging out and got to be pretty tight. I cannot for the life of me remember why. That is a lie; I do remember: it just came to me. Girls are so devious. I so just remembered. Well, the story is about to get better.

OK, well, I could tell that Kimberly was hot for you, and so I started talking to her about classes and law school – stupid crap and then some kind of way we hung out, doing girl stuff like spending the night at each other's houses. We started doing the girl-talk thing, and anyway I was right about some things; and so we both made embarrassing confessions and bonded over that. This is key: I AM THE ONE WHO STARTED THIS WHOLE THING. I told her first, and she was like, "He is cute," and some other stuff, but I don't want to say too much and blow your head up too much. So we would have fun and laugh and talk YOU.

Anyway, the funny part of the story is that Kimberly then started to like John too at this time – I think that's right. Anyway, she started giving me advice about what I should say to you. Through all of this stuff, we (me and you) kept talking about getting together to watch a movie (I'll die if you remember), and FINALLY it was about to happen. The whole time, Kimberly was like, "Just stay on him about it and be assertive," and all this stuff, and I was like, "I am trying."

So anyway, we made plans, and I asked Sal to stay and of course she was like, "Hell NO," but then she agreed. So then I was like, "I need to call my BFF, Kimberly, and tell her that HE (you) is finally coming over." Anyway, I started thinking, Well Kimberly likes him too, and she has listened to me a lot. We are friends, it's not a date, and Sal is going to be there, so I asked Kimberly to come as well.

Well, when I told Sal that Kimberly was coming, she was like, "Are you stupid or stupid?" She was like, "You like this boy, right?" I was like "yeah," and she was like, "Kimberly likes this boy too, and you invite her over as well?" She then says, "Do you think Kimberly would be dumb enough to invite you over if he was coming to her house to watch a movie?" I, being me, was like, "Yeah."

OK, so then you arrive, and Kimberly arrives, and I am just giddy – and Sal is looking at me like *You friggin idiot.* So the evening ends, you and Kimberly walk out together, and I am just in this ridiculously good mood. Well, about a half hour later, Kimberly calls me and is like, "Well, I asked Paul to go with me for coffee. Thanks for having me over tonight; it was really fun."

I am an emotional person and I feel first and then think, and so I didn't consider the "I told you so lecture" I was going to receive from Sal, so I burst into her room and told her the whole thing, and she just says, "Let me guess: she didn't ask you to come, did she?" So I guess this is why I still harbor some bitterness with my gal-pal, Kimberly. I don't really. I just think it is funny to bring up sometimes.

I have twenty minutes left on my lunch, so I will wrap this up. It is funny how you bury things in your mind, and then something random will make you think of it. Really, a lot of this started around that movie. I think that is where my infatuation began. We had that senior seminar class together, and we were in the same group, and I kept bothering you because I was scared about my part. You were so nice and patient with me, and anyway we were supposed to meet at the library to watch this video I had gotten from there (I still have that video; yeah, I suck as a renter). Anyway, the library had closed earlier than we thought so we went to mine and Sal's apartment and watched it.

Anyway, it was on the way the back to university to drop you off, you started telling me about the movie. For the life of me, I can't remember why that started. I really can't. You told me all about it, and then I was interested, and right when you got to the end you stopped and refused to tell me the ending and said I had to watch the movie. Isn't it strange how something so strange and small and seemingly so insignificant could prove to be, well, I don't know; but I guess something that wasn't insignificant at least to me. Gosh, that was profound (not). Anyway, this was supposed to be funny – not me attempting to be deep. And this is so all just about friendships, so don't dare think that I like, love you, or am in love with you or anything. Yeah, don't get it twisted; I would really hate to have to drive to Alansville, Mississippi, and bitch slap you over that mistake :)

Feel better soon!

Your friend,
Mary
--
Wishing You a Lifetime of Learning
                    - Mary 09/02/07

Mary: I seriously hate that I have no self control when it comes to you. I hate that. I really had every intention of letting you read all of the millions of emails I have already sent you before I sent another one. But DEAR LORD, I can't help myself. Is there anything that you feel you are not in control of? It is horrible if "no" is your answer, and you don't know which would make me feel even more pathetic. Maybe that question is best left unanswered. In my defense, I spend eight hours of my life five days a week in front of a computer. I guess I have that.

Oh, this is worth mentioning, the last time Sal and I went to Las Vegas we did not get to see Celine Dion and we were crushed. We didn't get to go because Rhoda did not want to go, so we saw Mama Mia, which was awesome but not Celine. Anyway, come December, Celine is not going to be in Vegas anymore, and Sal and I vowed that we'd get back before she left. Well, I got a call today from a friend asking me and Sal to go to Vegas in November. Wow! Of course, we will go. Oh, the cool part: they say they are paying for the room and other expenses, minus the plane tickets. I know the person is using us so they can cheat on their spouse, but I will still take the trip. Our supposed benefactor lies every time she opens her mouth, so I may need to keep my excitement down.

My good night nurse it is only 6:00 PM. I have six hours left. I won't focus on that. Oh, that Halle Berry movie we watched was TERRIBLE.

I don't think I have liked one of her movies since *Boomerang*, and that includes *Monsters Ball*. Anyway, we enjoyed Giovanni Ribose. Don't ask me why but me and Sal both like him.

When capped off the night with *Road Trip*. That is a classic. That's embarrassing. I mean, it is stupid and terrible, but it is funny. We put stuff on to fall asleep to, but we ended up watching the whole ridiculous movie. Have you seen it???? That brings me to another stupid movie we like: *Harold and Kumar go to White Castle*. That movie is soooooooooooooooooo RETARDED but FUNNY. I saw online the other day they are making a sequel. That is crazy to me.

Alright well enough for now!!!

--

Wishing You a Lifetime of Learning 09/09/07

Paul: I've probably told you before, but you should get Hugh Laurie's novel *The Gun Seller* if you're any fan. It's a lot of fun to read but probably not anything you're truly that interested in book-wise. It's a/an hilarious sort of international espionage novel about a self-deprecating agent, Thomas Lange. I loved it. Definitely start reading again, and shy away from People. Eeekk ... (I kid, but only just....)

Owen Wilson. Did you know that his story has for some reason troubled me terribly? I usually couldn't care less about celebs and their Idiot Lives as far as emotional response, but Wilson's undoing really affected me. *The Darjeeling Limited* looks brilliant, as usual for Wes Anderson, and I typically like the movies Wilson is in even when the movie itself isn't all that great, because he carries such an easy charisma. As usual, though, it's a case of the Funny Clown Who Was Sad Inside. Such a cliché at this point (maybe even a cliché of a cliché), but this whole suicide thing really got me down.

I saw *Balls of Fury* this last Friday. My pal Justin wanted to see it, so my sis and his husband (Olivia and Stephen) and I went to see it with them (oh, and our buddy Cal). It was GODAWFUL-BORING. It had exactly four chuckles. And 80 minutes of PLEASE KILL ME.

About *Harold and Kumar*: hilariously unexpectedly hilarious. The trailer, at least, for the sequel looks freaking great. I laughed throughout most of the 60-second preview. It could well be terrible and not live up to the cult-classic stupidity of the first one, but ... I might check it out if word-of-mouth is good.

There are 15 movies I need to see, yet it keeps not happening. Life.
Hope you're well.
Ta-ta!
S 9/11/07

Mary: Thanks for the suggestion. I will look into that. Glad you're doing well. 09/11/07

Paul: WOW! You're doing better! 09/11/07

Mary: Is that sarcasm, Mr. Hughes? If I didn't know better I'd say you were missing my long entertaining emails. 09/11/07

Mary: Paul:
I'm only writing you because I am on my lunch break and I am caught up with my reports and I am not eating dinner. I am über proud of myself this week because I have had a MAJOR crisis and I am not even telling you about it until like four or five days later. I didn't even tell you so you might feel sorry for me and call.

Well, I believe that everyone has phobias. Now, because they are phobias, it isn't a rational fear; but it is one nonetheless: I am deathly afraid of rodents – anything that remotely looks like a rat, a guinea pig, hamster, gerbil – you get the picture. Well, I was on my sofa a few weeks ago watching TV (shocker) and I heard this noise coming from the kitchen. I could hear items in cabinets moving, or so I thought. Well, I turned the TV down and investigated the sound and found nothing. I tried to put it out of my head.

Well, Sal came over that weekend and we camped out in the den. We were in there watching a movie and the sound started. Sal and I looked around and couldn't find anything. Sal then says, "I think you have a mouse." I went nuts, jumping on furniture. I cut the fool. Then Sal says, "Calm down, I was kidding." I knew she wasn't, and she knew, but we both pretended for the sake of my last little bit of sanity.

Well, this past weekend she was over and we were cooking in the kitchen and Sal stopped abruptly and told me to come and look at something. I was petrified because she wouldn't tell me what it was, and I was scared it was going to be a rodent. Anyway, it wasn't a rodent, but we found rat crap in the cabinet. I felt nauseated immediately.

I called the leasing office and had an ordeal convincing them this was their problem. I had the get down-right ignorant. When that didn't work, I called my mommy, and she handled it. It was unreal how accommodating they were with my mom. Anyway, they have found THREE MICE in my apartment so far. On Sunday, when I got home from work, I found more evidence of the rodent, so I called Sal at 1 AM and was like, "I am coming over," and I have been there ever since. See Sunday, I made muffins and I left one on the stove. When I got home, the whole muffin top was GONE. I called Sal hoping she'd say she did it. I left her at my apartment when I went to work. When she said "no," again I acted like a fool.

Anyway, so far everyone has indulged my fear, but now everyone is like, "Get over it." I am going back home tomorrow because I hired Merry Maids to come over and clean my apartment. I told my mom I wanted to move and she was like, "Now you really are being ridiculous." She was like, "Get over it. It is unpleasant, but it isn't the end of the world." Then she told me that one of the houses she lived in growing up had mice, and they had to set traps. Then Sal told me last night that she has lived in a house before that had mice, and lastly my cousin, Rachel, told me that she had mice before in an apartment. She has been the most sympathetic. So now I feel a small tad better about returning home.

It just really makes my skin crawl. I would be so much better if it were something else. I can deal with gross, but to me rodents are the epitome of gross. I would take roaches over rats, really. The bright side of things is that I haven't seen the little suckers because that would have been seriously traumatic for me. I know you are reading this and thinking "ridiculous" and "She is a drama queen," but for real I am terrified. I can't even stand to see rodents on television or in movies.

Now that I've gotten all of that out of my system, I feel better. How are you? I hope you aren't still battling with your virus (mono). Do you watch *Grey's Anatomy*??? Again, I only wrote because it is my lunch and I did have something important (important to me) to tell you. I am getting better. I have started journaling again, so every time I want to write you something I journal it and move on, and it seems to be working. I guess I will move on and find something to do for these last twenty minutes of my lunch.

--
Wishing You a Lifetime of Learning
- Mary 09/13/07

Mary: I'm moving. The situation at my current apartment has gotten worse. Surprisingly, I don't want to talk about it, because it has been such an ordeal. I just wanted you to know that I am moving and am not happy about it considering I haven't really unpacked from my last move.

I feel like I talk too much about myself when I talk to you. Sometimes I don't really know what to say, so I say everything. I try to think of things that you'd be interested in talking about, but I don't really know what that subject is at this time. I know nothing about video games, and I don't really enjoy playing them, but I know you do so I guess I could ask you more about that or you could just tell me because I don't know what to ask.

I don't want you to be angry with me or resent me because of the money I borrowed from you. I do remember it and think about it a lot and do intend to give it back to you sometime in our lifetime. I do have a plan for that and could tell you, but I'd just rather get you your money. I know at this point you aren't holding your breath, but I do plan on rectifying that situation. I really do have a plan in regards to that.

I know that it might not be apparent but I really do work very hard to keep myself realistic and balanced. I try REALLY hard to be in control of my emotions and not let them control me, like I have up until this point.

I have so much that I wish I could say to you and it would come out right, exactly how I would mean for it to come out, but I know that won't work and so I just try to say things to keep myself from saying other things. I know that made no sense, which in a weird way is my point.

I dream about you and that's strange and somewhat comforting at the same time. I wish I had control over that at times. Some dreams are better than others, but they all leave you on my mind way too long. I wish I were making that up, but it is the sad truth. I wish you could see my dreams: the good ones and the not-so-good ones. My descriptions wouldn't do them justice. I have nightmares a lot. They are very vivid and terrifying, but the worst dream I ever had was that I won the lottery. And just as that news started to sink in and I believed it, I woke up. As soon as I reached out to touch my money, I couldn't get a hold of it. I kept reaching for it and it kept moving further and further away until finally I woke up. For some reason, that was devastating.

I'm scared – really terrified – that I am living on borrowed time when it comes to you. Even though I have committed myself to not making the same past mistakes, I wonder at times if I am destined to. I try entirely too hard to understand you. I read way too much into what you write and when you don't. I know that isn't good. Sometimes you will say something/write something and for days I am thinking about it. I am trying to work on that. I think I do that because there is always so much behind everything I say and I automatically think that everyone else is the same way.

I sometimes feel like I am rarely honest. I know that is hard to believe because I know I say things at times and you are thinking, "That is way too much information," but surprisingly I don't feel like I tell the truth – and the saddest part of that is that I lie to myself the most.

I miss you a lot. I would like to see you, but I will leave it at that.
I am at work and so I guess this is as good as any stopping place.
Mary 09/19/07

Paul: Here we go:
My computer's hard drive (my beautiful Mac Book failed me for the first time; I was crushed) failed on Thursday night. I called Apple that evening. The next morning, I got a box and sent it back while the DHL guy was on my porch. It was fixed and sent back yesterday, but I was at work when the driver, this time a FedEx lady, came by. I'm now writing to you on my returned laptop, glad to have it back, but sad that it is going to cost about $330. But how was I here today to receive the package? That's part two.

Yesterday, my buddy Saul stopped by to play some XBOX and to watch some *Jeeves and Wooster*. He's living back at his mom's for a bit while he waits for one of her rental properties to free up after a lengthy eviction he's still going through; his roommate situation was very bad – long story. I made these, you know, breakfast burrito things, just some hot breakfast sausage, scrambled eggs, pepper jack cheese, salsa, and, um, burrito. They were really good, but they may or may not be the cause of some ridiculously bad stomach pains I've been through since late last night. In other words, I stayed home.

I would much rather have gone to work, believe me. As I type, my hands are trembling a bit, which doesn't seem all that good. I have another theory which involves this past weekend with my brother Doug and his wife and our buddy Milo at the ALABAMA Valley Fair, chicken on a stick, and a piece of raw chicken I found wrapped IN THE FOIL I was holding well after I'd eaten most of the chicken (that was cooked). I can't believe it's a total coincidence that I found raw chicken in my food on Sunday, got paranoid and looked up salmonella poisoning on the internet, and am now experiencing horrendous stomach pain. I've never known myself to be a hypochondriac, but I guess it's possibly psychological. I just really doubt it. I'm hoping it's just something I ate last night rather than salmonella. Ugh. If it persists, its doctor time; but I already know what it'll be at this point.

As I've said in times of Olde, *you are a silly girl.* I don't know how to respond to you half the time and you still wonder why I look past some of your remarks. I think that should be the best response at all; call it cowardly, but that's me. ;-)

The $300, or whatever it was. I told you long ago that I live by a very specific credo when it comes to lending, even in the face of Polonius's advice to "neither a borrower nor a lender be": when I lend someone money, I assume I shall never see its return. It's the only way to lend. That being said, I will plainly say this: if you can ever reasonably pay it back, with ease, without hardship, I won't deny it, but I will a) never ask you for it and b) never begrudge you a lack of repayment. Never.

Never wonder how to make your writings to me "more interesting." My interests are many, and I'm not so shallow as to become bored by e-mails that are centered on your life and events. What would the alternative be? You talked about me for 800 words? Please, spare me that. Haha ... One's epistles are inherently self-centered, and that's as it should be.

Whatever is going through your head when I don't write back in a timely fashion or even when I do, I'm going to just put something back on the table I thought was clear, probably naively: we are friends who knew each other a very short time almost seven years ago. I'm happy to keep our correspondences going provided you can live happily with it without doubts or worry or constant vacillation. Is our friendship, however casual or formal it is, able to be endured by you in a healthy fashion? If answer is yes, let us continue. If no, let us reevaluate one last time.

Breaking the numerical list for the end, I want to say that I hope you are at least slowly finding some point of contentment and joy (not cursory happiness, mind you, but real, deep joy), not clinging to the many negativities and doubts you harbor and manufacture (even in dreams), not worrying and gnashing about over. I do hope I haven't mistaken your meaning or your tone and added drama or worry where there was none.

Be well out there, and good luck with your unfortunate move; let's assume your next quarters will be even better. 09/19/07

Mary: Hey,

Well, I moved. It was exhausting, but we got it done. Surprisingly, I have gotten a lot unpacked. My mom is here helping and also surprisingly she *is* actually helping. Usually she comes and is just sort of here. Anyway, I think we could be moving faster, but I have the first four seasons of *Monk* and we love the show and keep getting distracted. The show is really funny but sometimes really moving episodes will creep up on you and it's like, "Wow, that was intense." I don't know if you watch, but I had recorded the season finale a week or two ago and didn't watch until yesterday, and I actually teared up. Well, I am also the girl who watched Fat Albert today and cried. Okay, that's weak, but the *Monk* episode was really good and not in a lame way.

I hope you are having a good weekend. I hope that stomach issue cleared itself up. Here's my new info, just in case – just in case whatever. Here it is: 7896 South Highland Pointe Drive, Campbellton, ALABAMA, 37200. 615-555-7337 (home); 615-555-3723 (cell)

Mary 09/22/07

Paul: Quick note:

Congrats! Hope you like it there. *Monk*? I've seen every episode. You're right, too. It packs a powerful punch when it changes gears. Remember that one episode where *Monk* found Trudy's killer, hooked up to an IV in hospital, and he said, "This is me, killing you. And this is Trudy saving your life." Something like that. I was blown away.

Stomach: almost the same as it has been (since Tuesday night), although today it has allowed me to eat with the reverse effect; instead of almost all food murdering my stomach, it has actually helped it out. I had toast and oatmeal this morning, and it was awesome. I didn't work after Tuesday. Fun! No money!

I'm pretty sure I had/have salmonella, contrary to your hopeful assessment.

Ha-ha...09/22/07

Mary: Not the first time I've been wrong. I watched that very episode last night. He said, "This is me turning off your morphine drip (dramatic pause). And this is Trudy, the woman you killed, turning it back on." I cried on that also.

Good night 09/22/07

Paul: I was actually leery about sending you that in case you hadn't seen it yet ... ha-ha. I thought surely you had. And at least I got the essence of it right, but I was way off on what he said... ha-ha. 9/22/07

Mary: I just felt like being a smartass; it wasn't that far off. It's the essence that was important. I keep hoping that Trudy won't really be dead. Then there was that one episode when they made you think for a hot minute she wasn't, and that was devastating, but it is just so sad to me that he loves her so much and she's dead. It's like, you want him to move on, and then you don't because you love that about him (well, I do). Rhoda watches *Monk* also and so she calls me Adrian and I call her Ambrose. Don't ask me why or how that started; I have no idea.

I am at work on my dinner break and I thought I'd write. I am glad to hear that you are doing better and sorry to know that my diagnosis was incorrect.

Take Care,
Mary
P.S. I should not even type this, but I can't help it. I have diarrhea of the mouth. In one of your emails you said that you could tell you were doing better because you were able to eat some oatmeal and toast.

That just struck me because I think oatmeal is the most disgusting stuff in the world and looking at it makes me nauseated, so it was funny to me that someone being sick at their stomach could eat oatmeal. My granny used to fix it and make me sit at the table until I finished it. I would sit there forever, and it would get cold and disgusting. Then I'd get tired of sitting and try to eat it, and I would throw up. This would happen every time I was over there. Oh, and to add insult to injury I would get a spanking, because she said I did it on purpose. I guess I just needed to let out that childhood trauma. Thank you for that. I feel better, and I have made peace with oatmeal.

P.P.S. This is cool. Last week, my mom had to go to this week-long conference in Napa Valley, California, and everyone there got an iPod Nano. And of course, that got passed on to me. I didn't think I'd ever have one because I would never pay the money for one. Anyway, I thought that was cool.

Night night. 09/23/07

Mary: How are things going? Things here are pretty good. I am excited that tomorrow is my Friday. I am looking forward to having some uninterrupted time to finish putting my apartment together. Sal and I are planning another one of our weekends: Movies and Karaoke! I know, we are dorks, but it's fun. We are watching *Knocked Up* this weekend. We are late. We tried to go and see it in the theater but it just never worked out. Sal and I love the *40 Year Old Virgin*. People keep saying that *Knocked Up* is funnier. I can't even imagine that. Hopefully people are right or it is just as funny.

What are your plans for the weekend? Are you better or are you still fighting your stomach issue (which was definitely Salmonella). My mom is still here in Alabama and that is driving me crazy. I think she is leaving on Saturday. I love her, but I am constantly going behind her and cleaning things up and that drives me nuts. She is just messy and she can't help it. I have almost completed my *Everybody Loves Raymond* collection. There are nine seasons in all and I have eight of the nine. The ninth season just came out on Tuesday. I cannot wait to get it. I keep talking myself out of it right now because moving was expensive, but I will probably break down and get it this weekend.

I started back with my online masters program yesterday. I hate myself for being such a slacker. Had I buckled down and stayed on course, I would have been done next month!! I get pissed at myself whenever I think about it.

I hope things are good. 09/26/07

Paul: REALLY FAST RESPONSE BEFORE I CRASH INTO BED:

Knocked up is one of the funniest movies in years, and at LEAST as funny as *40 Year Old*, I thought. Judd Apatow is truly one of my big, big heroes right now. Also, I died laughing through the entirety of *Superbad*. 09/26/07

Mary: Hey,

This email will be brief because I don't feel so hot but I had to tell you about *Knocked Up*. OK, Sal and I watched it last night, late last night, and IT WAS SO NOT FUNNY TO US. We are going to try and watch it again, because we thought maybe we weren't laughing because we were tired, but I didn't think it was just as funny or funnier than the *40 Year Old Virgin*. I mean, Sal was falling asleep. I thought it was an OK movie. It didn't suck, but in terms of laughing I think I laughed out loud maybe three times. It just wasn't that funny to me. Some parts were sweet. I really want to have a baby, so since I am going through that right now, that appealed to me; but in terms of peeing in my pants from laughing – didn't happen, captain.

Sal and I kept saying to each other, this person said it was funny and this person. We were like, "What are we missing?". What I said to Sal was that it was white-boy humor, more so than the other movie. I hope that's not offensive, but it was. Then I started thinking about everyone who told me it was good and funny, and they were white guys. It's kinda like, for the crowd that is entertained by David Chappelle. That is just my opinion.

That's all. I am home today ill so I am lying on my couch watching Justin Timberlake (speaking of white boys) on HBO. I think he is soooo cute – not in a sexual way, but sort of like if I was white what I'd want my son to look like. I feel the same way about Elijah Wood. They just have such sweet little faces. Oh, and also Shia LaBeouf. He is an absolute doll – so, so, so cute.

Well like I said before, I am home tonight chillin'. I already changed into my PJ's. I did get up and go to church today, and I placed membership. I was so embarrassed for some ridiculous reason, but I am glad I did. It is a nice church. Well so much for brevity. You should call me today and talk to me. That would make me feel better. Actually, the Percocet I took is doing a good job, but you should still call me. 334-555-8143 (new home phone number); 334-498-3752.

Mary 09/30/07

Mary: I finally figured out how to get the iPod to work. I was excited about this last night. I have been listening to it today. It is neat. I didn't know that you could keep pictures on there. It has these neat little functions. I have the small one so I can't imagine what the big can do. I just wish I could listen to it in the car. I mean, where it comes out of the car speakers. I feel too disconnected from concentrating on driving when I listen with headphones on. My cousin's car has some kind of neat thing where you can hook it up to that. I checked and I don't, so I guess that's it.

Rhoda's birthday is this weekend, and she will be thirty. I am trying to talk her into letting me throw her a party. She is hesitant for some reason. I think it would be fun and thirty is a big one, I think. She is supposed to be thinking about the party and getting back to me. I love to do parties. I hope she agrees. Rhoda's sort of laid back and doesn't like a big fuss (like someone else I know), so I won't be surprised if she says no. We might end up having dinner and then calling it a night.

I hope all is well with you. 10/01/07

Mary: The other night I was able to put all of the music on my computer on the iPod and that worked fine. Then today I got a bunch of songs off iTunes and tried several times to just add those songs. Well, every time I thought I was transferring the new stuff, it would erase what was already there and put the new items in their place. I've tried three or four times, and it just deletes everything. So I put all of the other stuff back on the iPod, but for some reason when I transfer everything the new songs are still not on there. If this made any sense and you know what I am doing wrong, I would be so appreciative if you'd enlighten me.

Frustrated 10/02/07

Paul: Dear Mare,

First off, somehow I totally missed this e-mail. I think when I'm clicking "newer" in Gmail, going through the newest mail, I click it twice or something at just the wrong enough time to cause it skip stuff. That's my explanation. Anyway, on to the Apple business.

The only thing I can think of is related to a problem I had back in the day when I first got myself an iPod. It involves syncing and manually updating your iPod. The average user prefers to have iTunes automatically update her iPod each time she connects the iPod to the computer. In other words, if you SYNC, iTunes examines both your library and your iPod to see what has changed since the last time you hooked in. It then adds all the stuff you've added to iTunes since last time. Sometimes, making big changes to your iPod causes it to completely re-write all the data on your iPod, which is what I think you're describing. So, I recommend check marking the option to manually organize your data, or whatever the option is. This means you'll have to hook in, highlight everything in your library (try holding CONTROL-A, for instance) and drag all those songs onto your iPod. Then you can drag the songs you've bought there, too. This shouldn't cause the problem anymore. However, I would start by formatting your iPod (if you have everything backed up in iTunes, and I think you do based on what you've said), starting fresh, setting it to MANUAL, and dragging all the music.

I have no idea if this a) makes sense at all or b) will actually solve your problem, but I have a real feeling that it's the auto-sync that's f'ing everything up.

Let me know vut heppens. 10/03/07

Mary: Ivory,

This is the second-to-last email of the night. I know I will write again when I finally make it in. That is, if I don't feel too bad. It is about to be 7:00 PM and I have to make it to midnight. I don't know how I will do it. I didn't think it would be this hard to come back. I should have, considering for the last month all I did was choke down pain pills and lie on the couch. I'm achy and I want to lie down so badly. I am hoping this will get better. I have this weird pain in my neck. I think it is stress. I am so old. All I can think about is getting home and rubbing this Ben Gay-like substance on my neck. I know you find that so sexy. Don't deny it. It smells horrible, but it works.

I just have to make through tonight and tomorrow and then Friday and Saturday I am OFF. I can do two days. What is two days? Right? Right!

Everybody has been very nice to me today and made me feel better about my return. I was even asked about what holiday time I wanted off. It about killed me to say that I wasn't requesting any. It burns trying to be mature. I figured working those days was the very least I could do seeing how they didn't fire me for being off a month. So I will be working Thanksgiving, Christmas, My Birthday, and New Years :(

I guess maybe you did make your trip today after all. I hope you have fun and think about me a lot and call me sometime in the near future, seeing how that is very important to me for some reason.

Ebony 10/31/07

Mary: Clyde Barrow,

Today was lovely. I was off and so I slept a lot and ran errands. I would have slept longer BUT my mom attempted to helpful and drove my car to the gas station and filled it up and locked the keys in the car. She then had to take a cab back here, and then we drove her cab back to the station and after than I went ahead to Jiffy Lube and other places. My mom had been really nagging me :) about having my oil changed, and so when I finally did she then told me I got screwed because I paid $66. How was I supposed to know??? All she said was an oil change and that's what I told the dude at Jiffy Lube.

Tonight is Sal's night to cook so I decided to bake yet another cake. I thought it would be nice because I am the lone soul who has enjoyed the German chocolate cake. Mom wouldn't touch it because of the coconut, and Sal doesn't really eat chocolate. SHE ate some but NOT a lot. I am the one that made love to the cake daily. I ate it for breakfast as snacks. Now there are a few pieces left and I just can't do it anymore. I am officially burned out on the cake. Rhoda is coming over tomorrow, so I am sending the rest with her. I am making a pineapple upside down cake now. That is not my favorite, but Sal and my mom like it so it gave me something to do this afternoon. Oh, and my mom is LEAVING tomorrow. She will be missed BUT it is solo time.

Sal and I have this crazy dream that one day we are going to open a bed-and-breakfast in Vermont, so every time we cook something delicious we write it down and save it for the bed and breakfast. We want that to be our hook – the delicious food. I must admit we have some pretty good stuff written down.

Well, I hope you have had a great day.... All the best.

You're Partner in Crime,
Bonnie Parker 11/02/07

Mary: Yes it is about 1:30 AM (my time) in the morning and I am up thinking about this. I am only checking on this because of our discussion on how intentions aren't always clear with email, especially when it comes to our interactions. Are you still harboring feelings of rage, frustration, aggravation, ennui, or whatever over the nagging issue? I thought that was resolved BUT maybe I misinterpreted that as well. I can't ever tell BUT I figure it is stupid to be afraid to just ask.

Anyway, that was on my mind, and I didn't want to keep sending you emails and stuff if you were aggravated and wanted me to stop. That's why I am asking. I really don't want to get on your nerves, Paul. I know maybe it doesn't feel like that to you BUT that isn't my intention, even though that might be the end result. 11/07/07

Paul: Things are cool, baby. I'm just really spread thin right now. Things should be back to the status quo soon enough, one hopes. Just take care of yourself and work hard. I'll write again soon. 11/07/07

Mary: If I make it to midnight tonight (my time), that is one whole week. After those two days last week, I didn't know, BUT it hasn't been too bad. I have actually felt pretty fine this week (knock on wood). I think I got dizzy once and that was like for ten minutes. Anyway, I hope your week has been a pretty good one.

--
Wishing You a Lifetime of Learning
- Mary 11/08/07

Mary: Well I have forty minutes and then I would have made it a WHOLE week. I know I should NOT pat myself on the back for such things (normal things, things I should be doing, things people do every day and don't give a second thought to) yet I do. Anyway I just figured I'd get that out, and I thought if I did it now I might actually get to tell you good night before you actually went to sleep. SOOOOO good night.

Sweet dreams,
Mary 11/09/07

Mary: It is 9:00 PM and I am BEAT. I was OFF today and I am yawning already. I was trying to put songs on the computer so I could add them to the iPod, but it is taking a little too long. Sal has her big COMP test tomorrow so she is studying ALL night. She is supposed to be, but she keeps popping out of the room to say stupid stuff. I think she is having a hard time focusing. Even though it was her night, I cooked dinner, which means she is supposed to clean up but I am sure that ain't gonna happen. I'm too sleepy to clean so guess that means tomorrow. I think I'll put the food in the fridge and then I'm out. I wasn't thinking and told Sal that I would wake up early and fix her breakfast before she leaves for the test. That is going to kill me. Of course, the silly girl wants pancakes :) I definitely talk way too much.

So sad I will probably be asleep by ten on a Friday night. Tomorrow after Sal's test we are going to a movie and dinner to celebrate. I can't even tell you how long it has been since I've done anything. I'll be glad to get out tomorrow.

A TENDER MOMENT SECTION: proceed with caution

I hope things are calming down in your world and you are not feeling spread so thin still. I know you have a lot on you – not sure what exactly, because you won't talk to me about it but I know it is there. Enough of that. I just hope things are looking up. I miss you (I guess).

Anyway, I am going to at least get in my bed and listen to music until I fall asleep.

Have Sweet Dreams, Paul (especially if I'm in them) 11/09/07

Mary: Good night for real - I got caught up with listening to songs. I am really about to pass out now. Oh, then Sal came in here wanting to be quizzed :)
Sweet Dreams 11/10/07

Mary: Paul,

I have had a not-so-good day today. Yes, this is a whining email. That was your warning. Sal had her COMPS today, and I was going to wake up early with her and make her breakfast to send her off and be productive today. Well, I woke up at 7:15 (too late) so that plan was out. So I cleaned the kitchen, made myself breakfast and then tried to watch TV. At around 9:30, I get a call from the on-call doctor in my doctor's practice. He tells me that the lab called him this morning about my lab work from yesterday. I take blood thinners and my range is supposed to be around two or three. Anyway, it is at nine, which is WAY TOO THIN. He is like, "Do nothing today. Stay on the couch all weekend and see Dr. Neese first thing Monday, and stop taking the blood thinner for now." Then he says go to the ER and get a vitamin K shot. So I start whining, "For real?" and he is like, "Yeah." So, grudgingly, I get dressed and go.

Then when I get there I mention I have a headache. BIG MISTAKE. They start freaking out, "She might have brain hemorrhaging." I'm like, "Dude, I get headaches ALL THE TIME. I see a neurologist for them. Look it up." He insists that I get it. Well, an hour and half later, BIG SHOCK: no brain bleeding. Then they insist on testing the blood again. I have to wait on those labs. OK, now the IRN levels are at ten. Then finally they give me the smallest pill I've ever seen in my life and let me go. Do you know how much that cost me? 50 DAMN dollars!!!!!!!!!!!!!!!!!!!! I was/am PISSED.

Then I spent $20 at the doctor's office and had to pay this bill yesterday that was delinquent. I wrote checks, knowing I didn't have the money. So, I had to ask my friend, Erin, to loan me money, and also my friend Constantine and my fake mom. So hopefully one or all of them will be able to help. I really hated to ask Erin because she is getting married and I know money is scarce. I feel like pond scum when I have to do that. So now I am depressed about that and sulking tonight.

Speaking about depressed, I don't why I am telling you this because you already think I'm insane for various reasons (I love you, I'm overly emotional, I take things to seriously, I take things too far, I email incessantly … etc.); but on Friday my doctor prescribed me PROZAC. Wow!!!! That was on a whole new level. I said I felt depressed and a little anxiety ridden, but for real? PROZAC? Sal told me I had too many negative stigmas against mental health (that's the masters gone to her head). Plus she thinks I'm crazy too. Hey, maybe there is something to this after all :)

When my mom was here, she washed about a million clothes for me and they have just been stacked up in the corner of my room. I am sick of looking at them so I am going to finally hang them up tonight (I hope). My plan is to listen to music and put up clothes. Sal's friend had surgery so she is visiting her. I get distracted when she is here.

P.S. I hope you're alright. You have been more cryptic than usual and that's scary. 11/10/07

Mary: Hey Guy,

Just wanted to say goodnight and send more encouragement your way. I am so curious and wondering what is keeping you so busy and feeling spread so thin. Are you in need of help of some kind? I mean, I really don't have much right now, but I am hoping that will change soon. If THERE IS ANYTHING I CAN DO LET ME KNOW, even if it's the littlest of things, let me know. I would love to do something to help you. I know you don't like to lean on people, but that's what friends are for; they even wrote a song about it. You've just been on my mind so much over the last couple of days. You like to send curve balls from time to time.

Sweet Dreams Sweet Boy 11/12/07

Mary: Good night Axel Hughes 11/13/07

Mary: Disclaimer: This is going to weird you out, BUT you will get over it. By now you know that I have no boundaries.

Quickie: Yesterday I came up with this idea, and I think it might be a good idea but it is in the beginning. In a few weeks, I may not think so, BUT I am excited. Anyway, I am trying to make a website for the idea. I want to tell you about it, but if you make fun of me at this point it will hurt my feelings. So after I have a little more time with it, I do want to tell you about. I just wanted to come up with something to give back to people who have helped me and others and also help myself get stable. (You needed to know this to get the next part).

The Dream: I dreamed last night that you and I had a baby (yes, US, Mary E. Jacks and Paul A. Hughes) and honey, that wasn't the weird part. The weirdness: 1) The baby came out and looked completely white and pasty. 2) It could TALK. 3) It knew stuff. Like, it immediately started calling me "mommy." It was very creepy. Oh and it could pick up things and hand me things, and it knew who you were, and it had heard conversations we had heard. 4) The baby was CUTE BUT not cuddly because of the personality, and it was rude. It didn't want to be held, or snuggled. It was kind of cold and distant. Then I felt bad because I didn't like my baby and I didn't want it, and then I woke up. So later when I remembered the dream I looked up dream interpretation online and this is what I learned about giving birth in dreams.

Interpretation:

To dream of giving birth or see someone else giving birth suggests that you are giving birth to a new idea or project. It also represents new beginnings or some upcoming event. A more direct interpretation of this dream may represent your desires/ anxieties of giving birth or the anticipation for such an event to occur.

To dream that you are giving birth to a non-human creature signifies you have an overwhelming (and unfounded) fear for the health of your baby. You are overly concerned that your baby may have birth defects. This type of dream is common in expectant mothers in their second trimester. If you are not expecting, then it refers to your fear of the outcome of some decision or project. You are trying to overcome difficulties in your life and achieve inner development. In particular, if you dream that you are giving birth to a monster, then it implies that your inner creative energy has yet to differentiate itself and grow into expression. You may hold some hesitation in releasing this "monster" for fear that others will judge your or that they will not accept your ideals.

I just thought that was spot on. I had to share that. I know you probably wish I hadn't.

Mary 11/13/07

Mary: I get off in an hour and a half. I am so glad. I am ready to go home tonight. Anyway, this is the goodnight email. I know you will probably be asleep or whatever at midnight my time. So good night. And again I hope things are well with you.

Mary 11/13/07

Mary: Goodnight...

P.S. You're not out getting someone else pregnant, are you? 11/15/07

Mary: I was told that a Bible professor at the university died of cancer today – Dr. Sales, my favorite professor. I just thought that was sad and you might want to know.

Wishing You a Lifetime of Learning
-Mary 11/15/07

Mary: Have you ever just haphazardly picked up something random and starting reading it to waste time, and the first couple of pages completely changes your life. This happened to me about 30 minutes ago. I was trying to find anything to read because I have an all day appointment, so I was packing a fun bag for myself. OK, the point: I grab this book and read the first couple of pages and feel utterly humiliated. I wanted to go and dive under something. I felt like the book was about me. This was just the introduction, but I felt so small, and the funny thing I also felt embarrassed. This, the COLD, HARD, BITTER, GUT WRENCHING thing I have unearthed from those couple of pages. To you, this is going to be repetitive; but for me this is invigorating and – I am hoping – freeing. I hope that more than anything else. There are so many things in this world that I suck at. There is almost nothing that I'll say I excel in, but I do a good job of loving and sincerely caring and being for those who are need.

The Epiphany: Disclaimer: I am ÜBER fine with email. I am not upset at all, so don't send me a hateful email, then followed by an email that I question if you wrote it due the vernacular.

The point, to borrow an overused quote and some pretty good advice, is that you are just not that in to me. Please excuse the street language, BUT that is right-on like an m***f*** (chickened out). That sums up everything. I have such clarity about this now, and it only took six or seven years. What the book showed me – and then slapped me rather brutally hard with – is that I would have to ask you to call, visit, etc. If there was a real chance for something to happen, anything, you'd want to see me too. The book also said that women have a tendency to make up excuses for men and that women will come up with anything rather than deal with the TRUTH: that he isn't interested. That part is right-on. I do that soooo much.

I was humiliated reading that back. I felt like hiding in my closet to read. You can't change your feelings any more than I can change mine. It's sad to me, but I get. I guess I keep thinking one day it will. So now that I am feeling a little more empowered and honestly know what I want, I feel this strange quiet peace and so tied up in knots all the time. All the energy and stress I put into analyzing what you say and whether you meant anything by it was exhausting. And from reading the book, I know now that I don't have to do that. If you wanted me to know something, you'd tell me. I have to believe that.

I am not upset just feeling introspective. Oh, and wondering if you are actually reading these ridiculous emails I send you. I still love you and think you should visit and call and – more importantly then that – want to do those things. What I should have picked up on is that when someone is into someone, they want to be around (no begging). I am finally on the right road (I know I have been here before) but this time I can't really explain it, but I get it. Something magical and beautiful isn't going to happen to you and suddenly change you so you are going to love me back.

Mary 11/16/07

(And Finally He Speaks) Paul: You may not have noticed, and perhaps it's just the fact that many of my friends and I just have different lifestyles than you and me, but you tend to put me in a very bad position.

You see, I don't see it as my duty as a friend to inform each and every one of my friends what I'm up to day in and day out. Sometimes, they hear about it, and sometimes, they don't. Part of it is privacy, sure. Part of it is my personal belief that I shouldn't be presumptuous enough to believe my friends would WANT that kind of detailed information on a regular basis. I just tend to do my own thing, based on my own beliefs and insecurities and respect for other people's privacy.

So, when, as happened this last week, I decided to drive up to Montana to visit my uncle and see my best friend Cooper and his wife Stella (and ended up staying there quite nearly an entire week, as opposed to what I had planned, which was a weekend), you no doubt started thinking about why I wasn't writing, especially since I had made a comment about feeling spread thin and anxious.

I really am grateful you're concerned, and I apologize for not being able to write you while I was away. But the bad position I mentioned is that because I don't inform you of so many things (that no one else seems much to mind, not counting certain things I neglected to mention to you that were obviously huge Life Moments that still somehow slip through the cracks of "Old News I've Probably Already Told Everyone 50 Million Times Yet Haven't"), and I, let's say, go out of town for a while, I return to see that things have gotten out of hand with your imagination.

Yes, you were concerned about me, and I appreciate that. But it's more than that, isn't it? You start questioning why I'm not writing YOU, and only you. You start wondering what signals I'm sending by not writing YOU. You sent me these e-mails, like 20 times before, that talk about how you're learning how to take me, how you still "love" me, how you understand I'm "just not into you." And on and on. Do you realize that one of the reasons it's so hard to give you anything in return is because it blossoms into so many other things in your mind?

After a period of perhaps writing every couple days, perhaps a week or two or three passes, as things happen and life gets in the way, you begin to wonder what might have caused it. You wonder what I'm thinking. You wonder why I can't just do what you want and make you happy.

You've put me in a position to be wary about almost everything I say to you, yet you never give me any leeway when I don't say much at all. You have to – HAVE TO – understand by now what's going on. I get home, boot up my e-mail program, and I see Mary Jacks all down the INBOX. Just glancing at the latter half, especially the latest, instantly tells me your frame of mind and what you're thinking about. My heart sinks.

Now, I think, I have to find some way to explain I've been gone without it all sounding like some big excuse. Because I'm always in this position. Because I didn't tell you what I was doing for a few days. Because your imagination gets perpetually out of hand, and there's nothing I can do about it. If I had told you I was going somewhere, I have no doubt that you would have, at least for a moment, thought, "If you can go there, why can't you come here?"

I always end these e-mails, KNOWING you're going to get totally ticked or sad or that you'll underplay something you've said or I've said or take something onto yourself as if I've done nothing wrong, or tell me to take something onto myself as if you've done nothing wrong, and I say something like, "Let's just try to take this for what it is," blah blah blah blah blah blah ad infinitum. It never, ever, ever ends. We can't have regular conversations, because you don't want regular conversations. We can't have a regular friendship, because you don't want a regular friendship. It has ALWAYS been this way, Mary, regardless of what else you might say; you've never simply wanted to be friends. I know that. You don't have to try wording it another way or say anything else.

If I'm wrong, you'll see now that my mind cannot be changed. Either I've misread six or seven years of what you've had to say or you don't want to be regular old pals. Period. And I know I haven't misread you.

I usually end these things with, "I want you to be well, happy, less worrisome, and calmer, more at peace, content." I don't know if you can be until we simply go our separate ways, Mary; and as hurtful as that sounds to you, it doesn't sound hurtful to me. I like and have always liked you as a funny, self-deprecating, and beautiful person, but if I had known that you would suffer for this long (AND YOU HAVE, I don't think I need to remind you) because of something unrequited, things might have been very different.

I'm not over-reacting here. I'm not speaking out of turn or without care or thought. If you believe nothing else, believe that.

P 11/16/07

Mary: I so would have responded a lot earlier but I have been at the hospital for the majority of the day and I am just getting in now.

I am sincerely sorry, utterly ashamed and deeply embarrassed about everything and that I have been so exhausting to you. I say that with no malice, sarcasm and with no hidden agenda. You are absolutely right about everything. I have no defense. I cannot express to you in any way how small, ridiculous, crazy and insignificant I feel.

I'm just really sorry, Paul, and I will try really hard not to bother you anymore because that was never my intention. I know you won't believe that, but emailing became obsessive for me and I couldn't stop myself at times. But that's not your problem; it's mine.

Mary 11/16/07

Mary: Paul,

Just wanted to give you a heads up that I'd be sending you some things in the mail. I had bought you some things around the Christmas when we fell out the last time, and I really don't want to hang onto them any longer. It's not a peace offering; it's sort of closure thing. And we aren't enemies or anything (at least I hope not). I am sending it to your mom's address because that's the address I have.

In closing, I just want to say I wish so desperately that things could be different, but I can't lie to you anymore and I can't lie myself any longer. I never wanted to be just your friend and I wasn't happy when I tried to pretend that was all I wanted. You were right on just about everything you called me on. Being just your friend is not something I am capable of doing. I'd fool myself or lie to myself into thinking I could do it, and then things would fall apart. I'd think something is better than nothing, but maybe in regards to me and you, nothing is better – or maybe healthier is a better word.

I would think that one day things would change. After years and years of the same thing, I would think that. In your email, you mentioned how you'd have to be careful with what you'd say/write to me because of what I'd read into it. That was very true. Reading that really did something to me, because I'd hope with each email there would be something to tell me to keep holding on and waiting, or with each email I'd send there would be something that would change everything for you. Then when you mentioned the whole thing about the inbox and all the "Mary Jack's" I absolutely wanted to die, and I knew it was true and I couldn't do anything but feel retarded and like a complete and utter psycho. (I'd like to interject here that I didn't know they were piling up. I thought you were getting them daily.)

When it comes to you, I am a psycho. I wish you could know me in any other circumstance and situation where I'm normal, charming and delightful. I hate that you know me like this. The other thing that struck me HARD is when you said that you didn't tell me that you were going out of town because I'd immediately think, "He can go there, but he can't come here." That was like "DAMN." That was a huge slap in the face, back to reality. Again that is exactly what I would have thought. YEARS, I have been BEGGING you to come here. That says something that I have been too stupid to hear.

The culmination of all of these things helped me see that you're right: I was lying when I'd say I want to be just friends. You have been telling me these things FOR YEARS, and I just wouldn't listen to you because I just wanted to believe that some way, somehow, we'd end up together.

I am a sick person. I mean that physically and mentally. I think I just needed someone to attach to and feel close to when I felt down and scared. As long as I felt like I "had" you, I didn't really have to have anyone else or have to try to enter real relationships. I spend a lot of time being depressed, and it was easy to just do this; but instead of our relationship/friendship being symbiotic, it was parasitic (one guess as to who was the parasite). As I said in the previous email I am so sorry for that.

I know that this is for the best. It is killing me. As I write this, I am hoping that you tell me that we don't have to do this. The fact that thought even entered my mind is more proof that friendship is out of the range of my capabilities. I don't know what's wrong with me, because I want to be your friend more than anything, but I guess I want something else more than that.

I know that I will probably miss you forever and wonder how you are and feel bad for a long while because of my weakness. At this stage of my life right now, I feel that I love you very much and maybe one day I'll meet someone else and I'll realize that I didn't; but as of right now, tonight, that's how I feel.

With Much Affection Always,
Mary

P.S. Merry Christmas (That will help with the temptation to email Christmas Day) 12/01/07

Mary:

We can't be lovers;
We can't be friends;

Where does that leave us?

You've said, I have been too much to take.
I have been left quivering in your wake.
This is far too much to make.

You saw through me and knew I was a fake.
What hurts the most is that this is all for my sake.

You have years of regret,
which make me easy to forget.
While I am haunted by an unexplained weakness
that won't allow me to.

I talk;
You walk;
I'm paralyzed by weakness;
You by closeness.
You have a determination to stay strong;
To prove to me that I am wrong.

Where does that leave us?

When I tell you how I feel,
You say, I'm mentally ill.
I tell you that the love I feel for you is strong
You say that something has to be wrong.

Redding says, "I've been loving you a little too long to stop now."
He croons in the song, "You've become a habit to me,"
which brings me to a new low.
This too shall pass, but the journey will be slow.

Desperately wanting you in my life
unsure how you can be without strife.

You believe this is for the best.
I pretend to acquiesce; just another one of life's tests that burn like hell.

We can't be lovers;
We can't be friends;

Where does that leave us? 01/28/08

Mary:
I've been loving you
Too long, to stop now
You were tied
And you want to be free
My love is grown stronger
As you become a habit to me.
Otis Redding "I've Been Loving You (Too Long Stop Now)"

I'm not writing you for sympathy. I also figured that at this point you couldn't possibly think any less of me, so I really have/had nothing to lose. I'll spare you the details, but I am sick and haven't been to work in a month so I have had lots of time on my hands. Anyway, that's dangerous for me. I am writing just because I feel like it, and I want to. I don't want you to write back because in my mind that would mean that you cared and I'd have china patterns picked out and kids names within the week. For a while, things were going pretty well not communicating with you. I had sort of made peace with things. I had an enjoyable Christmas (still have something to mail) and my birthday was alright. Then February hit and my health went downhill, and it seemed my resolve weakened.

At first, I took an AAA or NA approach and took it one day at a time. That worked really well, especially with the emailing. Good Lord, that was horrible. There wasn't anyone I emailed that much; everyone else I saw or talked to on the phone, so that was an adjustment. Then it seemed I would come into all these things that reminded me of you – not farfetched things that I had stretch and contort to somehow make them in some kind of strange other world relate to you.

Here are a couple of examples, I'd get a call from Alansville, Mississippi, ALABAMA, and the caller's name would be Paul or Hughes. Or it seemed that *Rear Window* was on an awful lot. Most recent occurrences: I was reading the paper or something and read that Wilco and somebody else were going to be here in Alabama in March. I thought I bet he is going to be here for that. Then today Sal and I went to CD Warehouse just so I could get out, and I saw they had this box set of Emmylou Harris, and I said to Sal, "I think Paul likes her." Sal then says, "What does she sing?" and I replied with "The hell if I know." Then we laugh and leave. Then there is thing with Elton John. I love Elton John and listen to him, and you said something about him YEARS ago that I still remember (sadly) and can't help but think about when I hear him.

I wondered whether us ending communication was a little a sad for you or whether it was it just this GIGANTIC relief for you. My guess would be the latter. That is such a bitter pill to swallow. I can't blame you for that, because ... well, I just can't. Like I said, I have had a lot of time on my hands. I started another journal. Sal's mom, Jackie got me one for Christmas. Anyway, that prompted me to pull out older journals. I started with one from 2001. As I read through it, I kept thinking, "I feel so sorry for this girl," and then it hit me that I *am* this poor girl. I have these same issues and feelings; I am just a lot older. I am still telling you the same things, having the same feelings, pissed at you for same things, and banging my head against the same wall. It was real; I don't even know what to say. 2001!!!

I wanted to end it all right there (that was a joke). One thing that I did learn from those earlier journals is that, as tired as you are of hearing how much I love you, how much I care and all of that stuff I say, I am just as sick of saying those things to you. And baby, that only took seven years! Now I'm almost thirty and have spent the better half of my 20's being an idiot. Now, if my health doesn't improve, that's how I would have spent my life. This is too depressing to continue.

I sometimes wonder if this is just because of me or whether it would have been with anyone. So this is me relapsing. This is me having no self-respect. This is me wanting you to know that I'm sad, scared and not quite ready to say good bye, even if it is for the best. And no, this isn't a ploy for you to write or call. I know what that would do to me and where my little brain would go. It just gives me some kind of sick peace to write you. I don't know what that means about me, and I am petrified to go deeper to truly find out. It all seems so unfair doesn't it, Paul? All this attention for just being a nice guy.

Things I would say if we were communicating: I would say I am very sad about the deaths of Heath Ledger and Brad Renfro. I feel very sorry for Brittany Spears. I would tell you that my mother has moved in with me for six months to help me out until I get well. I have to use a wheelchair for now. I am completely and utterly humiliated about the situation (I can walk), but I fall a lot because of this other long story. Anyway, so until that is cleared up, they don't want me to walk a lot.

I am even more embarrassed about this than I am about sending you thousands of manic emails. So basically, I am not going anywhere; so that's why I have time to do to this. I haven't seen any good movies lately. Everything I have seen lately has sucked. I desperately want to see *Juno,* but since I am cripple and not leaving the house, I can't.

P.S. We are so past the mystery of Christmas gifts. Two or three years ago I bought you a DVD for Christmas. Anyway, we stopped talking, and I put the gift somewhere, wrapped, and forgot about it. Anyway, my mom found it, and it was my intention to mail it but I didn't – and then I decided, well, I'll wait until next Christmas. I know that's ghetto. It had been awhile, so I forgot what DVD was wrapped. This year it was my intention to mail it to you. Well, it dawned on me this year that the movie is *One Flew over the Cuckoo's Nest.* I thought, "How appropriate. What a fitting end." 2/10/08

Mary: I'm feeling weak. 10/24/08

Mary: Am I really as crazy as I seem? Or, am I shockingly and terrifyingly right about a few things, or maybe about one or two very important things? Are you possibly as cold as you'd have me to believe? Or are you just shockingly and terrifyingly brilliant? I don't talk about you that much anymore because it is getting harder and harder to lie with a straight face. Sal has begged and pleaded with me to not do what I am doing right at this very minute. I think, with no doubt in my mind, I can say that she is embarrassed for me. I'll keep this to myself for a good week or two, and then with a whole lot of shame I will admit that I have broken. I know the minute you saw this you probably rolled your eyes and thought, "What now?"

I write you pretty sure that you aren't going to write back but still have this sick feeling in the pit of my stomach that you will and that you will be harsh (in that way that only I seem to bring out in you). I think it's strange how clearly my mind can see something or know something, but still I go in the opposite direction because emotionally I feel led somewhere else.

I have always prayed, but over the last year I have really gotten serious about my praying and my conversations with GOD. I feel very weak physically and of course emotionally, and I pray for strength. I also pray for you, believe it or not. My new prayer as of late has been to let go if you are not the direction I should be going in, and obviously that's the case. I don't feel strong enough or brave enough to stop caring on my own. Maybe that's harsh. I don't mean stop caring but to stop caring as deeply as I do.

Sometimes, I imagine that we have switched places and how I'd feel in your shoes. That is another road that I am not ready to travel. I continue to write you because I'm bored, I'm hooked, I feel connected to you when I write you (even though you don't write back). I've done so for so very long. I think your funny, you're so easy to think about, I've created so many little things that make me think about you, I like talking to you (when we are both not thinking about how I feel), and you frustrate me so damn much (I guess in some weird masochistic way, I like that). I know by now you (I wouldn't be surprised) probably have me blocked from even sending you emails, yet I still feel compelled to send them. I couldn't blame you for that, but again the part of me that keeps writing you would.

It bothers me so much that this isn't hard or a struggle for you. That means I have to face what a burden I must have been (and continue to be) to you and face the idea that I could have been (am) so off-balance and confused as to let you mean so much more to me than I did to you. I think about all the years and all the ridiculous things that I said and meant (sadly), and I wonder: did I go through all of these things, feel these things and am I now faced with letting these things go, all because you were being polite to me when I was scared to do my part in our senior seminar group?

That not only hurts but terrifies me on a level you will never truly comprehend. I can't even truly grasp the magnitude of that, because it is too life altering. I don't want you to forget about me, and not even in the psycho way it sounds but in the selfish way, because if I can't forget you I don't want you forgetting me.

Why isn't this easier for me? Please tell me how to not let another person have any effect on me and not be concerned by their feelings or lack thereof. I mean it. If you can tell me how you do it or better yet just pray that it happens for me, that would mean more to me than you'd know.

It's the strangest thing; I miss you even though I never really had you. 2/25/08

Mary: Have you seen *Becoming Jane*? Just so tragic, sad and inspiring all at the same time. 03/08/08

Mary: I'm sick, scared and alone tonight. I'm writing because my resolve has weakened. I've been ill so I'm missing work. My mom is on a business trip, and I am alone. The silence here is deafening and the TV isn't drowning the silence. I hear it clearly. I just feel drained and tired from thinking and feeling. Anyway, I hope everything is nice and in place in your life, world, and universe. I know how much that means to you. You continue to be in my prayers and thoughts. Don't worry; I don't have another bad poem in me tonight.

I miss you a lot, which is strange as I (and you) have pointed out time and time again. I just believe that things in this life happen for a reason and it is our job to find the reason hidden within these strange little moments that make a life. I don't know what's going on in your life, what keeps you awake nights; I'd love to, but that's not how you play this game. I wonder silly things like what kind of car you drive, what you're watching, listening to. Curious if you still write reviews and wonder where you are working. I wonder if your mom is doing well with her challenges. I hate things are like this. We weren't seeing each other or talking on the phone, but to lose emailing privileges – that is something.

Mary 03/10/08

Mary: I know I should not be writing you but I cannot help myself tonight. Things have been very hard these last few weeks, just with life, family and as always health. I seriously considered quitting my job and going on disability. My immune system is so weak and I have something new it seems every week. I just recently went back after being gone a month, and here I am at home tonight. I have some kind of vicious stomach virus. I have never had stomach pains like this before. Anyway, it makes me feel a little better to write, even though you don't write back and might not even read these things.

I think I told you that my mother had moved in to help me out while I've been so sick. Anyway, my health has been going up and down, and as it was beginning to look like she was going to be needed longer, we decided to just bring my dad here. It just felt like the right thing to do. Some days, I think about how I went from my own apartment, to living with Sal, then mom moved in, and now dad is here. The Jacks's are all together again under one (my) tiny roof.

I had some anxiety about moving my dad in, but then I saw how happy it made him when we discussed the possibility of it with him. It broke my heart that he was there and I felt that was crushing his spirit. Seeing the difference in him since he has been here has been so life affirming and every day convinces me that I did the right thing. I didn't picture that at 30 I'd be living with my parents again, but I realize there was a time when it looked like I would not have any more time with my dad.

I don't know why this makes me feel better, because you don't write back, email, call or visit, but for some unknown reason this is OK with me for right now. I hope you are well. Obviously, I do think about you a lot. I wonder what you are doing, were you are working, what you're driving, what new musical nightmare that has you enthralled with it.

I got a new iPod the touch screen. It is waaaaaaaaaay cooooooooooooool. It amazes me how fast songs accumulate on that thing. One of my dear friends, Nora, is getting married on Saturday. We have been friends since we were eight and graduated from high school together; she more family than a friend. Anyway, I am not going to her wedding. Ninety-two percent of the reason why not is my health. I haven't been cleared to drive yet, even though I snuck out once and went to Wal-mart. Then there is the 8% that is soooooooooooooooooooooooo jealous. GOD, I HATE THAT. I AM A HORRIBLE PERSON. I love Nora, and I'm happy for her – I am – but it stings because Nora was my person that understood, and now that part of our relationship – the lamenting over love unrequited – is gone, and I am a lone loser. I shouldn't be jealous. It was my decision to waste the better part of my twenties and now thirties chasing and fighting windmills.

I think about all these years and emails I have sent you over the years, and it all seems so ridiculous at times and then at others it makes sense to me. I did go to work last night. My mom takes me and picks me up (because of the driving). Anyway, this song was on, and I know it was Rob Thomas. I don't know if it was him solo or with Matchbox 20. Anyway, I had heard the song many times, but last night I really listened to the words. He said, "Just let me hold while you're falling apart. Just let me hold you and we will both fall down." I think it is called "Ever the Same." Anyway, hearing that encouraged me to get my iPod out and listen to some tunes. Then I started listening to

Elvis Costello. I starting liking him because of a CD you made me many, many, many moons ago. I'm actually listening to him now.

As always, I miss you, I DO LOVE YOU (go ahead get pissed get something). Well, I don't know what's going on with you and your family, but you all are in my prayers. I hope you are happy, Paul, and I'm sad that I can't be a part of that. It just all seems so unfair to me. I love you; why is that a big deal? Don't worry, I am not looking for answers from you. I just love you. I didn't ask you to marry me or father my children - it's just three words.

I know this has not worked in a decade so this might be futile, but I think we should see each other. I don't mean like next weekend, I mean down the road, maybe in May or June, and just talk in person. I think that is important. Just like last time, I will come to you - because that's what girls like me do. I just think the clarity would be better, and I think it will help me. I promise I won't try to touch you, I won't say anything about love or anything else that makes you uncomfortable (so we will just talk about me the whole time).

Right now, I am a little off balance because of some pills I took, so I may regret this when the calm leaves my body. One day, if you ever feel this way, from drinking, or meds, or at that place right before you fall asleep listening to Elton John's Sorry seems to be the Hardest Word. I hope I cross your mind.

No stronger, no better, no wiser,

Mary 04/03/08

Mary: Could you pretend this was a struggle?? I mean, just for a little while. I think I really need that. Anyway this is me attempting at something really anything.
Desperately Seeking Mary 04/09/08

Mary: good night.
--
Wishing You a Lifetime of Learning
-Mary 04/22/08

Mary: Paul,
The boys are too good this year!!! I don't know if you are watching, but *American Idol* is HOT this year. The guys by far surpass the

girls, even though I love Brooke. She has a kind spirit and she moves me when she sings. If you are not watching, you should check it out or listen on iTunes. David Cook is ridiculously TALENTED. HE is the resident rocker this year. He is sooooooooooooooooo friggin awesome. He has done soooo many great things this season. He kicked ass on Michael Jackson's "Billie Jean," Lionel Richie's "Hello" and recently Mariah Carey's "Always Be My Baby." That was hot!!!!!!!!!!!! !!!!!!!!!!!!!!!!!!!

I love him and little cutie David Archuleta who looks 14 but is 17. I refer to him as my little son. He is adorable. His voice is precious. Also, I love Jason. He is the white dude with the dreads. I am afraid that he may get sent home this evening. He tanked really bad last night – he and Brooke actually. One week, Jace this did version of "Somewhere Over the Rainbow" that was great. I heard that it was some take he had gotten from some artist off You Tube. Jason is the prettiest boy I have ever seen in my life. I mean it. He isn't the most attractive male I've seen, but he is just physically a pretty boy. He is beautiful in the face. His eyes, lips and face are just flawless and gorgeous. Anyway, it's worth checking out. Millions think so, not just me, if that makes it anymore appealing. Sir Andrew Lloyd Webber has even given AI his stamp of approval.

Do you ever watch this hilarious show *Two and a Half Men*? Anyway it stars Charlie Sheen and John Cryer. Well, if you don't watch it, you should check it out because it is FUNNY. Well, Charlie has this neighbor, Rose, who is obsessed with him and "stalks" him. Anyway, I finally came clean to my friends and family that I pathetically still email you to no avail, and I have now been dubbed "Rose." Just when I think I can't sink any lower.

Anyway, I guess you can say I am bored again. This makes week two that I am at home. I am having problems with the kidneys. I don't expect you to give a damn. I'm just here and stewing, and so this is what I am doing with my idle time. Still miss you like crazy, still crazy (joke) and wish we could be together.

No better, No wiser, No stronger
Your Rose 04/23/08

Mary: Miss u! Hope you are well. I don't want to be this person in your life, the problematic ex-friend you ignore. I've been in the hospital for awhile and did a lot of thinking. We have a lot of history,

Paul, and not all has been horrible. I hope I am not alone in thinking that. I am sorry for the stress I have caused you, but you have to know that you can be an infuriating, frustrating and complicated little man. I will promise to stop telling you how much I love you and believe in you and want to be with you. I know you know, and it doesn't matter for reasons I will never understand. I get it. I don't think you should give up on us yet. I know it has been hard and I am a frustrating and exasperating woman, but my intentions were always pure – although misguided.

I know I can't be in love with you forever, because I want a relationship and that can't happen with you. I know, good God, I know. Like a retard, I've invested in you for near a decade. I'm just asking that you do the same for me and give me another chance to be your friend. I hate that I'm this weirdo/psycho in your life. That's not who I want to be for you. I will take any place in your life you allow me to have. That sounds so pathetic and desperate, but it is truer than most anything else in my life. I just want to know how you are and if you teared up at the end of *Juno*? What weirdo music you are listening to? How wild are you finding this election year? I miss friend things, Paul, things I had before I let my hormones get the best of me.

I want to be able to tell you about all the shit that's happened to me over the last few months and know that you care, even if it's a little bit or as my friend. I just miss you, and I hate sending you these blind emails. I know that everything was completely my fault and I went too far, but that is what I do. Don't be so self righteous in your quest to save me from myself and continue to freeze me out. Give me one less thing to worry about. I pray this touches you in some way. I swear I will never tell you how I feel again, no hints, no songs and no parallels to other things in life.

Sent from my iPod 5/10/08

Mary: Goodnight and sweet dreams my friend.
Sent from my iPod 05/11/08

Mary: Paul,

I guess it is safe to assume that your continued silence means that you are not willing to give me another chance and try to be my friend. When I made the mistake of mentioning all of this to my mother, she said, "Good for Paul for not writing. One of you needs to be the strong one in this, and it's just not you." She continued to tell me a bunch of stuff I already knew and then said that this is a cycle I have with you that needs to be broken. She said I would never be happy with a friendship with you, because you can't give me what I want.

That hurt. It feels so bad that you don't respond and to have my own mother say, "Good for Paul" was indescribable. Of course, Sal concurs with my mother. She thinks this whole thing is sad; I'm sad and need to focus my energy and affection elsewhere to someone who can reciprocate them. I have totally accepted that no one understands me and with each failed attempt at contact I am making myself that much more pathetic. I've accepted it. The other night I heard this incredible story that made me hopeful and ignited my continued desire to have us communicate again. That is my explanation for the text message the other night.

What do I have to do, say, feel? Is there anything??? I'm sorry. I am sorry a hundred times over. I'm trying, Paul. I really am on so many levels. I just hate this and it makes me incredibly sad. I hope in some way this matters to you and you decide to talk to me again.

As always, I hope you are well. 05/17/08

Mary: Missing you. Wishing you'd reconsider this and acknowledge me. Stop making me beg. It isn't good for me. All I did was love you. Why am I being punished for that? Think about it.

Mary
Sent from my iPod 06/08/08

Mary: Hey,

What's new? Things pretty much still suck here. I managed to stress my way right into the hospital. I got out today so I am thankful for that. I still don't have job or know what I'm going to do, but whatever! I really miss chatting with you. I wish that were mutual. This is the first time in a while I've emailed with the computer, usually I use the iPod. Sal and I went to see that movie *The Strangers* not too long ago, and since then I have just had this really sick feeling of fear. I just feel fearful all the time. I don't think the movie caused it necessarily, but I think it brought it out. The movie was a real thrill ride for me. I personally thought that it sucked but it did manage to scare the hell out of me. I know that's not hard to do but still, that movie was pretty scary. I screamed.

I hope you are doing alright and are happy. I want that more than I want you to speak to me, so if ignoring me does that for you than I can't complain too much. I think about you all the time and wonder about things and what I could have done differently or lied about feeling differently. This haunts me in some ways. I hate that you're out there and I can't talk to you or you won't talk to me. It makes me feel so bad inside. I cannot explain to you how it feels; it just burns. So, what do I do? I keep whispering in your ear in the hope one day you won't fan me away.

Anyway, I miss you a lot and it would do a lot for me for you to acknowledge me. It hurts both ways, Paul, but this is worse than before, you know? Before, I at least had other emotions prior to the great brush off. I even miss becoming frustrated with you. Does this make you feel anything? Happy? A little sad? Regretful? Anything? I just need something.

I know I was crazy at times and I guess still am by the fact that I still write you and give a damn when you don't, but I know that I was a good friend some of that time too. I wasn't all the time a psycho bitch, you know that. I apologize in advance if this email does anything besides make you think. Yes, I am sober – just feeling and sharing tonight. I guess I knew that we needed space, or I did to get things figured out – and even though I said that no contact was best (and it was then), I never believed that we'd never talk again. I just felt that when the time was right, we would. We'd find out way back to each other. I don't mean that romantically; I just mean that in a real sincere way. Perhaps, this won't help my case or be the email that compels you to do something, but I have to try. It is who I am to try.

I wish with everything I am that things could be different, and I'll always feel that. I cannot help it. I know that I should be ashamed and stop myself from this, for my pride's sake, but sadly it just doesn't have that affect/effect (I never know which one) on me. Just one day, email me; send me a postcard; if hell freezes over, call; just don't be gone forever, OK? 06/26/08

Mary: Paul,
I hope the song plays. Anyway, I was supposed to see the Batman movie tonight, but things changed and so I am home waiting to watch

the season premiere of *Monk* and *Psych*. I am excited about seeing the movie, BUT as crazy as it sounds I feel haunted by Heath Ledger and I am a little worried about seeing him. I am so happy that there's this buzz about his performance and even Oscar talk, but it makes me so incredibly sad. It just seems so unfair. Life shouldn't be like that in my mind. I've done all this reading about how the role really got into his head and he was having trouble sleeping, and I can't help but to think about that and the pills. I don't know. It's crazy, but I'm torn up about it. On a better note, I am supposed to be seeing *Mama Mia* with my friend Justin and that will be great!!! I loved the play in Vegas and you know I love ABBA.

On to my favorite subject "us." This is so crazy. I know it; you know it. I mean, at least let me know if you liked the gift I sent you. I mean, did you keep it? Even get it? Give it away? Listen to it? I just want to know, Paul, even if it hurts. I saw it, and I thought about you immediately, and it didn't matter to me that you weren't speaking to me. I just wanted you to have it. A long time ago, maybe close to a decade ago, I told you that I loved your voice and that I wanted you to call me one day and read me some poetry. Of course, you ignored me, but I've always thought about that – and when I saw the collection I thought it was perfect, I guess that's what I thought. I wanted to give you something that meant something, and I hope I did. Life is just so short to feel like this and waste time in this way. I miss you and I don't know how else to say it.

Anyway, I am sure that you went to see the movie tonight or maybe even at midnight this morning. I could be wrong, but I think that. Please tell me I am wrong :) Tell me anything at this point, Paul. It's not easier, and if it's going to hurt I'd rather we'd be talking and know what was happening in your life and vice versa. I just want that, and if you can please respond.

I still think of you often and fondly and hope you are happy.

Mary 07/18/08

Mary: Paul,
I saw the *Dark Knight* last night. It really fucked with me. I knew it would, but I didn't realize how much. I'm glad I saw it, I think. I saw it with Sal, who has seen it now three times!!!!!!!!!!!!!!! I don't think I

could watch it again. I looked at most of it with my hand over my face. I am a wimp. I was scared. It's hard for me to sit through dark movies. I did see *Mama Mia* earlier this week and I LOVED IT. It took all I had to stay in my seat, but I didn't want to embarrass Justin. Rhoda is dying to see it, and we are supposed to go so I can act up with her. Rhoda has no shame about acting like a complete fool in public. I love her for that at times. I am still gainfully unemployed and stressing over what I am going to do about money and finances, BUT of course I'm doing the mature thing and going to movies I really can't afford. I always make the best choices!!

I thought my last email to you was incredibly good and moving. I guess I was wrong. I actually cried a little when I wrote it. I know that doesn't mean anything because I cry about everything, but I still thought it was very heartfelt. I can't stress to you enough how difficult things are for me right now and it would be one thing that turned out OK if you'd just write back. Just a "hello" or a "drop dead" would suffice. I promise I won't infer that you love me and that we are going to end up together, but rather that we are friends or that we were at one time. I shouldn't beg this way. I know it is so sad and pathetic, but this – you – means a lot to me, and so I persevere. I've gotten the point a hundred times over now, and I understand how you feel about the things that I say.

What are you doing with all of this? I am as sincere and desperate as I know how to be and perhaps that is the problem. I guess my desperation to talk to you or have contact with you is a bit daunting. I don't know what to say to that, other than it's honest. I just want to be able to hear from you once in a while and know what's going on with you. I miss knowing that (what I did know). Now that I know nothing, I appreciate what I did have with you. I never thought I'd say that, but I have; and I actually mean it. I really do. I have given up on hoping for something romantic with you. I'm just going crazy over losing my friend.

I'm not going to hassle you about visiting or calling or any of that stuff. I just want the occasional email, like before. It's funny how things can change over the course of a few months. Still dying to know whether you kept the CD's or listened to any of the poetry. Just you answering that would mean a lot. You answering anything would mean a lot at this point.

Sorry to be such a broken record, but when it comes to you and this, this seems to be the only song I know. Again, maybe that's the problem. Who knows???? You've won. I am weak and pathetic, and I couldn't last a few months without contacting you. I am a failure, a complete loser and – sadly and pathetically – that's alright with me. I don't want to rehash this past shit with you. I don't want to discuss what went wrong and why this can't work I just want to pick up from some healthy place and start there. I don't want to talk about your inability to open up about things and how often you should write and why you never call. I don't want to do any of that. I'm tired of that.

Sadly, that last email I sent you before you got pissed off was what I was trying to say. Then, I was trying to say that I got it, and that I finally understood our relationship and where it was going (nowhere). I wasn't trying to stir things up and enrage you, just enlightening you on this clarity that I had.

Maybe that was the wrong thing to do but at the same time I don't think it was. I think it was the straw that broke the camel's back, and it didn't have anything to do with what I actually said because that email was nothing compared to some of the ramblings I have sent you in the past. (Exhale) I feel better. I've wanted to say that for awhile.

I just want to be able to email you and tell you things that occur that are weirdly important to me and vice versa. I want to be able to share with you when I discover great songs like "Thirteen" and have you tell me how late I am in my discovery or that the guy singer you like who killed himself sings a version of the song. His name escapes me right now. I just want to be able to say how scared and sad I am over my life right now and have you say, "I'm praying for you," or, "It will work out." All the things that you say when I tell you that I am sinking.

Something that I don't understand made you important to me and that's never changed and won't ever. I'm not the same person I was a few months ago. I guess I'm just still dealing with the side effects.

There's this book, *Man's Search for Meaning,* by Viktor Salkl, and there's this quote that I love. It says, "A man who becomes conscious of the responsibility he bears toward a human being who affectionately waits for him, or to an unfinished work, will never be able to throw away his life. He knows the 'why' for his existence, and will be able to bear almost any 'how.'" That means something to me and so I pass it on to you, and I hope it means something to you as well.

Affectionately Yours,

Mary 07/27/08

Mary: Just checking in to see how you are doing. I hope you are well. I miss you.

Mary
--
Wishing You a Lifetime of Learning
           -Mary 09/27/08

Mary: Hey,

I'm feeling weak today and so you get an email. I hate this so much, Paul. I'm not sure if it's my weakness when it comes to you or the fact that you won't write back and don't care that bothers me more. I feel like this is the only thing in my life that is unresolved, and it just kills me. I finally settled things with Patrice and we are rebuilding are relationship (slowly). I made the first move in that even though I was still angry, because I don't want to feel bitterness against someone I love so much. She drives me absolutely crazy and pushes all of my buttons, which is one of the reasons I moved out, but she means something to me, and in the long run that's all we have. Luckily, she loves me back, and we were able to build on that and try to have a relationship again. My relationship with her and my relationships with you was the only issues with people that were haunting me.

Rhoda asked about you about a week ago and I told her that you still were not communicating with me but I still wrote you in the hopes that you'd reconsider. She laughed this huge laugh, and I had to laugh too because it was so utterly pathetic and amusing in a sick way. I can't let myself believe that you don't care. I know that in your mind, you're doing the right thing and cutting me off because I can never get what I want from you – and not to mention I was driving crazy right before we decided not to communicate. I get that. I know that probably everyone agrees that me not hearing from you is for the best and that one day I'll sober up and stop and just let go. I know that I've held on too long. But like Patrice, you mean something to me, and it is hard for me to feel that and not try. I know it is possible to maybe realize that a relationship with you isn't good for me and that

I can continue to care for you and not have you in my life. I know all of this rationally, but emotionally I'm not there. It's hard.

Whenever your name comes up – and yes, it still does – I try to laugh it off and act like it doesn't just rip me to pieces, but I know I am not convincing. What's funny is that the whole time I had you in my life, I kept wanting you to tell me that I meant something to you and that you loved me. It took you being gone or distant for me to realize that you just being there at all meant you cared. With Patrice, I felt such blind rage towards her for things that happened and for things that were said. With you, it's just this void and this sense of regret. At times, I hate that I was honest with you. I wish that I had lied a little longer or a little better. Honesty is so overrated.

I know things with the two of us move in cycles or at least had in the past, and so that had to be broken. I want to be with someone who wants me back; I sincerely do. I know that you will find someone to feel that way about, if you haven't already, and I know that person isn't me. I know that, and I am not holding out for that any longer. I just hate how things are. I hate that I, for the most part, caused this. God, if you'd just write back once to say that you're fine and a line about what you're doing now and that you don't hate me, that would move mountains for me.

Just recently, I got to the point where I could listen to Amy Winehouse again. I know that too is pathetic, but it made me think about you for some reason and that just felt too bad. Maybe that's progress – just a little. A lot of things make me think about you, but only a few things make me hurt: Winehouse was one of them. I still can't listen to "Trouble" but I'm working on it. Paul, I don't miss constantly seeking reassurance from you and re-evaluating our friendship and having new epiphany's every other week concerning you. I miss being able to talk about this election and the economy and all the crazy things going on in this world right now.

I want to know who you want to win this election. Good Lord, I hope that it's Barack Obama, but if not I want to be able to know why not and tell you why you are soooooooo WRONG to want John McCain to win this election. I don't even know what you do for a living now. It is my hope that whatever it is, you are happy with it. I wonder if you're an uncle yet or if your mom is doing alright. And yes, I wonder if you ever think about me beyond these desperate emails and the fact that I owe you $300. By the way, I owe everyone I know money at this point in my life due to my lack of employment. I have been so blessed by my friends, and I lump you into that category. Things have been hard and very close in terms of money, but my friends just help and help. I hope one day that I get on my feet and pay everyone back. I don't know why I got on this. I also wonder if you write anymore.

Saturday, Sal and I were feeling stressed, and because of my mom's Marriott bonus points we were able to get a hotel room gratis. Anyway, we just talked, went swimming and got in the hot tub. We talked a lot, and she brought you up. Most times she is incredibly disappointed that I continue to write, but this time she just asked if I still did, and then she said, "Well, in the next one, tell him I said hello." That doesn't sound like much but that's HUGE. I can't tell you how many times I have been shamed about this. But it was like she finally got how important this is to me, and I don't care how it makes me look. Maybe I should but I don't.

I write you always in the hope that you will write back, but I don't if my emailing you helps or if it just hardens your resolve. I just know that it makes me feel better than doing nothing. Sometimes I think that is what it is about: feeling better. Not having you communicate with me makes me feel like ... I can't even describe in words what it makes me feel like; but it is a feeling that I don't wish anyone.

I know that you probably think that if you give a little gradually I'll start to want more and more and we will end up right back here, so what's the point. And honestly, I can't argue with you, because past behavior is the greatest determiner for future behavior. I can say forever that things are different and I'm different, BUT why should you invest in that? I don't know. I wish I had something witty, poetic and compelling thing to say that would make you change your stance, but I'm not that good of a writer. All I know is that I want you to talk to me again and I accept that friendship is all I can have with you – that is, if I'm lucky enough to even get that. I hate that so much time is wasted with these words and hopes, but I just keep hoping things will change and that you will change. I know nothing I say comes as a surprise, because I never really stopped talking to you, but I still delve into self-help and listening to any and everything on relationships, and I know that the worse thing I did when we were friends was not listen to you. I never heard you when you said friendship was all you could give. I kept hoping that I'd change you or change that thought. I know that was stupid.

Here is a little tidbit I listen to *Hannah Montana*. I actually watch the show. I'm actually listening to it now. In my defense, I started listening with Madison (age ten) and sort of started to like it. Since I'm not working, I got on this weird schedule where I sleep all day and am up all night like until five or six in the morning. Anyway, last night, I watched this movie with Edward James Olmos, *American Me*. It was totally not my type of movie. It was this train wreck, but I got sucked into it. The weird thing is that I watched the entire movie and I am so at a loss as to what I watched. I didn't get it. It wasn't avant-garde or anything like that, but I just didn't get it or understand why certain things happened. I guess I didn't follow it well. I know it is probably futile to ask, but have you seen it?

Until next time...

Wishing You a Lifetime of Learning
- Mary 10/08/08

Mary: Well I am going to Indiana to knock on doors for Barack Obama next weekend. I'm nervous and a little scared but excited. I am worried about the mean people I might encounter, and I've never been to Indiana so I don't know what to expect. I know you have, but since you are not talking to me that doesn't really help me. I think I am going to dinner with Jake and Gloria sometime in the near future. I am looking forward to that. For a split second, I actually thought you might have called me. I like to assign people ringers and I couldn't remember what I assigned you, and my phone rang and I couldn't find it, but it was a song that never played and so I thought "Who would I assign a ringtone to that I never hear from?" Obviously that would be you, right? The call didn't register and I couldn't see who called because my phone is a piece of crap.

Anyway, I hoped so bad it was you, but when I looked you up I quickly realized it wasn't your ringtone. After I thought about it, I realized that you probably don't have my number anymore, since that time Sal called you from my phone, you answered. I know you probably wouldn't have done that if you knew it was my number. If we start talking again, I swear I'm not going to start emailing and telephoning you every day. I just hate the distance and the fact that I can't talk to you. This means a lot to me more than I can say. Will you just trust me enough to try????? 10/14/08

Mary: Paul,

I knew I wasn't your favorite person, but I had no idea that you hate me as much as you do. I've tried everything including begging and you are unyielding on this. I looked at Facebook as an opportunity to try once again to reconnect with you. I had no idea that it would bother you to the point of removing yourself so that I would leave you alone. Maybe I'm narcissistic to think that is because of me, but I think it is a safe bet. I'm sorry you felt like you had to take it to this extreme to get me to leave you alone.

I still feel the exact same way about you, but my resolve has weakened. It kills me every time I reach out and you won't even try to meet me half-way. You mean something to me and that is why I am unrelenting (not sure that's a word) and kept trying to get you to give me another chance. I'm here and I want you in my life, but I can't force you to. I can't make you care; I never could. You've won. I am destroyed, and I will leave you alone. You know I'm here and willing, and the rest is up to you. You're this brick wall that I've grown accustomed to banging my head against. I made myself laugh about the whole situation, hoping that it would make it hurt less, but I was fooling myself.

I know you have your reasons and maybe I'm not supposed to understand them. Perhaps I do and it hurts too bad to be that honest with myself. If it had to end, I didn't want it to be like this; I at least wanted a goodbye. I'm not angry with you, just hurt and confused and a whole bunch of other melodramatic feelings. I'm here, and if ever that's good enough for you just do something, OK?

Mary 10/19/08

Mary: Paul,

I am really ill right now and so wish that this could be over and we could be friends again. I have to have chemo now for my lupus (long story), but I feel like crap most days and this still weighs so heavy on me. Please forgive me and just talk to me. All I have getting my through are my friends and your absence becomes even more poignant to me. I'm too sick to cyber stalk you and call all the time, but every now and then would be really good. And yes, I'm using my condition to gain your sympathy. That's pathetic, but it doesn't make it untrue. Please try ...

Mary 03/09/09

Mary: Hey,

I'm not exactly sure where to start to make this email any different, better or more compelling than the last few hundred that I've sent BUT I'm going to try. All night, I had these weird series of dreams that were very unsettling. I think I might have had at least five different dreams over the course of one night. There's only one that I wanted to share with you.

I dreamed that I went on a trip to the beach with six or seven of my closest girlfriends, and I had managed to go off alone and was sitting on the beach with a laptop. I don't know what I was doing with the computer, but it was there. I then dreamed that I saw people from your family on the beach, and suddenly I felt so sick to my stomach, because I knew you were there somewhere. I kept wanting to get up and leave and go back to my room and be with my friends, but I couldn't move; I just sat there.

Suddenly in the distance I see you, and I still can't move because I am hoping against hope that something will be different and you'd at least acknowledge me. Finally, you get close enough to see me, and you STOP dead in your tracks with this look that is nothing but pure horror. I immediately get up and go back to my room and to my friends. I then tell them the whole story, and my friends being my friends say "Leave it alone. Don't try and talk to him. Just enjoy the trip and forget he is here. If he wanted to talk to you he would have."

Of course, me being me, I can't; and so I wallow in it while my friends go to the beach. When they return each of them tells me at some point that they spoke with you. My first friend says, "He was nice and couldn't believe this happened, but he wants to be left alone." The next friend comes to me and says, "I know this is hard, but you have to let it go and realize it is what it is, and he wants to be left alone."

Then finally Sal comes in and was like, "I talked to him, and he wasn't rude – just firm. He did ask about you and seemed to genuinely want to know but was firm in wanting to be left alone. He had a moment when he thought he should maybe say something to you but then he could see from your expression and overreaction to him that it still wasn't what he should do." Sal then looks at me and says, "It's time for you to let this go and stop. It's not funny or cute anymore; it's just sad." In the dream, I become sooo MAD at Sal, not because she was so dry about it or because she was right BUT because she didn't get it. She didn't get me. Then I woke up sad and a little mad.

My whole life I have had this issue with letting go and accepting what I don't want to hear. My mom says it is because I am an only child and am spoiled and used to working on people until I get my way. That might be very true, because I rarely accept a *no*. I keep trying until that *no* is a *maybe* and then I work even harder until that maybe is a *yes*. This is how I have been my whole life, and I guess, you know, it has worked for me, because it's what I do; it's who I am.

I guess I should say it worked until I met you. I know you are thinking, *How she can possibly be even more honest than she has been over the course of this freeze out*? My whole intention since I met you was to change your mind about me. I kept thinking that something would change and we'd feel the same way about each other. So I was willing to say whatever or do whatever to make that happen. This included saying things I didn't really mean or saying I had feelings that I really didn't have. This last time when we started talking "again" and I said I've changed and that I'm not secretly pining away for you and just want your friendship, and that I'm over the romantic part of it – OK, that was a BIG OLE lie, and I knew it was. I wasn't even lying to myself; I was lying to you in the hopes that you'd believe me and open up the line of communication again, and I would set out to convince you – unbeknownst to you – that I was right for you. Sal tells my daily that I'm not clever, slick or discreet. She tells me that it is funny to her that I pride myself on these qualities and possess none of them. OK, so she is right. I admit it: I am transparent.

I kept wanting this deeper connection with you and it consumed me. What kills me right now today is that I had what I needed from you, and I couldn't see it until you took it away. I really realized this about a month ago. I started looking through old emails and writings, and I came across something you wrote about me. It was one of those daily reminder things. I had told you about Sal's cousin drowning and my challenges with health, and you wrote about that. You referred to me as your friend and asked your other friends to not only pray for

Sal's family but also for me. All that heartbreak going on with Sal's family, which did and should have far surpassed me and my daily drama, and you thought about me. Right there was proof of what I really wanted and needed, and that was a friend.

But of course I was too obsessed with something else to see that and appreciate that. I know it is far too late to say this, but thank you for that. I'm sure at the time I said that, but I'm not sure I meant it the way I should have or understood how great that was. I've also apologized millions of millions of times just in the hopes that one day it would mean something and you'd talk to me. But I know now what I owe you an apology for, and that is for not respecting you and your choices and for not believing what you said about what you wanted. I was terrible at listening to you and taking you at face value. I always looked around what you said or under it, trying to find out the meaning. Which was sooo dumb, because you told me and it wasn't what I wanted to hear, and so I didn't listen to you. I'm sorry for that.

I have a hard time seeing out of my realm and I relate everything to myself and how I feel. In my head I kept thinking, *No one wants to be alone. Everyone wants to meet that perfect fit and be happy;* and for me, romance and love equates to happiness, and it didn't make sense to me how that couldn't be so for everyone. I understand now that it's not for me to understand – that is your choice, your life, your happiness.

I have learned that I can't convince you to talk to me, care about me or acknowledge me. That is a leap of faith that you have to take, and I can't strong-arm you with daily emails and pleadings. That won't convince you. There is this trust that you have to bestow once again before I can show you.

While I'm addressing everything, I know that was a new low to try to contact your mom via Facebook. At the time, it seemed harmless enough, but I know that was wrong and I should not have tried to bring her into this. Again, not the most subtle move on my part. I cannot tell you how much hell I caught over that from my mother and Sal. They were humiliated and thought it was my most pathetic move to date, which says a whole lot. I think what really nailed that in was when I asked my mom how she would have reacted if the tables were reversed and you had contacted her. She said she wouldn't have responded and would not have gotten into the middle of something between me and a friend. She asked me whether I really thought in my head that "his mom would defy his wishes to send you an email. Do you really think she'd do that to her son when she knows how strongly he feels about it?" I guess I really hadn't thought about it. It was impulsive and I did it, but I shouldn't have.

Finally in closing I must say that I want you to take that leap of faith in me and just email me and say, "I got your note," or, "This was way too long," just something so I know that you haven't given up on me or our friendship; BUT I also know that if you decide to continue with this I have to let go – not just because that's healthy and right but because I'd be respecting your wishes. Believe or not, that is important to me. It's just so hard, Paul. I try and try, and then something I read, watch or dream brings me back here, writing you and hoping that you will reconsider and be my friend again. It's not even that I want to discuss this history with you; it's all the new stuff that's going on. I want to be able to talk about last night's *House* with you, or the fact over the weekend my mom got me a Wii and a Wii Fit, which is very nice and cool but I have no idea what to do with it.

I wish I could talk to you about my chemo, not for sympathy but just because it helps to have friends. I don't believe that you're angry with me and just hanging on to a grudge because you are stubborn. I know it's deeper than that and maybe it's because you think this is better for me in the long run, or maybe your just tapped on me, or perhaps it's both and more than I can even begin to understand.

I miss you as my friend, and if somehow you can find a way to trust me again, I will show you that I can be the friend you deserve; BUT, by the same token, if you decide you can't take that leap of faith it is my job to trust you and your decision and finally and completely let go.

Mary 04/07/09

Mary: I did something weird today. I was going through various email accounts, and I just read through all the emails I have sent you and that you've sent me over the years. That was quite a roller coaster. I can so see why we are here now, but at the same time it's hard to see that we won't ever be back to being friends again. I was a psycho at times. I so see that. I also saw how, in my delirium, I read certain things into what you'd write. I kept reading and reading, and even though I knew how the story ended I kept wishing I had made smarter decisions and said/wrote better things to you. Gosh, you were so patient, but when you were pissed at me you were really pissed. It was hard to read some of what you'd written to me when I had pushed you to your limits.

I must say that after I read the emails one last time, I deleted them. Part of me resisted, but all reading them did was lead me here, writing you and feeling regretful and sad that you won't respond. I know this might sound like an insane and ridiculous question, but do you want me to stop? Is that what you really want? I know I should know this, but my head and heart have never been connected when it comes to you. I keep feeling as if you are still there and that if I really need you, you will stop this; but it is breaking me.

I guess I can deal with you being pissed at me because eventually that will go away, and I know that, BUT just being done with no feeling involved means this won't ever end. I know things in our relationship were always different for me so it is so hard to see this through your eyes, so I need help – help from you, I mean. It doesn't help me to guess what you are thinking. I know in the past I didn't listen to you and that I went on for almost a decade not listening to you and hearing what I wanted to hear; but I need to hear from you. I need you to respond to me and to all of this and tell me that you're pissed or tell me that you are just done. I need something.

Paul, I'm tired of this and I know that it would appear to you that if this were true I'd just give up and let you be and let myself be, but obviously I can't do that. I'm still invested in you. I've never in my life had someone just stop being in my life, especially when I wanted them there. I know it doesn't seem like it, but I am trying. Please forgive me. I just need that. I don't know if you can move past all of this so that we can be friends because I don't know that you can trust me, but I just need you to respond once and give me a fraction of what I need from you. If there is even the tiniest part of you that wants to respond, please listen to that voice and do so.

I've always wanted to know what went through your mind when it came to me. Some days I am so scared to know, because I can't imagine what you must think about me, and then other times it is all I can think about. Is everything about you and me negative? Do you regret knowing me all together? Like I said, this is me whispering and hoping that you don't wave me away this time.

04/29/09

Mary: PAUL,

I feel like the wind was knocked out of me. I have totally degraded myself trying to redeem myself in your eyes. Throughout this whole soap opera I have confided in Sal. She knows everything that I have done and felt. I can't believe that you would ignore every attempt I've made to be your friend again and you'd talk to MY best friend. I know I'm not your favorite person but this hurts more than I can say. I can't dictate her or your friends, but can a little part of you understand why this is devastating.

PEACE! 07/01/09

(After months and months of silence he speaks)

Paul: I haven't talked to Sal and don't know what you're talking about. You need get on with your life and leave me alone. Do not respond to this. I'm so freaking sick of having to defend myself against your perceptions. If this is because Sal sent me a friend request on Facebook, then you can take that up with her. She never gave me any reason not to talk to her, but I knew it would be trouble when I accepted her request.

Please, please, leave me alone. 07/09/09

Paul

Paul: You are a douche!!!! Don't tell me what to do. Don't fucking read this if you don't want to? It's your preference (that is up your alley). I've sent you lots and lots of emails since this all started, and nothing. Then you choose Saturday's email to write back. Not sure what about that email got your panties in a wad that you felt had to be responded to. I have had several low moments since I met you, but last night took it to an all time LOW. You are such a friggin genius to deduce from no communication with me that my life is somehow stuck and not moving due to you. Yes, Paul, my whole world stops unless I am writing you, thinking about you.

Thank you so much for acting like an asshole and making this easy for me. I mistakenly took your self-deprecating wit for charm. I do owe you an apology because I should have been stronger and stopped doing this a long time ago. I feel so foolish and stupid that I am 30 years old and still doing this with you. You're tired of defending yourself??? You don't have a monopoly on that.

I must give you credit for being consistent. I wrote that email on the 1st (I think) and it took you until yesterday to get around to telling me off – Paul Hughes style. That is classic! As far as taking my issue up with Sal, that was done way before I even considered writing you. Sal and I can communicate as friends without one of us being a martyr and the other a stalker. But sincerely, thank you for the advice suggesting I talk to my best friend. I am so sorry that a girl liking you and wanting to be your friend aggravated your little world. Why don't you go and fuck your typewriter from the early 1800s? I know this won't be the first time.

Mary

Please, please, please consider yourself left alone 07/10/09
*I didn't really send this one, but I did write it.
OK, this is was the actual email that I sent several months later.
Paul:

How do I start an email to you? Any beginning sounds ridiculous, right? I will get to the point; I at least owe you that. Gosh a lot has happened, and I think some of that I should share with you. I am bi polar. Probably no big shocker there, but actually it was sort of a shock. And because I am precocious, I have bipolar with a mixed state. I am still trying to figure all this out the way I did when I was diagnosed with lupus.

Anyway, I was resistant to this initially because of what little I knew about the condition; I didn't see myself as having manic episodes. Now with meds and three weeks of partial day hospitalization things are starting to clear up. These changes were of my own volition; nothing happened that sent me to see a PSYCHIATRIST except that I was depressed a lot. My shrink rocks and I am so pleased with him. Yeah, the point ... You were or are part of my mania or manic episodes. I so see that now. At the time, I felt totally victimized by you and, believe it or not, by another friend who got similar drama from me regularly. Like I said, this is all about a month old, so I am just at the beginning of a long never-ending road; but now I feel somewhat hopeful.

I am sorry, for whatever that's worth, but I'm doing OK. I'm now writing things other than letters to you. I finished that book from so long ago. It is now a memoir with changed names and events, but with the same feelings I had while writing it. After the very last email I got from you on the whole Facebook deal, I immediately clicked to reply and I think I called you a douche and some other choice words, and then I couldn't send it. I didn't know it was a literal mental disorder that caused me to act out, but I knew I had to stop. So I wrote the email and then I deleted it. That was the first time I had ever done that. Something really caught a hold of me through your words. I felt anger, frustration, but it was the desperation that I felt came across from you of you wanting to be free of me. That did something.

Anyway, I just wanted to say these things and tell you I'm working out my issues with meds and counseling – not just with regards to you but life in general. I am about as happy as bipolar people get, I guess. I hope you are great too.

Best,

Mary

> I remember that time that you told me, you said
> "Love is touching souls"
>
> Surely you touched mine
> 'Cause part of you pours out of me
> In these lines from time to time …"

It has been a few years and few things have changed. I say a few things, but I neglected to say "a few important things." I'm in my early thirties now. After that final email I wrote to Paul, I haven't heard anything from him. I've managed not to write him or call. I still consider myself in love with him, and somewhere inside I still believe this is temporary and he will come around and admit that he does love me too. He haunts my dreams at times. There are times when I wake up and for brief moment, I let myself forget that things are the way they are between us. So much time has gone by and so many words have been typed in an attempt to move past all this and to understand myself better. I'm not so sure that happened, but it helped. I was able to confess things here that I would never have been able to, to anyone else.

I've been back for a few years, and it seems to be one of the best decisions I have ever made. Sal and I are back to our usual mischief. Currently there is no one in my life. I am looking and receptive, but I am trying to not let it consume me.

I had to stop working due to my lupus. I went through a round of chemo to try and get the lupus that was attacking my kidneys under control. I've been diagnosed as bi-polar within the last few months, which probably explains the majority of this book and how and why it was written. Sadly, the meds I have to take have a wicked side effect of weight gain and I have put on 100 lbs. Obviously, I am dealing with esteem issues.

As far as Alistair goes, we never see each other anymore. He has not changed at all but I guess in this case I have. I still love and care about him, but I guess I finally got tired of chasing him. With Alistair, I never felt good enough. I was always too fat for him not sexy enough, not woman enough. These were not things he put on me but how I made myself feel when he came around. I'd tell myself, "He can't really love you because you're fat." Just being in Alistair's presence made me feel so horrible inside. It was weird that thinking about him was better than actually being with him. I call Alistair every so often, every blue moon and he calls me every other blue moon (if he needs something).

Health wise, I am taking life a day at a time. There are ups and downs, good days and bad days. I survived chemo for a few months to get my lupus under control. I worked as a volunteer on the Obama campaign as much as I could. Life is good. I feel as if I've lost a lot on this journey of self-discovery, but what I have gained, no matter how miniscule, has been immeasurable.

I'm still single, still living life with lupus and looking for love.

"There are places I remember all my life,
Though some have changed,
Some forever, not for better,
Some have gone and some remain."

CPSIA information can be obtained at www.ICGtesting.com
Printed in the USA
LVOW041043140112

263758LV00002B/108/P